D1522903

"Emilia"

The darkest days in history of Nazi Germany through a woman's eyes

"Do not look for my heart anymore, the beasts have eaten it."

- Charles Baudelaire, "The Flowers of Evil"

Chapter 1

The weather that day was especially windy. Emilia stood outside her house, pulling the collar of her overcoat closer to her face, scowling. Her father, Oskar Brettenheimer, was trying to reason with the Untersturmführer in charge, inquiring about compensation; the latter kept spreading his arms nonchalantly and shaking his head. Emilia smirked slightly and shook her head as well, but only at her father. Poor old man, he still had faith in the rightfulness of the German people.

He had always prided himself in being a German and even welcomed that madman Hitler's appointment as chancellor, saying how farsighted the man was and how he'd make Germany a strong country once again. He did; only it seemed that there wasn't a place for their family in that new country anymore. That had become clear after a new law was issued in 1938 for all Jews to register at the immigration department and to start wearing a yellow star sewn onto their clothes.

Oscar had gone gray in the course of a month, collected all their savings – luckily in time, before it was announced that all Jews were stripped of their citizenship – and moved his family to Poland, hoping to reopen his jewelry store and wait until it was safe for them to return home. Even then he was still certain that it would all pass.

They bought a nice small house in Gdansk, a city close to the German border, which had a predominantly German population. The Brettenheimers lived there quite comfortably for three years, until Germany attacked Poland a year after Emilia and her family moved there. The new occupants, roaming the streets in their gray uniforms, became a usual sight, but even then Oskar tried not to lose his optimism; or maybe he just didn't want to admit to himself that he was wrong and they were defeated.

"We're Germans, first and foremost," he kept repeating when his wife, Hannah, pleaded to move away someplace safe, to the United States or England at least. "We have lived in Munich our whole lives, our families lived in Munich their whole lives, and their families before them. Besides, they're after the religious ones, and we aren't considered religious by any means. We only go to the synagogue once a year for Yom Kippur, that's how religious are we! No, Hannah, I'm telling you, if we just comply with what they tell us, we'll be just fine. They have been in Poland for two years now and they've never bothered us. And forget your wild fantasies about England! Neither of us speak their language, so how would we survive there? No, we're staying put right here, where we are. They won't hurt us, you'll see."

Only a week after that conversation, Untersturmführer Weisner knocked on their door with three uniformed soldiers behind his back, introduced himself, tipped his cap and gave them an order for eviction.

"But this is our house! We bought it! We're the rightful owners! It's paid off!" Hannah screamed, while Oskar just stood there, fondling the paper in his hands, crestfallen and mute. "How come you're evicting us from our rightful property?"

"I'm very sorry, Frau Brettenheimer." Untersturmführer Weisner even tilted his head to one side, although his subordinates were already taking their clipboards out to make a list of the furniture and all of the Brettenheimer's possessions. "This is a high order. Poland is the territory of the Reich now, and, therefore, you aren't allowed to own any property. This house is being confiscated by the Reich. I'm afraid there's nothing I can do."

"So, you're just throwing us out on the street?" Oskar barely whispered, finally bringing himself to look in the eyes of Untersturmführer Weisner.

"No, most certainly not, Herr Brettenheimer." The young officer motioned to one of his subordinates and took a paper from the folder that the man held out for him. "Here's your new placement order. You are allowed to take several suitcases with you, but bear in mind that the things that you are allowed to take must not include anything of the value to the Reich. No jewelry and no money – only thirty zloty for a family is permitted."

Emilia moved away from the table when one of Weisner's subordinates smiled and pointed at the big silver menorah behind her back. She watched him put that on his list as well. Oskar thoroughly read the paper, with Hannah looking over his shoulder, wringing her hands.

"But it's in Krakow." Oskar glanced at the officer again. "How are we to get to Krakow from here?"

"Do not worry about that, Herr Brettenheimer, we'll provide you with transportation." Another formal, but at least polite, answer followed. "The trucks that will take you there, together with the rest of the people from your area, are already waiting outside. When you're finished packing any approved items, you may proceed to take your place in one of them. Only, don't forget to give your names to the receiving officer."

Less than an hour later, Emilia went outside to guard the two suitcases which her mother had already packed, and watched her father begging Untersturmführer Weisner to let them at least keep their family jewelry. Judging by the officer's look, it was in vain.

Emilia peered into distance, ignoring the looks which the soldiers supervising the eviction in their area kept throwing her way. One of them stopped indecisively in front of her and asked if she was Jewish. Emilia put her hand into her pocket, took out the armband she had been given, which had a blue star on it, and silently pulled it onto her sleeve.

"I'm sorry, I forgot," she replied, with absolutely no emotion in her voice.

The man only nodded and hurried away from her. Emilia was already used to such confusion by now about her family's background: her whole family had fair looks, and her own ashen blonde hair and gray eyes had saved them from the usual harassment that the darker looking Jews had recently been subjected to. One day, walking from the grocer with her older brother Ariel, she saw a group of soldiers posing for a picture that one of them was taking. Laughing and cheering, they surrounded three Orthodox Jews and began cutting off their payos and beards with their army knives, putting the cut hair on themselves and laughing even harder at that. Ariel had grabbed Emilia's elbow protectively and rushed to lead her away, before the soldiers noticed them and their armbands.

Emilia didn't know what to feel now. Being the only girl in the family, she was used to the dotting attitude of her father and her brothers, and throughout her entire, short nineteen years of life she had been sheltered from all the troubles and horrors of the world; only now, that horror had come to their house and slapped them right in the face. They were to be thrown out of their house, herded together with their religious and non-religious neighbors, which, as it turned out, made no difference to the Nazis at all, and would be forced to go to the other side of the country, where they barely spoke the language. Emilia kept looking at the sky, feeling completely empty inside.

"Fraulein."

Emilia lifted her head to see one of the soldiers, who was standing inside the nearest truck and holding out his hand for her, to help her get inside. Emilia pointed at the suitcases at her feet, but the soldier only smiled and motioned once again for her to get inside.

"Don't worry about you luggage, I'll help you with it in a minute."

Emilia looked back at her father, still pleading with Untersturmführer Weisner, and at her mother, who carried another two heavy suitcases out of the house, and she gave the soldier her hands. He easily pulled her inside the truck and laughed.

"You're as light as a feather! Let me go get your suitcases, fraulein."

He jumped down, picked up the luggage and effortlessly flung it inside the truck, where Emilia immediately arranged it under her feet. The soldier gave her another wide grin, before an older woman fumbled with the high step and accidentally brushed his shoulder, to which he roughly pushed her inside, his whole demeanor changing completely.

"Get on with it, you fat cow! Isn't it enough for your lot to feast on our hard earned money! You'll lose all your weight soon, you'll see!"

The woman stumbled again from the rough shove and fell on her knees, then brought herself to stand by Emilia to dust herself off. The soldier, meanwhile, broke into another beaming smile, as if nothing had happened.

"So, what's your name, fraulein?"

"Emilia," she replied quietly, intimidated, but not wanting to antagonize the soldier at the same time. "Emilia Brettenheimer."

"I'm Rudi. I'll be transporting you today."

Emilia gave him another faint smile, not knowing what to say. The woman took a place opposite her on a wooden bench and began throwing her hostile glares. Emilia just wanted to look away from them both and pretend that she wasn't even there, but she noticed her mother struggling with suitcases behind her new acquaintance's back. Fearing the same violent reaction from him, Emilia quickly jumped to her feet and crouched by the step, holding her hands out to her mother.

Surprisingly, Rudi helped her mother up into the truck in the same gentle manner as he had done with Emilia and, after handing them the rest of their suitcases, winked at Emilia. The big woman, sitting across from them, openly snorted with contempt.

"Where is Ariel, Alfred and Martin?" Emilia whispered in her mother's ear, trying to get rid of unwanted attention from both Rudi and her new neighbor.

Her brothers were working at one of the factories in the center of the city, and Emilia was afraid that they would lose each other in the rush of the forced eviction.

"Herr Weisner said that everyone who is registered with their office is being transported to Krakow today. He said that the boys will be transported right from the factory, and that they'll meet us in Krakow. He assured us that they will be given the papers with the same address as ours, so we'll all be living together in the same place."

Emilia nodded. It seemed that Herr Weisner's word was the only thing they could count on at this point. Nothing else was certain anymore.

Krakow ghetto, January 1942

Emilia hurried away from him again. Unterscharführer Richter's laughter behind her back was a sound she was used to by now. Since they first arrived here, to the former Krakow slums that had been made into a Jewish ghetto by separating them from the rest of the city with a tall wall with barbed wire on top, he seemed to enjoy picking on her – although, picking wasn't quite the right word, but Emilia didn't know how else to call it – every time she passed by his assigned post as she went to work and back.

"Emmi!" He would call her name as soon as she approached the steps of his "office," (that's how everyone called it), which in reality was a more or less decent house made into SS guards' barracks. Most of the time he sat on the steps of his "office," smoking, with his machine gun lying casually by his side. "Emmi, why don't you love me, Emmi? Come into my office for a minute, I have tea and *dampfnudel* for you. Or even a ham sandwich, huh, Emmi?"

Emilia would only lower her head even more and rush past by him and his comrades, who were also chuckling at their friend's remarks. One time, however, he managed to catch her alone, without the rest of the women that she worked in the hospital with, and whose company she preferred to walk in. That day, when she was sent to get the doctor who was tending to one of his patients in their home, she was almost knocked off her feet by the tall and broad-shouldered SS guard Richter, when he had almost jumped out at her from around a corner.

"Did I scare you, Emmi?" He laughed, catching her by the shoulders.

"Yes, you did," she admitted, trying to worm herself out of his grip. He wouldn't let go. "Please, I need to get the doctor, a man is coughing very badly in the hospital…"

"The man will die anyway," Richter replied nonchalantly, his gloved hands still firmly gripping her shoulders. "Why don't you have some tea with me instead? You must be cold and hungry. Look at you, so pale and thin. Now, that's not good."

Emilia fought the desire to look around, in the hope that someone would appear to break the heavy silence and make Richter let go of her. Instead, she kept peering into his dark brown eyes, frowning and hoping that her pursed lips and a scowl would help. It didn't; the SS guard was very well used to it and wasn't put off by such expressions.

"Come, don't be afraid." He was already pulling her around the corner closer and closer to the doors of the barracks. "I don't bite."

Unterscharführer Richter finally let go of her arms, fixed the machine gun on his shoulder and ascended the stairs. Emilia threw another desperate gaze around the deserted street – even his comrades weren't on their usual post today – and followed the SS guard inside, not even knowing why she did so.

Inside the barracks, he motioned her to follow him along the long corridor to the kitchen, where he hanged his machine gun together with his overcoat and a uniform cap on the back of a chair and invited Emilia to do the same.

"Sit, sit, Emmi, don't be so shy. How long have we known each other for you to be so shy around me?" Richter relieved Emilia of her coat despite her weak protests and moved the chair up for her.

Emilia threw a quick glance at the machine gun, casually hanging off the chair within her reach, while Unterscharführer started fishing something out of the small cupboard. His actions, but more than that, his intentions, were of the utmost mystery to her, especially after he put the kettle onto the gas burner in the corner. Emilia was more than certain before that, when he had dragged her here, he had in mind something other than offering her tea. He turned around and smiled, fixing his thick dark mane with one hand.

"So, Emmi. Tell me about yourself."

"What do you want to know?" She barely whispered. Witnessing the brutal treatment that most of the habitants of the ghetto were subjected to daily, with random shootings on top of that, she tried to stay as far away as possible from the guards; having tea and a pleasant conversation with one of them was definitely the furthest thing from her agenda.

"I don't know. It's not an official interrogation." He laughed at his own jest, while Emilia kept eyeing him suspiciously. Even though Richter wasn't doing anything worse than really making tea, she still felt very uneasy in the SS guard's company. Why had she even followed him at all?

"I really have to go get the doctor, Herr Unterscharführer…" Emilia's voice trailed off despite her attempts to keep it firm. "Can I come back later, and then we talk about anything you want to?"

"Now, don't be silly. The tea will be done in two minutes." Richter motioned his head to the kettle and started arranging a few items on a platter. "Aren't you hungry?"

Emilia didn't reply, but only threw another glance at the heavy weapon that was so close to her that she could outstretch her arm and grab it in case… What case? She was afraid of all weapons, and she wouldn't even know how to shoot it anyway.

"What do you want from me?" Emilia asked in a straightforward manner, clasping her cold hands on her knees.

Richter turned around and lifted his brows in surprise. "What do I want? Nothing. I'm only being nice to you, aren't I?"

He put the platter with two ham sandwiches, several crackers and even sliced cheese in front of her. Emilia swallowed involuntarily. For almost nine months her family had had to eat whatever scarce rations they were allowed, which mainly consisted of potato soup, very little bread, and dried meat if they were lucky to get it on the black market once a week.

She didn't dare touch anything on the platter, even though her mouth was watering and her stomach was rumbling, much to her embarrassment. Richter put some tea into two mugs and filled them with steaming water.

"Eat, eat, don't just stare at it," he encouraged Emilia, placing one of the mugs in front of her. "You must be starving."

"What are you doing this for?" Emilia asked once again, well aware of the fact that the only free cheese offered in this place was in a mousetrap. She wanted to know the price, so she knew what she was getting herself into.

"Again with your suspicions!" The SS guard made a desperate gesture with his hands and laughed cheerfully. "I'm trying to be your friend, that's all."

"Why would you want to be friends with a Jew?"

"Jews can be very useful in many ways, Emmi. Please, no more talking until after you eat something."

"How much is it going to cost me?" Emilia asked flat out, getting a bit irritated with his games. The SS were never nice, and they most certainly didn't want to become friends with the likes of her.

"This? Nothing."

Emilia still didn't move a finger, until he stopped smiling and barked out, startling her, "Eat!"

She jerked in her seat, quickly picked up a ham sandwich and took a bite, trying not to look too terrified.

"It wasn't that hard, was it?" Unterscharführer Richter leaned back into his seat, picked up his tea mug, and broke into a grin again. "Why do you Jews always make everything so difficult for yourself? We're just trying to help you, but you're making our job so very hard. And then you wonder why one of your lot got beaten or shot again. You should just do as you're told."

Emilia nodded and kept chewing on her sandwich, afraid to anger her host again. He moved her mug of tea closer to her.

"Do you want sugar in it? I have sugar, too."

She nodded indecisively, more to please him than craving sugar; she hadn't tasted it since they'd been forced into the ghetto and got more than used to drinking regular, watered down tea or ersatz coffee. Richter reached into a small pot where the guards kept cubes of sugar, took one out and dropped it into Emilia's mug.

"Thank you," she whispered.

"My pleasure, Emmi." He eyed her for some time, sipping his tea before leaning forward to peer into her eyes. "You could eat like this every day, you know. You and your whole family. How many of you are there? Five?"

"Six," Emilia replied, wondering where he was leading with such a remark.

"Six!" Richter exclaimed and tsked several times, shaking his head, his sympathy being everything, but natural. "You must be all starving there. And what happens when your father or brothers get so sick from malnourishment, or your mother, God forbid… They won't be able to work anymore. I'd have to put them in the truck."

"No, not the truck!"

Emilia bit her tongue, but the guard smiled slowly, catching onto her fear. Everyone in the ghetto knew what those trucks meant: permanent resettlement, as the SS were calling it. In reality, everyone knew that the ones who got into one of those trucks, never came back.

"Well, then you have to take care of them, don't you?" Emilia froze under his steady, piercing gaze, with sandwich near her mouth. "Eat, eat, Emmi. It would be a shame, if a pretty girl like yourself got sick too."

Emilia took another bite, trying not to burst into tears.

"Are you afraid of me, Emmi?"

She barely nodded, without looking up.

"Why? You shouldn't be. I'm trying to do the right thing by you."

A heavy pause followed, disturbed only by the clock ticking on the wall and Unterscharführer sipping his tea.

"I don't have any money to pay you," Emilia uttered at last, just to break the silence.

"Most likely you don't. But, after working here from the very first day of this place opening, I've learned a lot about your people, Emmi. You aren't stupid, that I have to give you. I know that you bring a lot of things with you that you shouldn't be bringing. Jewelry, diamonds... You understand, what I mean. Only, it's all useless now, believe me. You won't be getting out of here anytime soon. The chances are bigger that you'll die starving in the next few years, if you don't catch typhus or any other disease. I'm not saying it to frighten you by any means; I'm only saying it how it is. I know you're a smart girl and realize what's going on. Why don't you take a bigger chance than the rest of your lot and at least feed yourselves while you still can? I've helped many of you already, and they have all been more than grateful. Some did get resettled, some died, but... that's not my fault, really. I've only been doing the right thing. So, what do you say? Get your chance while you can, because you never know when they might transfer me someplace else, and then you're all done for. Let's help each other while we still can."

"We don't have anything... My parents weren't even allowed to keep their wedding rings," Emilia muttered, fearing his reaction.

Surprisingly, Richter only smiled widely at her and nodded. "I've heard that before, too. Drink your tea, finish your meal, and come to me when you 'remember' that you actually have something hidden in your floor. Or the wall. Or sewn into your clothes."

He laughed again. Emilia couldn't taste her food anymore and had only one wish: to get out of there and to never come back.

Chapter 2

Krakow ghetto, May 1942

"Well, maybe we should bring it to him. What would giving away one ring do really?"

"Hannah, no! Then they'll know that we do have jewelry on us and they will wreck the whole apartment looking for it. I've seen them do it many times before. And we'll get shot for concealing it!"

"Ari needs medicine, Oskar, and the SS most certainly have it, or can get it for that matter. We should use Unterscharführer Richter's offer and ask him for it."

Emilia was listening to her parents argue for the third day in a row, while tending to her sick brother. The doctor had reassured them that Ari had caught the flu, not typhus thankfully, which was what they feared the most. The doctor was an old man who was kind enough to have come to their apartment when it became obvious that Ariel wouldn't be able to make it to the hospital on his own. Although it was just the flu, without proper treatment and, obviously, with their lack of food, Ari's chances weren't so good.

Emilia flipped the wet cloth on her brother's forehead – the only thing she could do to relieve his high fever. Ariel had always been her favorite brother, maybe because he was closer to her age – only seven years older than her – while Martin and Alfred were well into their thirties. Ariel was the one who had always been willing to give her piggyback rides when she was just a child. He was the one who had always agreed to play dolls with her and who had always, every single day, waited for her on the school porch to walk her home – especially when she got older – so no boys would bother her.

Emilia chuckled. Boys had always bothered her, as long as she could remember. Even *Hitlerjugend* boys in school, despite the fact that she was Jewish, and everyone was very well aware of that. They sometimes used to encircle her in the hallway, before she could walk out, and try to talk to her about something so very insignificant, like the weather outside or Frau Meyer's last class. It made her wonder sometimes what they wanted in the first place. One time they didn't talk at all, but just stood around her in a tight circle of black uniforms, to just stare at her. Emilia tried not to walk anywhere alone after that particular incident.

Ariel moaned in his half-conscious sleep, and Emilia rushed to take his hand and rub it slightly, as a gesture of her silent support. She felt so miserably helpless, but even more, she feared the moment when he'd wake up at last and look at her with those eyes, full of tears and agony – that was the worst part. She could never stand anyone whom she loved to suffer from pain that she had no means to ease. Or did she?

"Papa, I think Mama is right." She addressed her father without leaving Ariel's side. In their tiny apartment she knew that he'd hear her from the small kitchen, where he was whisper-arguing with her mother. "We should take a ring to Unterscharführer Richter. He won't do a search on our apartment, because if he did he would have to list everything he finds and give it back to the *Reichsbank*. He doesn't want that. He wants to pocket all of it for himself. It would be silly for him to search us. He'll still get everything we have, only one by one, item by item, and we'll give it all willingly, so he won't even have to go through the pains of searching and interrogating us."

Oskar walked into the room and looked at his young daughter in surprise. "And where did you learn such fine deduction, young lady? Reading all those English books about that French detective, no doubt."

"No." Emilia shrugged. "I learned it here. Life is the best teacher. I look around and make conclusions, that's all."

"You're too young to talk about such matters, *mein herz*." Oskar approached the bed, which used to be his and Hannah's before Ariel got sick and they'd put him there. The rest of them slept on makeshift mattresses on the floor, huddling next to each other to keep warm. It was lucky that spring had come, for winter in the ghetto without any heat available, besides from a small gas burner, was indeed brutal. Martin and Alfred often said that they couldn't wait to get to work because they could keep warm that way. "How is Ari doing?"

"The same. The fever is not going away. The doctor left some aspirin for him, but…" Emilia spread her arms in a helpless gesture. What good would aspirin really do?

"Ach, what can we do?" Oskar sighed heavily.

"We can talk to Unterscharführer Richter." Hannah used the pause to try and persuade her husband once again. "If Emilia says she knows him—"

"I don't want Emilia to deal with that man!" Oskar interrupted her sternly and frowned at his daughter as well. "Emilia has no business with the SS! I don't know why she spoke to him in the first place."

"I didn't want to speak to him, he wanted to talk to me."

"Well, there won't be any talking between the two of you anymore!"

"Papa, but what about Ari?"

"Ari will be fine."

"He'll die!"

"Stop saying such things! He won't die!"

"He will and you know it perfectly well! I work in the hospital, I see tens of people die daily from things far less serious than the flu! One man got a splinter in his finger and in just two weeks without treatment he died from sepsis! A simple splinter!"

"I said no, and that's the end of it! I'm still the head of this family, and I make the decisions here, young lady!"

Emilia didn't reply, but pursed her lips defiantly. She knew by now that there was no reasoning with her father, yet she still set her mind on getting her way. Her brother wasn't going to die like those that she tended daily in the hospital. Her father was stubborn, but she was his daughter. She was stubborn too.

"Where does he keep it?" Emilia cornered her mother in the kitchen as soon as her father left for his work at one of the factories.

The SS main office, that managed the ghetto, made good profit out of the Jews, lending them to the factory owners. The Jewish laborers cost far less than the gentile Polish ones, but the workers themselves didn't even get the money – the SS office did. The Jews were lucky to get their ration cards weekly – the Jews that could work that is. The ones that couldn't were put in trucks without further consideration or sometimes shot on the spot so as not to waste gasoline.

"Keeps what, Emmi?" Hannah turned to her daughter, wiping her hands on her apron.

When they were packing their belongings before the eviction they had wisely decided to take mostly dark clothes with them – they looked cleaner than white clothing would have. There was no hot water in the ghetto, but both Emilia and Hannah managed to keep everything neat and clean, warming the water on the gas burner and washing their garments daily in a small basin. There was a communal bathroom on their floor, but it was so old, rusty and dirty that the Brettenheimers spent what little money they had to buy a bigger aluminum basin for themselves, and they washed in that instead. They were lucky to get soap also, because Martin and Alfred did some smuggling on the black market, even though they never openly admitted it to neither their parents nor their sister. They sometimes bought items that were almost impossible to get otherwise.

"The jewelry. The jewelry that he hid in the lining of our coats. Where does he keep it?"

Despite Oskar's hopes for a safe return to Germany, even while they lived quite safely in their old house, common sense did prevail in the man, and he had decided to hide some of their possessions in different items of the family's clothing; mostly jackets that had a thick lining and trousers with double lining in the belt area.

Emilia had only found out about it not that long ago, after she told her parents about the strange conversation she had had with Unterscharführer Richter. Hannah had accidentally blurted out that maybe they should use one of their hidden things to buy some food.

"Emmi…"

"Mama, Ari has been moaning all night and all morning. He's obviously in horrible pain. He keeps turning and twisting and I can't take his whimpering anymore. He never whimpers!"

"Emmi, don't you think I don't hear it? He's my child after all!"

"So tell me where Papa keeps it! We'll only take one ring, he won't even notice. And even if he does, he'll thank us later, you'll see."

"Emmi, I don't know…"

"Mama, I will start opening up the floorboards with this very knife if you don't tell me." Even though Emilia's tone when she pronounced those last words was unemotional and leveled, the look of deadly determination on the girl's face, together with a big butcher's knife she held in her little hand, assured Hannah of her daughter's intentions.

"It's in the vent, not in the floor," Hannah finally replied, pointing at the small caged opening near the ceiling. "Pull up a chair, open the gate and carefully put your hand inside. There's a small piece of wood that is stuck like a shelf in between the two walls. The handkerchief with jewelry in it is on top of it."

Several hours later Emilia was on her way to meet Unterscharführer Richter.

Krakow ghetto, October 1942

"This is the last one," Emilia said in barely audible voice, handing Unterscharführer Richter a small round diamond earring.

Its sister made its way into the SS man's pocket two weeks ago and bought the family a weekly supply of margarine, bread – the real one, not the type that tasted as if it was made of sawdust – sugar, some *kielbasa,* cheese and even a little milk and morphine, which the Brettenheimers decided to store in the apartment just in case, afraid that another family member might fall ill in future. Almost six months had passed since Ariel had gotten better from his flu (thanks to the much needed medicine, which was shamelessly "confiscated" by Richter from a local hospital for gentiles and even more shamelessly sold to yet another Jewish family in need – their family), and since then Oskar had come to terms with the new order, set by his daughter and backed by his wife. He had begun to accept that they had to live in the moment, and in order to survive in that moment, they had to be healthy enough to pass each inspection, regularly scheduled by the SS main office, which aimed to weed out all unable workers and send them for "resettlement," enabling free space in the ghetto to be acquired for the new working force, herded and transported from all the occupied territories. Oskar did try to protest at first, but after watching their neighbors, who occupied the same floor, being put on a truck – the whole family, parents, their son, daughter-in-law, and their three small children – he finally gave in, and handed Emilia the first, and the least valuable, golden ring.

Emilia recalled how her hands had trembled when she headed to Unterscharführer Richter's office for the first time, with the ring she had taken from the vent. It was almost curfew time, but she had to make sure that it was too dark for any of their neighbors to see her walk in the direction of the office. It would certainly raise a lot of unnecessary questions, especially if anyone from *Jupo* – the Jewish police, which were sometimes worse than the German Gestapo in their desire to sell each and every one of their kin just to keep in the good graces of their new Aryan masters – stopped her for questioning.

Emilia stopped indecisively not too far from the SS living quarters, pulled the ends of her thin overcoat closer together and frowned at the guard, who was lazily leaning on the wall near the entrance, smoking. Emilia stepped a little closer, into the light of the lamp hanging above the door, under which the soldier was standing on guard. He noticed her at last, and after looking her up and down with a scowl he barked, "What do you want? It's almost curfew time."

"Unterscharführer Richter told me to come see him…" Emilia replied quietly, fondling the ring inside her pocket.

"What?" The soldier leaned slightly forward, scowling deeper. "I can't hear what you're saying, speak louder!"

"Unterscharführer Richter!" Emilia repeated louder this time, afraid to be chased away. Her brother needed her help, and she had promised herself that she would go through with the whole enterprise and not leave without medicine, no matter how terrified she felt inside.

The soldier snorted for some reason, but nevertheless opened the door and yelled something inside, probably telling one of his comrades to call his superior. He didn't speak another word with her afterwards, just kept eyeing her up and down, and even though Emilia looked at the ground under her feet, having learnt by now not to stare in the eyes of the guards so as not to provoke them, she could still feel his heavy gaze scrutinizing her frail frame. She was almost relieved when Richter came out onto the porch and spread his arms in a mock welcome.

"Emmi! You finally honored our modest house with your presence! Come inside." The last words sounded more like an order than an invitation. Emilia took a deep breath and obeyed.

Inside the living quarters she was met with cheerful banter and occasional bursts of loud laughter coming from the kitchen, together with the faint smell of recently consumed dinner, a much stronger smell of alcohol and heavy smoke from the SS guards' cigarettes. Richter opened the door to one of the rooms for her and for a second she locked eyes with one of the SS men, sitting by the table in his undershirt, like several of his comrades. He leaned towards his neighbor, whispered something in his ear, nodded toward Emilia, before they both burst into laughter. She slid inside the room as fast as she could, instinctively lowering her head.

Richter locked the door. It was quite a spartan room, although it looked like a palace compared to where Emilia and her family had to live. He walked over to the desk in the corner, above which hung the portrait of the Führer, to where a small black radio sat. Unterscharführer turned it on rather loudly and walked over to Emilia, closer than she wished him to. Yet, she found enough strength in her not to step back.

"Here," she said, taking the ring out of her pocket and holding it in front of her host on her open palm. "I need something to treat flu with. Morphine preferably. Something for the high fever. Anything you can get."

Richter chuckled, picking the ring up and inspecting it with his eyes slightly squinted.

"This cheap, tiny thing will only get you half a vial of morphine, Emmi. Now, if you want me to get you the good medicine and pills that we treat our people with, you bring me something worth my effort, preferably diamonds. I'm sure you have some of those in that hiding place of yours, where you fished this little contraband from."

Emilia couldn't believe his nonchalant tone, nor the cold calculation in his words. She stood quiet for a moment, trying to form indignant words.

"But this is the highest quality gold, Herr Unterscharführer! In Germany this golden ring could feed our family for a month!"

"Only, we're not in Germany anymore, are we, fraulein?" Richter arched his brow with a smirk, playing with her family ring by throwing it up in the air and catching it without taking his black eyes off the girl. "The prices are a bit different here, and so is the market. You should be grateful I'm dealing with you at all, and just because I have a kind heart."

Kind heart?! You're the greediest pig I know, feasting on other people's misfortunes, stripping them bare before sending them off to certain death! Emilia wanted to scream, but she bit her tongue inside her mouth, and nodded slowly, even though she still showed defiance in her eyes. Richter noticed it, most certainly, because he smirked too obviously.

"Can I have morphine now and I'll bring you something else tomorrow morning, on my way to work? I'm afraid my brother won't make it through the night."

Unterscharführer eyed her for a while, then turned to his desk and, after shuffling through one of the drawers, in which the ring immediately disappeared, he took out a small glass vial and handed it to her.

"It's only because of our special friendship that I'm doing this, Emmi."

Emilia couldn't help shooting him a hostile glare in response to the obvious insincerity of his words, quickly hiding the small vial in her pocket.

"You're feisty." Richter chuckled once again. "I like that."

"Can I have a syringe, too?" Emilia asked, ignoring his previous remark.

"What am I, a medical ward?"

"But how am I going to administer it?"

"That's not my problem. You're the nurse here, you think of something." He followed his words with a shoulder shrug.

"Thank you, Herr Unterscharführer," Emilia mumbled, already knowing that any pleading would be in vain.

"See you tomorrow, Emmi." Richter went to the door to unlock it, but paused. He again leaned in too close to Emilia and whispered in her ear, "And don't be greedy. Bring something really valuable, and I might give you some food for your brother as well. He needs it just as much as medicine."

Emilia nodded just to get away from him, and almost ran along the smoke-filled corridor to the welcoming darkness of the night. On her way home she kept rubbing her ear, trying to get rid of the shivers that Richter's warm breath had sent along her spine. She promised herself that as soon as Ari got better, she would change her route to work just to stay away from Unterscharführer; he reminded her of those silent, but menacing *Hitlerjugend* boys at her school, only now she didn't have anyone to protect her from him, except herself.

However, despite all the promises she made to herself, Emilia continued her meetings with Richter every other week, which helped her family keep safe during the selections, held at least once a month, and kept them somewhat fed and much better off, compared to their less fortunate neighbors. However, in a very short few months the Brettenheimers had run out of their scarce hidden possessions.

"It's the last one," Emilia repeated after the earring made its way into Richter's pocket.

"Well, that's very unfortunate," the SS man replied, handing her food wrapped in the local newspaper. She had to rely on his good graces and honesty concerning what goods she was getting from him. Sometimes, he was generous enough to casually drop a few cubes of sugar in her pocket, one by one, all the while smirking at her. Emilia learned not to show her temper; after all, food at this point was much more important than one's hurt pride. "Another selection is coming up, and this one will be a serious one."

He paused for dramatic effect while Emilia searched his face, trying to decide if he was just trying to extort more inexistent money from her, or if he was speaking the truth. She could never tell, with his constant jests and half-hearted replies.

"They will be cleaning out most of the ghetto. Only essential workers with permits will be allowed to stay. The rest – out." Richter smiled, observing Emilia's reaction.

"Well, my brothers are all essential workers. Most certainly we'll be allowed to stay," Emilia protested.

"Your brothers – yes. Your father is not an essential worker, though. Neither is your mother." Unterscharführer Richter flicked a lighter and finished his thought. "And neither are you."

Emilia stood in front of him silently, trying her best not to break down or start screaming accusations at him. *All this time you were sucking our blood, throwing us whatever pathetic leftovers you had from your own table, calling it a decent meal, and now after we have run out of our resources, you're going to throw us in the truck?! What kind of a human being are you after that?!*

"I'm sorry, Emmi." Richter smiled again, spreading his arms in a helpless gesture. "I really do like you. But it's business. You're Jewish, you should understand it better than anybody."

"Business." Emilia nodded several times, frowning. "So, I'm going to be resettled, together with my parents."

Richter shrugged thoughtfully, raised his brow and squinted his eyes slightly, giving Emilia an evaluating look up and down.

"Not necessarily, if you have something else to offer me."

"I just told you, it was the last earring we had," Emilia repeated, this time with unmasked anger in her voice. "I have no money to pay you. You took everything."

Richter took a long drag on his cigarette, pondered something and then motioned his head in her direction.

"Open your coat."

"What for?" Emilia frowned.

Unterscharführer shrugged nonchalantly and went to his desk. "Go to resettlement then, what do I care?"

With those words he picked up a piece of paper and started writing something, as if completely forgetting about the girl's presence in his room. Emilia glanced at the door, then at Richter and then at the door again. She could just walk out of there and hope that fate would be merciful to her and her parents. *To me, maybe,* she thought. *I'm young and still strong, and I can work. My parents on the other hand...*

Papa's heart is weak, and Mama... Mama has never worked a day in her life. What will happen to her?

She had witnessed too many times what happened to those who were of no value to the Reich; sometimes they were executed right here, inside the ghetto, in front of everybody's eyes. Emilia couldn't run the chance of this happening to her parents. She slowly lifted her hand to the top button of her coat and, one by one, undid them all. Richter didn't seem to take any notice, though, as he devoted all his attention to the paper in front of him. Emilia knew that he was doing it on purpose, just to humiliate her even more with the uncomfortable wait for him to acknowledge her action.

"Herr Unterscharführer." She finally called him quietly, trying to hide the sense of resentment from her voice.

He turned in his seat at last, lifting his brow in mock surprise. "You're still here? Hm."

Emilia looked away under his scrutinizing gaze and jerked slightly at another request from him. "Open your coat."

She sighed, but did as she was told, still looking at the floor. She noticed ugly brownish paint covering the wood, worn out with time, the unevenness of one of the boards, scratches left by the chair on the floor and every insignificant, and so very irrelevant, detail, just to shut her mind off from Richter and his stare. It didn't help when he spoke once again. "Lift up your skirt."

Blushing to the roots of her hair, Emilia fumbled with one of the buttons on her coat, not able to bring herself to do as she was told, frantically thinking of fleeing these God forsaken SS living quarters once and for all, and come what may. No, not this, this she could never do. Trading jewelry for food and safety was one thing, but this... Not a single person had seen her indecent before, not even her own mother since Emilia turned twelve and suddenly became too aware of her changing body. She was even too ashamed to change into her night gown if her mother was in her bedroom. Her mother... *Laying in a pool of blood by the wall together with the rest of the executed Jews in less than a few days...* the thought flashed through Emilia's mind without warning. She pressed her tongue against her clenched teeth, inside her tightly closed mouth, concentrated all her attention on a little splinter in the board under her feet and slowly lifted her long woolen skirt just above her knees, to expose her grey stockings, which Martin, her oldest brother, got for her and her mother on the black market, in an attempt to keep them somewhat warm.

"Higher."

Emilia swallowed hard and lifted the skirt a few centimeters higher.

"Higher." Richter rose his voice slightly, giving way to irritation. "I want to see what I'm buying before making a deal."

Trying her best to contain her tears, Emilia moved the skirt up to her thighs with shaking fingers and froze where she stood, silently hoping that the earth would swallow her in that instant and end her sufferings. Richter's contemptuous snorting only added to the insult.

"A little too skinny for my taste, but… oh, well." He waved the girl off and turned back to the paper on his desk. "Meet me this Saturday at the corner of this building, at 19.00 sharp. Now off you go!"

Emilia ran out of the room, crashed into another SS guard walking along the corridor in her direction, apologized brusquely and rushed outside, shaking, with bitter tears flowing freely down her face. No, she would never come back here. Never.

Chapter 3

"You need to run." Martin raked his ash-blond hair with his never-healing, calloused hands and nodded several times, as if in confirmation of his own words. "All three of you."

He glanced at Emilia, sitting on the mattress next to him and then at his parents, who were holding hands sitting on the only bed. Alfred sniffled and Ari couldn't stop biting his nails.

"I can set everything up for tomorrow night," Martin continued. "I'll take you to the sewers from where people from the *Armia Krajowa* will get you out on the Aryan side. Too bad that we didn't save anything from Richter, as I had no money to pay for your papers, but I managed to secure clean clothes for you, so you won't cause suspicion at first."

"And how far do you think we'll get without money and papers?" Oskar sighed, voicing everyone's thoughts. "Yes, luckily we do look like gentiles, but it will only take us so far. Where are we going to live? We can't even rent a room without proper registration. We can't sleep in the street either, it's the first and foremost giveaway sign. We'll just get arrested and transported here again... or worse. No, I say, we stay here instead and see how it goes."

"See how it goes?" Martin leaned forward, trying not to raise his voice too much. "They're cleaning out the whole ghetto, Papa! Everyone without an essential worker's card will be put in the truck, and then that's it. Resettlement."

"Maybe resettlement is not so bad after all," Emilia's mother chimed in quietly.

"What are you saying, not so bad?" Alfred seemed to awake from his brooding. "The people that go to the working camps never come back! There's only one way out of there – to the trench on the side of the road, or wherever they're dumping the bodies."

"Stop it!" Ariel nudged his brother with his shoulder. "Mama and Emmi are terrified as it is, and here you go, with your bodies!"

Emilia though didn't even stir at the comment; a comment that would normally make her break into a cold sweat. She'd been living in the ghetto far too long, seeing those very bodies Alfred was talking about – in the streets and in the hospital where she was working. She'd seen them all, stricken by diseases, emaciated, beaten by the guards, bloated from water they kept drinking to at least somehow fill their stomachs when food wasn't an option, dying of hepatitis, typhus, kidney or liver failure… No, dead people weren't frightening to her anymore, it was living people who she had to be afraid of, that she knew very well by now; the same people who she grew up with in one country and who suddenly declared war on her whole race: her fellow Germans.

"No, Mama and Papa are right. Running alone without money and papers is not an option," Emilia said, twisting the end of her braid in her fingers, looking without blinking at the bed, on which her parents were sitting. "Martin, your people from the *Armia* won't help us either. They need to be paid as well, just like the SS. They won't do anything for free, and we'll be left stranded and we'll just get arrested. No… We better stay here."

"And just surrender to them?" Martin hissed. "Let them take you away to the camps without even trying to save yourselves? That's their perfect strategy, making everyone so obedient that they won't even put up a fight until the very last one is slaughtered. But this won't last long, you'll see. We're already gathering weapons and ammunition to give those SS a little taste of their own medicine, and see how they like it!"

Alfred shushed him under Oskar's stare.

"Marti, what are you saying? You aren't getting involved with those partisans from the *Armia,* are you?"

"No, no, Papa, he's not," Alfred rushed to reassure him, but Emilia still caught on to the falseness in his voice. "It's just a common fantasy our working lot here like to talk about. It's nothing, really. Just talk. Keeps our spirits high."

Oskar slowly nodded, choosing to believe his middle son. *Poor Papa,* Emilia smiled inwardly, *always trying to persuade himself to what suits him best. Maybe it's better that way though… Saves him heartache.* Her thoughts started trailing off, back to the old carefree days in Munich, with trips to the lake every summer, with ice cream after school, with the first SA troopers goose-stepping at the parades that her father took her to, all dressed up and with big bows in her hair. Oskar wanted to believe that the new regime would save his country from their external enemies, but till the very last day it seemed he would refuse to believe that he and his family would be announced as internal enemies of that very state. That his daughter, who he had lifted up in his arms so she could give flowers to the passing SA troops, would be stripped of what was supposed to be the happiest years of her life and quite possibly die at the hands of those soldiers; soldiers who had kissed her smiling cheeks just several years ago.

Emilia leaned onto the wall and soon started nodding off, exhausted by the hard work in the hospital and the heated family discussion. Used to sleeping with one eye open, just in case, she heard how her parents wished her brothers good night, leaving their decision for the next morning, and how, later, when they had fallen asleep, Alfred chastised Martin in quiet whispers that he shouldn't have been opening his mouth at all concerning their Underground business. From their whispering, Emilia understood that not only were her older brothers most certainly the partisans that her father was in such awe of, saying that they would only anger the SS even more and have them all killed for sure, but that they wanted to keep Ari out of their affairs.

"You think they'll have a chance out there?"

Emilia continued breathing deeply, not indicating that she was awake, hoping to hear the truth from Martin and Alfred, not sugarcoated for her and her mother's sake, at least for once in her life.

"I don't know. I really don't." Martin sighed heavily. "I'm more afraid for Emmi. They have a sixth sense when it comes to anyone in hiding."

"The *Jupo?* "

"Yes, the *Jupo,* but their snitches are even worse. I don't know if she's better going to the resettlement. This way she'll at least die almost instantly."

"Don't you say that!"

"What? What do you think those rats outside will do to her as soon as they learn that she has no papers, and that she's a Jew on top of it? They'll sell her right back to the Gestapo for their fifty zloty, but not before they have their share of her."

"Martin!"

"She's too pretty for her own good."

Emilia swallowed her tears silently before she heard them starting to snore evenly, and only then she allowed herself to weep soundlessly, clenching the mattress with one hand and pressing herself into the wall so as not to wake up Ari with her body, shaking with hysterics. Her young mind just couldn't understand how she had become trapped inside this nightmare, from which there was no escape, not outside, nor inside the ghetto. After she'd cried till there were no more tears left, she made up her mind. She'd never met these "*Jupo* snitches" as Martin called them, and she had no intention of meeting them. Richter was at least a familiar evil to choose. He wasn't the vilest of human beings, compared to some that she'd met. Instead, he was just a common opportunist, and at least he had treated her fairly well so far, even though it was only due to her money. He was clean and not that bad looking either. And what was more important, he was alone, and not one of God knew how many of those people outside that Martin was so worried about. Emilia wiped away the last of her tears and sighed almost contentedly, wondering casually whether some people felt the same calmness, ready to accept their fate and face it, when they were condemned to the gallows.

———————

Emilia kept hiding her face from any passing SS guards, fearing that maybe Richter had changed his mind and wouldn't come to the corner at all. She turned her face away every time she heard approaching steps, afraid to be seen by the *Jupo,* or worse, someone who could tell her brothers or family that she was loitering by the SS barracks without any seemingly good reason. Emilia stole another glance at the hand-watch that she had been miraculously allowed to keep due to it being pretty much worthless, and lifted her collar even more, starting to bite her already red finger relentlessly.

"Ach, here you are."

Emilia nearly jumped, startled by the voice behind her back. She turned around to see Unterscharführer Richter's smirk in its usual place.

"Hello, Herr Unterscharführer," she muttered softly, lowering her eyes to the ground and feeling the heat burning her cheeks with shame. Maybe she shouldn't have come here at all, maybe she should've taken her chances outside the ghetto or maybe it would have been better to let them take her to the labor camps and get it over with. Only, they wouldn't kill her off at once, she knew with certainty. They would almost certainly kill her parents first, and she wouldn't be able to live with that kind of guilt on her conscience.

"I was almost certain that you wouldn't come." Richter flickered his lighter, looking the girl up and down. "After you ran out on me like you did."

Emilia shrugged slightly with one shoulder, or actually jerked it in a dismissive manner. *So, it means that you were of a better opinion of me than what I really am,* she almost told him. She didn't know who she was anymore. The old, good Emilia would have never agreed to anything like this. This new person was a stranger to her, with a plagued mind and a frown that seemed to be forever stuck to her otherwise pretty face, and Emilia didn't like her at all.

"All right then. Come," Richter commanded and started walking in a direction away from the barracks, not even caring to check if she followed him. He was sure that she did, and he was right.

Emilia kept her head low, concentrating on the iron glistening on the soles of Richter's heavy boots with every step he took. The sound of that iron on the cobble road reminded her of her grandfather's – or *Opa* as Emilia fondly called him – chronometer, which he bought from some clock master a long time ago and had cherished as one of his most prized possessions. He had enjoyed collecting old clocks and chronometers, and would often invite little Emilia to the special room that he kept especially for his priceless collection, telling her with his soft voice about the origin of each and every item, about their previous, famous owners and the family secrets that the object related to. And later, after some tea with milk, that little Emilia liked to dip her cookies into, he would wink at his favorite granddaughter with a conspirator's look and open a chess board and allow Emilia to choose the color of her army. She always chose white…

"Come inside."

Deep in her memories, trying to distract herself from the inevitable, Emilia didn't notice how they had made their way to a deserted part of the ghetto, no doubt already cleaned out during one of the latest *Aktions*. Richter actually held the door open for her. Emilia glanced at him once again and slid inside a dark corridor, doing her best not to brush him accidentally with her shoulder.

"Go up to the third floor. There was a decent bed there last time I checked."

The casualness of his voice, and the shuffling of his overcoat behind her back now that she was walking in front of him, made her hands tremble even more than they were before. Emilia noticed her shaking hands with hatred, and railed against her weakness, as she held onto an old wooden railing along the steps.

"Where to?" She hated how meek her voice sounded when she stopped on the third floor, looking at the four doors near the staircase.

"This one." Richter pushed the door open to one of the apartments, motioning with his head for the girl to follow him inside.

Don't do it, don't do it, don't, you won't be able to fix anything once it's done, the old Emilia kept pleading with her inside her mind. *There must be some other way! What would Opa say about his little girl? You'd break his heart!*

He's dead! Emilia shouted back at the pleading voice inside her mind and almost stumbled upon an old rug as she followed Richter inside. *Stop doing this to me. Please, stop talking. I can't think about anything now. No, no thinking anymore. All the words don't matter anyway. This does. This needs to be done to save us all. It's still better than death. I'm not scared. I'd have to do this with my husband anyway. All women do. There's nothing to be afraid of…*

My husband… Maybe it would be better to pretend that he's my husband, Emilia thought, lifting her eyes for the first time to look at the SS guard standing in the door of the apartment's bedroom. Richter smiled at her encouragingly and made a mocking gesture with his arm, as if saying, *after you, fraulein.* Emilia walked inside. Yes, there it was, a "pretty decent bed" as Richter called it, even made up by someone, who was either already dead or still working in the labor camp "for the prosperity of the Great German Reich." Emilia looked back at Richter again, who was undoing the belt of his overcoat, which had the words *"Meine Ehre heißt Treue"* on it. *My honor is loyalty. Honor…* Emilia swallowed hard and started unbuttoning her overcoat with fingers that refused to listen to her.

Yes, I'll just keep thinking that he's my husband. We just got married and this is our beautiful new apartment in Munich. And he loves me and cares about me. And I care about him. Yes, I'll just keep thinking this way…

Richter meanwhile didn't rush to get rid of the rest of his clothes, after dropping his overcoat and his belt with its holster on an old Viennese chair. He unhurriedly lit another cigarette and nodded at Emilia, who stood motionless in front of the bed.

"Well? Are you going to undress or are you waiting for a dinner with flowers first?"

Emilia looked at him with reproach, slightly tilting her head to one side as if asking a silent question, *why are you making this even worse for me? Don't you feel any compassion for me at all? I came here to give you my most precious possession, and you mock me on top of it? Is there anything human in you at all?*

"I've never done this before," she finally whispered, looking at her feet again.

"I figured as much." Richter chuckled, stubbed his unfinished cigarette out with his heel and walked over to her. "I don't even know why I agreed to this. You won't even know what to do."

He took her coat off her and unbuttoned the jacket under it, while Emilia stood staring with unblinking eyes at the ribbon going through the second buttonhole of his uniform.

"Turn around."

Emilia silently obeyed and jerked instinctively, feeling his warm hands undoing her blouse against her neck.

"Lift up your hands."

She did as she was told and let Richter take the top off her, leaving her in a simple white cotton slip and a skirt. He unbuttoned the skirt too, and it slid easily down her hips, too narrow from malnourishment.

"Take off your shoes, stockings and underwear," Richter commanded, getting busy with his own uniform and boots. "You can keep that slip on. It's too cold anyway, and besides I'd prefer to imagine that I'm in bed with a woman and not a twelve year old boy. And I bet that's exactly how you look without it."

Emilia felt a sudden surge of gratitude that she was at least spared from the humiliation of being absolutely naked in front of a man who she barely knew. She quickly got rid of the rest of her clothing, besides the slip, then quickly got under the covers which smelled of stale sweat and chlorine. Richter also decided to keep his undershirt and underwear on, either not to scare Emilia even more or just because it was indeed freezing cold inside the apartment. Most likely it was the second reason, Emilia thought as he got under the blanket with her, immediately pressing her into the thin mattress with his heavy body. Emilia froze immediately, all the horror stories from her school friends coming back in all their vividness. She overheard girls a couple of times, when they were whispering during recess, rolling their eyes and saying that "there was really nothing to it, only it hurt as hell and it wasn't fun at all, like Hans had promised it would be."

"Will you kiss me at least, Emmi?"

Emilia forced herself to open her eyes and after a second's thought planted an awkward kiss on the corner of his mouth. Richter replied with a hard glare, clearly getting annoyed with her inexperience.

"For Christ's sake, don't tell me you've never kissed a man before." After Emilia didn't reply, squirming slightly under his weight, he put his hand firmly on her neck, making her turn her head towards him. "Come on, open your mouth."

Emilia tried to hold her breath as long as she could while he was almost gagging her with his tongue, bitter from cigarette smoke, but then couldn't take it anymore and inhaled sharply with her nose, all at once allowing into her lungs – more cigarette smoke, sharp pine aftershave and something else, gunpowder or gun oil that she couldn't quite place. Up close, he smelled exactly like she imagined he would, like any of them, the SS, would – of smoke, wool and death. Until her death, Emilia would never erase that smell from her memory.

Richter grabbed her barely shaped breast under her slip and moved her legs wide apart with his knee. Emilia jerked once again when she felt him move his underwear down his hips and press his hard flesh in between her legs. *No, this is wrong, this is not how it was supposed to be,* she thought feverishly, pushing against Richter's chest in a sudden desperate attempt to escape.

"Please, let me go." She didn't even understand how she mustered the courage to plead with him, trying to move away from under his body, but it didn't seem to have any effect on the SS man.

"Where are you going, Emmi?" He smirked nonchalantly, firmly holding his victim in place. "You can't bring a man to the table and expect him to get full just by looking at the food. Doesn't work that way, *mein herz*. Now, better you relax and stop squirming, or it'll hurt even more."

Emilia stopped moving altogether, almost paralyzed with fear from his words. She fought the nausea rising in her throat, and tried to do as she was told, as Richter positioned himself in between her legs and entered her. Emilia only inhaled sharply, but didn't even whimper to her own surprise; strangely, but it wasn't half as bad as she had feared it to be. It was quite painful for the first two seconds, but then, as Richter started rhythmically moving inside her, it felt more like someone was insistently brushing her skin that had been burnt in the sun – quite unpleasant, but at least tolerable.

Emilia opened her mouth to his when he wanted to kiss her again, hoping that her compliance would make it all be over with sooner. Only, Richter started moving harder instead, hurting something deep inside and making Emilia wince a few times, as she tried to somehow shift positions so as to alleviate the pain growing in the abdomen. Taking her writhing for something different, Richter dug his fingers deeper into the skin on her hips, lifting them up even more, while he started to breathe faster. Emilia cried out at the especially painful thrusts, not able to tolerate the torture anymore, but it seemed to excite Richter even further. After another disgusting wet kiss, he whispered in her ear, "You like that, don't you?"

"Yes," Emilia whimpered, praying to all the gods for it to finish. If he, thinking that she was enjoying his performance so much, would end it all faster, she would just go along with whatever made her torturer happy.

Richter buried his sweaty face in her stiff neck, and after another minute that seemed to never end, finally groaned with pleasure and collapsed on top of his barely breathing victim. Emilia managed to draw in long labored breaths under his weight, glad that at least she would soon be free to go. He was still inside of her, but at least he was not moving anymore.

"Not too bad for the first time," he joked, just as Emilia had begun to think that he had fallen asleep. He pressed himself into her chest, getting up from the bed. "But I expect next time to be better."

Emilia got up from the bed, standing up on her feet not too steadily, and they both started dressing in silence.

"I'll send a man for you and your family later tonight. Be ready, with everything packed." Those were the last words she heard from him before he picked up his machine gun and walked out without looking back at her. Only then did Emilia allow herself to slide down the wall to the floor and weep.

———————

Unterscharführer Richter did keep his word, and one of his SS men knocked loudly on the door when the family was arguing inside, whispering of course, about what they should do next. Needless to say, minutes prior to his arrival, no one really paid attention to Emilia's suggestion that Richter would transfer them later that night into a section of the ghetto which would be safe from the upcoming *Aktion*.

"And why would he do that?" Martin was the first one to snort with contempt at what seemed to be the naivety of his little sister.

"He told me he would. I met him after work and asked him to help us, and he said he would," Emilia muttered, paying all of her attention to the potato she was peeling. "We gave him a lot of money after all…"

"He's just playing with you, and you're listening!" Martin raised his voice with unmasked hatred in it. "You think that they remember that you gave them something? They're ungrateful pigs, who take everything from us and then kill us, don't you see it by now?"

"What were you doing near that man again?" Oskar joined in, making Emilia only purse her lips tighter. "Didn't I tell you that you have no business talking to him?"

"I'm just trying to help us all," she replied defensively.

"Help! It's a man's duty to help and protect his family."

"And sometimes men fail miserably."

Oskar gasped and even stepped back, shocked by his daughter's words.

"Emilia!" Hannah made huge eyes at her as well. Emilia threw the potato down into the pot angrily.

"What, mother?!"

"Don't you dare blame us in this." Oskar made a circle around himself, obviously indicating their desperate living situation and the party policies that had put them in the ghetto. "I was trying to do my best to shelter all of you from all of this for as long as I could—"

"By refusing to immigrate to any country that was accepting refugees like us?" Emilia raised her voice at her father for the first time in her life. "By preferring to believe that your beloved fellow Germans would spare you and your family because you're such a faithful patriot?! Or because you were afraid that because you don't speak the language of the country that was ready to offer us asylum you would lose your status, and God forbid, live in poverty?! You all, telling me that I believe them! You believed them first! How are you better than me?! You should have thought better if you wanted to 'protect' me from them, father, because you did a lousy job!"

Emilia threw the peeling knife on the floor and stormed out of the room, trying not to burst out into tears in front of her family. Ari, who was fixing the sole on his shoe in the other room, rushed to his sister's side, as she hid in the corner between the bed and the wall.

"Emmi..."

"Don't touch me!" She angrily shrugged his hand off her shoulder. "Leave me alone, all of you!"

"Emilia, what did you do?" She heard her father's shaking voice barely mutter the words behind her back.

A loud knock sounded on the door and could have spared her from replying. The knock was followed by Richter's SS man's shout to come out with their suitcases. Emilia got up from the floor, brushed past Oskar, who still stood in the middle of the room clasping his throat as if he suddenly couldn't breathe, and said bitterly before opening the door, "Only what had to be done, Papa."

Chapter 4

Emilia was washing her hands in the hospital where she still worked, wondering how long it would take for someone to discover the truth at last. They had already started asking her all sorts of questions on the day after *the Aktion*, as soon as she walked inside the unusually silent hospital. The SS had shot almost all the patients, and the medical staff were forced to remove the bodies from the street, where the guards dragged them off by their limbs, indifferent to all the pleading and the doctors' reassurances that some of them would be walking in just a day or two. Emilia wasn't there to witness it herself, as Richter, having buttoned his pants, had "kindly" warned her to stay home that day, but she heard the other nurses exchange tired remarks that at least the SS didn't shoot them inside the wards and therefore there was no need to change the sheets at least.

"Where were you hiding?" the nurses asked her as soon as they saw her walk inside the staff room. Unlike them, qualified medical personnel who all had an "essential worker" card, Emilia was just a volunteer and therefore everyone immediately thought she must have waited out the *Aktion* in some hideout. It appeared that it puzzled them as to why she came back at all, considering that it put her at risk of being discovered and deported anyway.

"They didn't touch our section," Emilia replied warily, going to the sink to wash her hands and proceeding to put on her white gown. "I couldn't come to work yesterday because the SS wouldn't let anyone in or out."

They only nodded slowly with suspicion, but didn't proceed with their interrogation. Now, a whole month had passed and Emilia was starting to catch more and more glares behind her back, and she couldn't help but notice how the room went quiet as soon as she stepped through the doors. The problem wasn't even so much that she still worked there and never got bothered by the SS, even though everyone without papers had long been gone from the ghetto; it was more that she was now taking a different route home from the rest of the nurses, most days of the week at least, and they of course eventually took notice.

"Shall we wait for you or are you going to see your boyfriend again tonight?" Greta, the most talkative nurse of them all, had asked her this a few days ago, when they were getting ready to leave after their shift.

"I don't have a boyfriend," Emilia replied, feeling everyone's eyes on her again.

"Where do you go all the time then?" The head nurse, Lina, confronted her as well, crossing her arms on her chest. "Or, do you have something to do with the Underground maybe? We don't need problems with the *Jupo* because of you."

"I don't have anything to do with the Underground."

Lina looked her up and down, frowning, and then before she headed toward the door she said, "You're not stealing supplies for them, are you? I heard that your brothers might be connected to them. If I find something missing, don't even doubt me – your head rolls first. I'm not going to cover for you and deal with the *Jupo* or even the Gestapo for that matter. It's not the good old Weimar republic anymore; here, it's everyone for himself."

The nurses left and Emilia kept washing her hands for more than a few minutes, completely immersed in her thoughts, wondering how long it would take for them to discover the truth.

It took much sooner than she had hoped it would. In less than a week, Lina left the patient she was caring for and, seeing Emilia enter the ward at the start of her shift, almost dragged her out of the hospital by the scruff of her neck.

"Give me that gown back, and don't you ever show up here again," Lina hissed, roughly yanking the medical gown off a stupefied Emilia. "We don't need your help here anymore."

"What did I do?" Emilia tried to protest weakly. Even though she wasn't a qualified worker, she was still eligible for a ration card from the *Judenrat* just like the rest of the medical workers, and she couldn't afford to lose it.

"What you did?!" Furious, Lina towered over her, her fists butting her wide hips. "You dare ask me, what you did?! You open your legs for the SS, you filthy whore, how about that for a reason?!"

Lina spat on the ground next to Emilia's feet, making her move away instinctively.

"You thought no one would find out?! You're even worse than those who do it for the *Jupo!* Those are at least Jews, like us, but, no, you're obviously too good for that, aren't you?!" Lina continued contemptuously moving towards Emilia, who in turn kept stepping away. "You want the SS, the purebred Aryans, don't you? What is it, a uniform fascination, or are you just one of those field whores, who just like to support the troops' morale, huh?!"

As Lina almost barked the last word, Emilia turned around and ran. She ran away from the head nurse with her face red with anger, and she ran from the hospital, pockmarked from the recent *Aktion*, with blood splatters still covering its walls. She wanted to get far away from the words that burned her more than the shame itself; shame about what she'd done, and the shame of what she was still doing day by day – because it was the only way that she, and her family, could survive.

Emilia ran through the streets of ghetto without even knowing where she was running, until a sharp pain in her side made her stop to catch her breath. She walked over to the closest building and leaned on it with one hand, holding her side with another. Biting her lip relentlessly, she tried to ponder her options. It was still early morning and no one would be home besides her mother – but less than anything she wanted to explain why all of a sudden she was dismissed from her position in the hospital.

Her whole family knew about her 'relationship' with Richter by now, but thankfully they kept quiet about it, tactfully evading the subject every time she came back later than usual to silently unwrap a couple of cheese sandwiches or a pack of crackers. From time to time, Richter was kind enough to supply his pet Jew, as he himself 'lovingly' called her, with food. He always made a big deal out of it of course, puffing his chest and reminding Emilia daily how lucky she was that he had chosen her out of hundreds of others. Emilia always nodded in agreement and even managed to smile.

Feeling a little lightheaded from running, Emilia squatted by the wall, pressing her back into it and wondered how life would have been for her if she had been born into an Aryan family. She wouldn't even look at a man like Richter then, even if he gushed over her and got out of his skin just to get her attention. She would find herself someone better. That thought cheered Emilia up a little and even brought a faint smile on her face, which changed into a deep scowl right after; find herself a better who? A better Nazi? She couldn't look at them anymore without instinctively pulling her head into her shoulders. No, she wanted someone good and kind, like her Ari was. If she ever met a man who had as kind a heart as her brother's, she would marry him right away.

Emilia hid her face in her hands, concealing her bitter expression from herself. Who would want to marry her now? All the good boys with kind hearts wanted good girls to be their wives, not someone who was… spoiled goods, like she was now. Even Martin, her own brother, still refused to talk to her and only pursed his lips and left the room with a huff every time she entered. The only time Emilia had tried to talk to him, Martin had yanked his hand out of hers with a disgusted look on his face and pushed her out of his way with unexpected rudeness, talking through gritted teeth as he passed her by. "Don't you ever touch me again! You're a disgrace to the whole family. Pray to God that no one finds out, or I'll throw you in the street myself." How could she explain to him later that night that Lina had told her to never come back to the hospital? Would Martin really follow through with his threat and throw her out? Emilia smirked sadly; they almost lived on the street now, so where else could Martin possibly throw her? She'd just go and find another free apartment. Maybe the one where Richer took her all the time. After all, it did have a decent bed…

Emilia rubbed her dry eyes and noticed with a sense of indifferent curiosity that she didn't cry too much recently. It was as if she had cried all the tears that were possible for her to cry throughout her whole life and there was nothing left anymore. She was only twenty years old, and look what had become of her: sitting in the street of the ghetto, thinking of going to live in the place where she had lost her innocence to her enemy, who she continued to see almost daily to trade her body for temporary safety and scarce leftovers that he condescended to throw her, like a bone to a stray dog. She was probably less than a stray dog to him. *A pet Jew.*

Emilia pushed off the wall, slowly got up and took the already familiar road to the SS barracks. With some inward disgust, Emilia admitted that out of the whole world around, Richter was the only person who she could go to and ask for help. An SS guard, for whom Emilia had become a familiar face by now, only nodded as she appeared before the entrance and asked in her usual quiet voice for Unterscharführer Richter.

It appeared that the head of the guards was still having his late breakfast – alone, as he had sent the rest of his subordinates to patrol the territory, and being in an exceptionally good mood, he even put a whole *knackwurst* on her plate.

"There is a rumor that I'm being promoted soon," he announced with unmasked pride on his face, as he chewed on his sausage and motioned for Emilia to do the same. "Go ahead, eat, while no one can see. I'd feed you like this every day, Emmi, but I can't. You have to put yourself in my shoes too, I can't keep sneaking out food from under my soldiers' nose, everything is accounted for and I'm stealing as much as I can for you as it is."

"Thank you, Herr Unterscharführer," Emilia replied mechanically, hungrily stuffing the thick, juicy *knackwurst* into her mouth before someone could come in where Richter would most certainly take it away from her or, even worse, throw it in the garbage in case, God forbid, someone found out that the Unterscharführer was feeding a Jew.

He nodded and winked at her. "You're hungry, huh? So, what are you doing here? Missed me so much?"

Emilia threw him a glare while feasting on her unexpected treat and took another bite, choosing to forget about manners and talk with her mouth full rather than taking the risk of the meat being taken away from her. She had almost forgotten how heavenly it tasted.

"I got thrown out of the hospital. The head nurse found out about me."

"What did she find out?"

"About us." Emilia stopped chewing for a second, catching herself thinking how strange and alien it sounded to say "us." Richter put down his fork as well and knitted his brows together. Emilia lowered her head and bit into the sausage again. Even if he got angry and decided to punish her for being so careless at evading her fellow nurses' eyes, she'd at least be full. He had never hit her or hurt her physically before, but she had seen him do it quite a few times with others.

"What exactly did she say?"

"She said that she knew everything about me, that I..." Emilia paused for a moment, thinking of the best words to use, and hid her eyes in the plate again. The *knackwurst* seemed to make everything much better. "That I go with the SS, that's all she said. She didn't say your name, though."

Richter was pondering something, with his fist under his chin and his black eyes fixed on something in the distance. Emilia finished her sausage just in time, before Richter got up and reached for his uniform jacket.

"You'll come with me and show me that woman," he ordered before going to his room to take his machine gun.

Emilia shifted from one foot to another while waiting for him, twisting a button on her coat in her hand. She followed him silently to an open military car, which the guards sometimes used for inspections. She stole a couple of concerned glances in Unterscharführer's direction, but didn't dare ask anything. His impassionate face didn't give away much as well. On the way to the hospital, Richter picked up three of his subordinates and less than a few minutes later the car stopped at the entrance of the hospital, where a red cross was painted above the doors.

"Order all the medical personnel out," Richter barked at his subordinates and motioned Emilia to exit the car as well.

He lit a cigarette and was smoking nonchalantly leaning on the car door, as the nurses together with the doctors came running out of the hospital with their hands up just in case, rushed by the screams of the SS and their machine guns pushing them in their backs. After all the medical staff, which consisted only of twelve people, were lined up in front of the building, Richter took another drag on his cigarette, shifted his machine gun on his shoulder and addressed his soldiers.

"All of you have probably met fraulein Brettenheimer and are familiar with her, as she comes by quite often to see me."

Emilia threw a worried look at Richter, wondering where he was going with this.

"Some of you probably wonder what a Jew has to do with the head of the SS guard squad, whom is responsible for this particular sector. So, I think it's time I tell you that our good friend, fraulein Brettenheimer, has been helping me greatly in finding filthy, ungrateful rats, who badmouth the SS, and more than that, those who support the hostile mood within the ghetto, and in some cases even help the Underground." Richter paused for effect and then continued, strolling along the line. "Apparently, one of these rats got wind of fraulein Brettenheimer's collaboration with the SS, and threatened her in the most malevolent manner. Such behavior will never go unpunished, and I, personally, will always take charge of punishing such perpetrators. Today will be the first lesson which all of you will remember for the rest of your lives – if you want them to be fairly long, that is. Emilia, point out the woman who threatened you."

Emilia jolted slightly at the mention of her name and caught a collective pleading look from her former colleagues, all of whom were still standing with their arms raised. She finally understood what he was about to do and swallowed hard, unable to utter a word.

"Emilia!" It wasn't a request anymore, it was an angry, impatient shout.

"Her." She pointed at Lina without looking at the woman or Richter. She was too terrified to think about what was going to happen next. She had witnessed several shootings already, but she had never been the reason for one. Emilia started shaking slightly.

"On the ground, face down," Richter commanded the pale faced nurse, in a cold, leveled tone.

"No, please, Herr Unterscharführer, this is not true, there has been a misunderstanding—" Lina tried to plead with the SS man, folding her shaking hands near her chest, as if they could protect her from his bullets.

Another shout interrupted her before she could finish, "Face down, I said!"

"Please, don't do it," Emilia whispered, barely moving her lips, speaking more to God in the hope that he would hear her if Richter didn't – Richter likely wouldn't listen to her anyway.

Lina got down on her knees, openly crying and wringing her hands. "Herr Unterscharführer, she can come back here any time she wants, I just misunderstood what someone told me. I'm begging you, please, Herr Unterscharführer—"

"Down, you Jew bitch, now!!!" Richter yelled, stepping towards the woman and pointing the machine gun to her head.

"Herr Unterscharführer," one of his orderlies called out to him, making Emilia hold her breath. Maybe he'd talk him out of it. Lina was the head nurse after all, and it would be a mistake to kill an essential worker. Richter could even get in trouble for it if the murder wasn't justified, that much Emilia knew. But the soldier only pointed at the kneeling woman, saying, "The gown…"

Richter nodded; white medical gowns were a bigger rarity than the ones wearing them. New nurses would likely arrive soon with a new transport, and there was a shortage of gowns, so there was no need to ruin one.

"Take your gown off," Unterscharführer commanded.

Lina started struggling with the ties in the back with her trembling hands, swallowing tears and breathing in panicked short breaths. Richter ran out of patience, yanked the gown off the woman, pushed her down to the ground with his boot, adjusted a setting on his machine gun to single shots, and fired one in the back of her head.

36

Emilia clasped her mouth, partly not to scream and partly because she felt that she could get sick any moment now.

"You." Richter pointed at one of the doctors. "Who was she in immediate contact with?"

The man shook visibly as well, chewing on his lip, which was invisible under his white beard.

"Answer me or I'll shoot all of you!"

"The nurses. She had five working under her charge, fraulein Brettenheimer included."

"Point them out to me."

The doctor stepped forward and pointed at the four women, who instinctively clung to each other, already knowing their fate. One of them, Greta, looked Emilia in the eyes and whimpered sheepishly, "Emmi, please, tell them, we didn't know anything, she never spoke to us, only about work, Emmi, please..."

"She's right." Emilia turned to Richter at once, feeling that she was hyperventilating again, but she desperately continued talking, trying to get a hold of her breath. "Lina never spoke to anyone, these women didn't do anything, Herr Unterscharführer, please..."

"Gowns off. Face down, all of you." It seemed that Richter didn't care to listen to their pleadings, nor to Emilia's.

"Herr Unterscharführer." Emilia tried to catch his sleeve as he was passing her by to collect the gowns, but he paid no attention to her whatsoever. In less than five seconds all four women were dead as well. Richter threw the gowns into the doctor's hands and motioned his soldiers to get back in the car.

"Clean up the mess here," Richter told the doctor, who followed him with a petrified, unblinking stare. "Oh yes, one more thing. Fraulein Brettenheimer is your new head nurse. Make sure you listen to her, or I'll come back here again."

Emilia kept quiet all the way to the SS barracks, where Richter let his soldiers out, and she only spoke when he drove off to give her a ride home.

"Why did you do that?"

"You said it yourself, that she knew about us. Neither of us need problems with the Gestapo, *herz*. And dead people don't talk."

"Why did you make me their head nurse then?" Emilia muttered after a pause.

"You need a ration card, don't you?" came the casual reply.

"I don't want to go back there. They all hate me..."

"It doesn't matter. What matters is that they will listen to you and obey you." He pulled up at the back of the building she lived in, stopped the car and gave her a dirty wink, unbuttoning his pants. "Now, how about you show me some appreciation for helping you again?"

Ten minutes later Richter waved goodbye to her and sped off, leaving Emilia on the corner. She made several uncertain steps and then grabbed the wall, bent in half, and threw up.

Chapter 5

Her mother was the first one to notice that something was not right with Emilia.

"Emilia, are you pregnant?" she asked, while the two of them were making breakfast in the small kitchenette.

"No," Emilia replied coolly and continued stirring watered down porridge without looking at her mother.

"You get sick almost every morning…"

"So what? I can't get sick just because?" Emilia brushed her mother off once again. She had had her own suspicions for quite a while, but someone voicing them, as if making them real, only irritated her, for she hated to admit the truth even to herself, and more than that, to people around her.

"People don't get sick just because," Hannah said softly, taking the spoon from her daughter.

Emilia gave her an annoyed one shoulder shrug and went to the sink to fill the kettle. "Yes, they do. Here people get sick all the time. It's because I'm hungry."

"When did you last have your period?"

Emilia pursed her lips, as Hannah didn't seem to want to let go of the subject. "A year ago. What does that tell you?"

"If you didn't have it before it doesn't mean that you can't get pregnant."

"Will you leave me alone?!" Emilia put the kettle on the gas burner angrily and started setting the table, almost throwing the utensils down.

"I just want you to talk to the doctor in the hospital. Maybe he will—"

"What? Help me out? After what happened? First thing he'll do will be to call the Gestapo!"

Oskar showed his unshaven face through the door. "What's the matter? What are you arguing about in here, Hannah?"

"Nothing, Oskar. Call the boys, please, breakfast is almost ready."

Emilia looked away and whispered after several seconds of heavy silence, "Thank you, Mother."

"I just want to help you, Emmi." Hannah turned to her daughter and tried to take her face in her hands, but Emilia wormed herself out of her embrace. Recently, she resented any kind of physical contact with anybody and preferred to just be left to her own devices. Hannah seemed to understand as she stepped away, giving her daughter necessary space. "You need to do something about it."

"I know. I'll talk to Richter today. He'll think of something."

Hannah went quiet for a second, worry furrowing her brow. "He won't…"

"No, Mama, he won't hurt me or kill me, don't worry." Emilia smirked and noticed how cynical it sounded. "He actually said he'd marry me if I was Aryan, can you imagine? How romantic."

Later that evening, when Richer was smoking in bed next to her – a habit that he had recently adopted instead of running out like he used to do before, she tried to muster up the courage to bring up the subject, but she couldn't seem to form the right words. Suddenly, Richter lifted her head and put his arm under it, smiling at her.

"I'm getting used to you, Emmi," he confessed abruptly, blowing out another cloud of gray smoke. "You're like my field wife here."

He laughed at his own joke. Emilia simply lay next to him, afraid to move, stupefied at such unexpected intimacy. Such sorts of cuddling, for some reason, caused more aversion in her than what usually preceded it. She was somehow used to him using her body for his pleasure and leaving her afterwards, but now *this*… Emilia couldn't even describe why she suddenly felt such a surge of repulsion towards him, as if it wasn't enough for him to own her body; now he wanted to bring "feelings" into their twisted relationship, by domesticating it and making it look normal, like that of a regular couple. It only added to the insult in Emilia's eyes.

"You know, I didn't lie when I said that I would have married you if you were Aryan." He continued, oblivious to the girl's stiff posture. "I really would. You're a very pretty girl. Even prettier than my Heini. Henrietta, my fiancé back home. She's not bad looking, but she's not like you. She is much curvier, though, but you're still prettier. You wouldn't look good curvy. I didn't like it at first, but now I do. I like that you look so… fragile, delicate. Such a shame that you're a Jew."

She couldn't bring herself to tell him anything that evening, and only nodded in gratitude when he handed her two ham sandwiches and a few cubes of sugar.

"For my sweet girl." He winked at her and brushed her cheek with his gloved hand, before heading towards his car. As soon as he turned his back on her Emilia wiped her face with her shoulder, getting rid of his touch. On her way home, she felt something squirm inside and stopped for a second, bringing both hands to her belly, fighting nausea again. This was not what she had imagined it would be like. In her distant, girlish dreams, when she used to put lace pillow covers on top of her head and walk around the house talking to imaginary guests pretending that it was her wedding, it was so very different from her reality now.

She had always pictured her husband as being tall, blond and handsome; like the lawyer's son, who lived across the street from them and who always looked so serious, as if he knew some very important secrets. Emilia liked spying on the young man when he came back from his studies, with his briefcase squeezed under his arm. But one day he came outside in his new black uniform, waved goodbye to his parents and Emilia never saw him again. Oskar once mentioned that he had supposedly moved to Berlin to work for the government.

Emilia didn't mind the uniform back then, so she still held onto her childhood crush and hoped that one day he'd come back when she was all grown up and pretty, that he would fall in love with her and they'd get married and have many beautiful children. When she was just a teenager she sometimes wondered how would it feel to carry a child, to feel it move inside and then to have it in her arms. She always imagined it to be something magical and always knew that she would make a wonderful mother. She thought she would love her baby from the moment she felt it move inside for the first time. Emilia looked down at herself again; she didn't love this child. She didn't want it and, moreover, she couldn't imagine actually bringing it into the world, having to care for it for the rest of her life. No, she would have to tell Richter everything tomorrow. It was just as much his problem as it was hers, so let him deal with the consequences of his actions for once, Emilia thought angrily as she started walking towards her house.

Only, that conversation never happened. The next morning, in the wee hours, the Brettenheimers were awoken by loud screams outside, shouted out in German. They sat up slowly, exchanging anxious looks as soon as they started hearing the unmistakable sound of tens of iron-lined boots on the cobble road. Martin was the first to rush to the window and soon the rest of the family joined him, watching the soldiers lining up outside, with dogs barking and their commanders yelling orders, all of it echoing from the walls in the mist of the early morning.

"What's happening, Marti?" Hannah was the first to voice the question that occupied everyone's mind.

"Nothing good. Looks like another *Aktion,* and it seems like they'll be cleaning out our area this time."

"No, Unterscharführer Richter would have told me," Emilia said, watching the soldiers in disbelief.

"Well, maybe your lover is not as high and mighty as he pretends to be," Martin replied spitefully, turning his face towards his sister. "Or maybe he got tired of you and found himself a new Jewess; one a little fresher and prettier than you."

Emilia hit him across the face and yanked her hand back right after, cradling it as if afraid of her own temper. Martin just eyed her for a few moments of stunned silence and then spit out through gritted teeth before rushing out of the room, "Whore!"

Emilia bit her trembling lip as Ariel wrapped his arms around her protectively.

"He didn't mean it, Emmi. He's just angry, that's all."

"Let's pack suitcases before they chase us all out." Alfred sighed, turning his back to his siblings as well.

Hannah and Oskar had just opened two old suitcases to quickly throw their meager belongings into, already knowing the drill, when they heard loud shouting outside.

"Martin!" Oskar jumped to his feet and rushed to the window.

"What is he doing?" Hannah watched her husband while twisting a jacket in her arms that she was supposed to be packing. Alfred immediately ran towards the door and rushed downstairs not even closing it after him.

"He's screaming at the soldiers, God help him!" Oskar mumbled, brushing past Hannah as well and hurrying after his son.

Emilia and Ariel exchanged looks and ran downstairs, their mother trailing after them. When they ran outside, Emilia gasped in shock at what she saw: somehow her enraged brother had seized control of one of the soldiers' machine guns and he was now shielding himself from the rest of the SS with their comrade's body, holding him at gunpoint.

"Martin! Put the gun down and let him go, son, I'm begging you!" Oskar screamed, clasping his hands on his chest in a pleading gesture.

"Oh God, what is he doing?" Emilia heard her mother whimper behind her back.

Alfred, meanwhile, rushed to his brother's aide, but got hit by several machine guns firing upon him before he could reach Martin, and fell in a bloody heap on the cobble road. Hannah let out an inhumane shriek and ran to her dead son's body, not thinking twice about throwing herself in the line of fire. Seeing his brother die only steps from him, Martin seemed to completely lose it as he pushed the soldier away from himself and shot him, before opening fire at the rest of the soldiers in front of him. His bullets barely grazed a few of them, as he was immediately gunned down by more than ten machine guns.

Emilia rushed to her mother, who was hugging and weeping over Alfred's body, and tried to cover her from the soldiers, who she knew would most certainly shoot them all just out of retaliation. Their commander, who had just rushed to the scene after hearing the sound of gunshots, interrupted their shouting and Emilia's screams as she pleaded with them not to kill her mother. His whip landed on her shoulder, burning her skin even through her the clothes.

"Stop yelling, you stupid bitch!"

Emilia stopped, too shocked from the violent blow and too terrified to say another word anyway. She lifted her eyes to him, as he stood over her in his long overcoat, a deep scowl painted on his propaganda poster-perfect, vicious face.

"I can't hear what my men are trying to report because of you," he said in a very calm tone, as if explaining why he had to hit her. His sudden personality change from that of a violent assailant to someone with a completely calm demeanor within seconds petrified Emilia even more.

Making sure that he was leaving her silent and too afraid to move, he slowly turned back to his soldiers and motioned one of them to speak. "Report."

As the soldier started speaking, Emilia turned back to her wailing mother, shushing her, trying to pacify her in case her cries might provoke the commander. She was shaking herself, not able to comprehend how she had just lost two of her brothers at once, and still too stunned to even cry. Her father and Ari, as it seemed, were in the same state as she was: pale, wide-eyed and drawing in air in short gasps.

The commander's whip caught Emilia's chin again, turning her head towards him and away from her father and brother.

"Are these your brothers?" he asked as calmly as before, still holding her head high at a very uncomfortable angle, nodding at the dead bodies of Martin and Albert.

"Yes." Emilia swallowed hard. His steel blue eyes were boring into hers with the coldness of a scientist, who might pin a live butterfly onto a sheet of paper even though its wings were still battering.

"Is this your mother?" He gave another nod at Hannah, who didn't pay any attention to anything around her, too consumed by her grief.

"Yes." Emilia somehow managed to gather her strength and started speaking in a quiet voice. "Please, don't punish her because of them, Herr Officer. She's just an innocent woman, she didn't do anything, please, I'm begging you, sir, please, don't kill my mother, I'm begging you…"

Tears finally found their way out and flowed freely down her face. The commander scrutinized Emilia even longer this time, then slowly traced one of the tear lines on her cheek with his whip and smirked slightly.

"I like it when you beg."

He turned his gaze towards Oskar and Ariel, who was hugging his father most likely supporting him from fainting. The old man was breathing hard, his right hand over his chest, clasping his heart.

"Are these your relatives, too?"

"Yes, Herr Officer. This is my father and my brother. They're both good people, they won't give you any trouble and both can work, sir—"

"Shoot them both," he commanded to his squad, not even allowing Emilia to finish the sentence.

"No!" Emilia shrieked and hid her face in her hands, shutting her eyes tight, not able to watch the execution of the rest of her family. Even after the gunshots were replaced by a lingering silence she still refused to uncover her face; maybe they were both still alive if she just didn't look.

"Look at me."

Emilia felt the tip of the whip move on top of her fingers again. She knew he'd just hit her again if she didn't comply. She slowly lifted her wet face to him.

"Why are you crying? I'm letting your mother live, just like you asked. You should be thanking me."

"Thank you, Herr Officer," Emilia squeezed the words out of herself, afraid that he might change his mind. Her mother was the only family she had left now, after losing the other four members of her family in a matter of just minutes.

He stared at her for quite a while, playing with his whip. "What's your name?"

"Emilia. Emilia Brettenheimer."

An evil smile tugged the corners of his lips upwards. "I'll see you around, Emilia Brettenheimer."

Emilia started shaking uncontrollably as he walked away. For some reason she felt that what he had said wasn't a simple joke and that she would meet him in the future, somehow, someway, but she would, and it wouldn't be a pleasant meeting.

In less than a few minutes, Emilia and her mother were rushed to the main street, where lines were already forming. With typical German efficiency the *Judenrat* officials were sitting at their tables, each with an SS guard by his side making sure that there was no mistakes made or that any bribery could occur, as they sorted out the essential workers from the rest. Emilia noticed Richter standing next to the *Aktion* officials. He locked eyes with her, giving her a hopeless look, shaking his head slightly, as if to say that he didn't know about the executive action. Emilia just shrugged and looked away. What did it matter now? She felt absolutely numb inside and didn't even flinch when a *Judenrat* worker pointed her to the line next to the awaiting trucks. She waited for her mother to be pointed the same way and wrapped her arm around her, leading her towards the trucks. *The sooner it ends, the better, she thought nonchalantly.*

The trucks took them to the railway station, from where they were herded into cattle train cars. Emilia was lucky to be one of the last ones to be put on the train, and after the door was locked, she grabbed the bars on the small and only window and spent the rest of the way watching the scenery outside, which was as bare and bleak as her mood. They didn't ride for too long, which wasn't a good thing, according to one of the elder women, who was speaking quietly to someone, who Emilia didn't bother to look at. According to the woman, a long ride meant Germany, where the food portions were supposedly bigger and work not as hard. She said she knew that from the very few postcards she had received from one of her relatives, who was incarcerated in Ravensbrück, an all-female camp. No one ever got any postcards from their relatives in Poland, and whatever were the reasons, they couldn't be good.

The train finally came to a stop. Emilia was one of the first ones to see a small wooden platform, where SS guards – both male and female, something that she never saw in the ghetto – and scrawny men in striped uniforms, pulled the small steps up to the doors of the trains. No one was eager to get off the train, and Emilia involuntarily stepped back as the door opened, but a skeletal hand, almost black with dirt, reached for her and grabbed her wrist, yanking her outside.

"Out, out, everyone, now!" A man in a striped uniform yelled in Polish, but she understood the words now, after living for so long in an area which spoke the language. She looked back to find her mother, who had stumbled upon uneven wood and almost fell on the ground next to a viciously barking dog.

"Watch your step!" Another inmate, who was armed with a wooden baton, yelled at her, pulling her upwards and pushed her roughly to the platform. "Get in the line, move!"

Her indifference for her fate soon changed into something more frantic, more terrifying as the reality sank in. A physically sickening anxiety made her grab her mother's hand tightly and pull her close, as the woman, who had finally caught up with her daughter, looked around with distress and kept asking her the same question, "Where are we, Emmi? What is it this place?"

Emilia didn't answer, as she had as little clue about what was going on and what was about to happen to them, as everyone else who had just came off the train. People were talking in hushed, worried voices, instinctively clinging closer to each other, as the inmates with batons pushed them into one straight line, surrounded by guards with German shepherds. The dogs were crazed with fury, spraying saliva at anyone who had the misfortune to come a little too close to them and their uniformed handlers.

Holding her hand over her stomach protectively – a gesture that she didn't understand herself as soon as she noticed what she was doing – Emilia approached two uniformed SS guards, standing on the little wooden podium. It seemed that they were sorting people out in front of her. As Emilia and her mother's turn approached, one of them locked eyes with her for a second, looked her up and down quickly, before then pointing his whip to his left.

"Both, right."

A female guard took charge of them from there, pointing them to the small paths in between two walls of barbed wire, separate from the ones that men were sent to.

"Walk all the way to the disinfection building. You'll undergo the delousing process, you'll be handed new clothes and assigned to your barracks."

Walking towards the small concrete facility, Emilia turned around a few times, wondering where the other ones were going; the ones which the officer with the whip had sent to the left.

Inside the facility, there was a strong chemical smell, and Emilia immediately felt sick. Another female guard, in the same even and unemotional tone, kept repeating the same lines for all the newcomers. "Take off all of your clothes and put them over there, by the wall. They may be contaminated with typhus, so they will have to be destroyed. After you undress, form a line over there, by the doors that say "Disinfection." After you undergo the decontamination process inside, you'll come out from the other side and you'll receive your new clothes and barrack assignments."

Trying to fight nausea, Emilia watched another guard counting women out as they disappeared behind the doors of the "Disinfection" room. Emilia noticed that the woman stopped each time she reached fifty. After that, she locked the doors and motioned to another guard. In less than a minute, the smell grew even stronger, and Emilia, afraid to throw up right on the floor in front of these new guards who, most certainly, wouldn't take it too well, ran outside ignoring their angry shouts and emptied her stomach right by the entrance. A tight grip yanked her upwards, and Emilia found herself facing a very furious looking SS female guard.

"Who told you that you can run around as you please, huh?!"

"I'm sorry, frau, I got sick..." Emilia wiped her mouth with a shaking hand. "The smell inside..."

The woman squinted her eyes slightly and immediately shifted them onto Emilia's stomach.

"Are you pregnant?"

Emilia just opened and closed her mouth, too afraid to answer. The guard didn't hesitate and reached for her clothes, pulling her top out of her skirt and yanking the skirt down to expose the small mound on Emilia's belly.

"Pregnant." She confirmed her guess and pulled Emilia's hand, holding her firmly by the wrist and grumbling as she dragged her back to the disinfection facility. "We don't need your Jew-bastards here. There's enough of you as it is, but you go and make more of your vermin."

Emilia barely kept up with the guard's long strides, when suddenly the SS Helferin stopped and called out to another guard, "Karla! Watch my post, I'm taking this one to the medical block."

"Emilia!" She heard her mother cry out behind her back. Emilia threw a desperate gaze over her shoulder as she was dragged away by the woman towering over her with her strong build. She saw two female guards grab her mother by her arms as she tried to run after her daughter. They pushed her back in line, holding the pleading, naked woman in place with their batons. Emilia turned her face away and swallowed her own tears.

Are they going to kill me? It was the only thought that occupied her mind as her hand started hurting from the uncomfortable position and the unnecessary strong grip of the guard. It wasn't like she could run away anyway, as the place was a true maze of paths with barbed wires, with each exit and entrance guarded by an SS guard with a dog, and watchtowers with men with rifles walking inside leisurely, watching everyone from the height of their towers like eagles watch their prey, ready to strike at a moment's notice.

Soon they approached a separate building with a red cross above the door. The medical block, Emilia guessed, and she started shivering again, fearful of what was to come. Maybe she should tell them that the child was from a German? Maybe they would spare her life then? Or, on the contrary, that might prove to be her death sentence, for committing a *Rassenschande,* race-mudding crime. Emilia decided to keep quiet for now.

The *SS Helferin* stopped in front of the door and knocked on it, still holding Emilia by the wrist.

"Herr Doctor? I have another one for you."

The door opened and a young man came out, wearing a white coat on top of a uniform, with a cigarette in his hand, clearly discontent at being disturbed. The guard saluted him and reported sharply, "She just arrived with a new transport. A Jew. She's pregnant."

The doctor only nodded and dismissed the guard with a wave of a hand. "Thank you, I'll take it from here."

The guard disappeared after another salute and a click of her heels, and the doctor smiled at Emilia. The last thing she remembered was his comforting smile and soft voice, as he said something reassuring to her while she lay absolutely naked on a cold gynecological table, the drug that he had shot into her vein earlier clouding her thoughts. The doctor was good… He wouldn't hurt her… The doctor had come to save her from this hell… Only, barely an hour later, Emilia soon realized she had woken up in a real life hell.

Chapter 6

The first thing that returned was pain; excruciating, searing pain all over her abdomen that felt as if her intestines were on fire. Emilia moaned, unable to open her eyes, but tried to shift her body that didn't seem to listen to her commands too well, into a less painful position. It seemed that moving only intensified the pain, and Emilia whimpered slightly, bringing both hands to her stomach.

"The first few days are always the worst," a woman's voice said, tearing through this new nightmare. "It'll get better later. Try not to move too much."

Few days?! This will go on for days?! Emilia did the impossible and forced herself to turn her head to the voice and open her eyes. Her mouth was completely dry, but she still managed to whisper, "I never thought abortions were so painful."

"They're not." The woman had a scarf on her head, and lay on the medical cot next to her in the same white camisole that Emilia was dressed in. The woman smiled weakly. "It's the chemicals that hurt. They put them inside of you after….to sterilize you."

Emilia thought that she misheard her, that's how savage the words sounded to her.

"To do…what?" she asked again weakly, with disbelief.

"To sterilize you," the woman repeated quietly. She reached out and patted Emilia's hand slightly. "No more children for us."

"No more?" Emilia was staring at the woman with her eyes wide open, tears already stinging them. "I don't have any children… That was my first one…"

The woman lowered her eyes and sighed, taking her hand away. "I'm sorry, girl."

Emilia lay silent for some time, touching her painful, swollen abdomen, tears rolling down her cheeks more from the emotional pain than from the physical one.

"But… They never warned me that they would do that… How can they do that to a human being? Without asking my permission? I wanted children in the future! I wanted so many children and a husband… How could they do this to me? I'm not a dog to sterilize! I'm a human!"

"Oh, shut it, you!" A harsh voice from a different cot interrupted Emilia, who was openly crying now. "You're not the only one here who had to go through this! There's nothing you can do, so stop your whining. Some people are trying to sleep."

"Stefka!" Emilia's neighbor shook her head scornfully. "How can you say that to the girl! As if you didn't cry when you just found out!"

"I cried because it burned like hell, not because of what they did. They did me a favor to be truthful; I left six of them, bloodsuckers, at home. They didn't take them, as they're half-breeds, my lot. Their father was a German, only we weren't married as he had his own family at home, but that didn't stop him from coming to me in Krakow every now and then and making me another kid. He was a railway inspector of some kind, only he was inspecting me far more than the railways!"

Stefka, a sturdy woman of around forty with the round face of a typical, healthy and good-humored peasant, laughed at her own joke and addressed Emilia, who was sobbing quietly, covering her face with her hands. "Stop, stop it, girl! Why kill yourself about something that might never happen anyway? You have to think about surviving now, and in this place, let me tell you, it's not easy. We all might get sent to disinfection tomorrow, so what's the point with all the tears?"

"What disinfection?" Emilia took her hands off her face and glanced at Stefka with concern, suddenly remembering her mother, who she had left at that very disinfection facility.

Stefka looked at the door and continued in a quiet voice. "That's the basement where they take you to supposedly undergo a delousing process. Only, the ones who enter, don't come out. The capos drag them out, all mutilated because of the gas. I know one of them; the corpse carriers the SS call them. He told me their faces change color and they have foam on their mouths and blood still dripping from their noses and ears—"

"Stefka!" The woman next to Emilia hushed her again. "Stop it with your stories! You'll scare the girl to death!"

"My mother was sent to disinfection…" Emilia barely whispered, covering her mouth with trembling fingers. "As soon as we arrived…together with me…"

"No, don't fret, girl, that's a different disinfection." Stefka made a dismissive movement with her hand. "That's the real one. I went through that one, too. They just spray you with some chemicals and then send you to the shower, and from there – to the barrack. If that was the basement, they wouldn't have bothered to pull you out of line; why go through all the pains of saving you and doing surgery on you if they could kill you right away? No, they need you to bend your back for them first, and then…"

"Then what?" Emilia couldn't help by ask, even though she already knew the answer.

"Ach, God knows what." Stefka shrugged her round shoulders. "You know what, girl, you should find yourself a protector here, then you'll last longer. You're a pretty girl, you won't have difficulty securing yourself a warm spot under some capo's wing."

"Who are capos?"

"Capos are the inmates who help the SS. They have authority over the rest of the inmates and keep order for the guards, report any suspicious activity and what not – if someone steals food, or if someone's visiting a lady friend at night, that sort of thing. They're the men with batons, who you must have seen at the station."

Emilia frowned as she recalled the rough, calloused hands grabbing her arm and stale, rancid breath that hit her nostrils when one of them yelled at her to stay in line.

"They aren't so bad," Stefka continued as if reading her mind. "And they get bigger food portions than the rest of us. If you're nice to them, they'll gladly throw you a piece."

Emilia couldn't hide the disgust on her face and turned away, thinking about Richter. He was at least clean and somewhat attractive, and even if she felt like a lowly whore with him, selling herself for food, she wouldn't be able to live with herself if she ever went with one of those capos.

"At least they won't rape you one by one until the whole barrack is done, like the SS do," Stefka concluded calmly. "And they won't torture and kill you afterwards. I saw those poor girls' bodies myself, just thrown in the street like garbage in the morning. They always cut their breasts off for some reason…"

Emilia looked around the barrack that she had just been transferred to, after almost three weeks of thorough observations and tests done by different doctors. She was walking almost normally now, even though shooting pains kept returning from time to time, making her bend in half and clutch her lower abdomen with both hands. But at least urinating wasn't causing her such immense pain as it was in the first two weeks. Every time it had brought tears to her eyes and barely audible prayers for it to end, as her hands clenched into fists and her knuckles turned white.

After a female guard simply pushed her inside the barrack in the evening and told her to find herself a bunk, Emilia just stood in the entrance, wondering how she could possibly find herself a bunk when all of them were overflowing with women, most of whom didn't even pay attention to the newcomer. Some glanced her over with unmasked hostility and Emilia looked away, deciding not to challenge them.

"Hey, you! You, blondie!" A surprisingly cheerful voice called over from the other side of the barrack. Emilia looked up to see a pretty redhead hanging off the top level of a three-level bunk, waving at her. "Yes, you! Come here, you'll sleep with me!"

Emilia didn't want to move away from the entrance, which was somewhat ventilated, as the smell inside the barrack, which had no windows, was nauseating. It was a mixture of stale sweat, rotten flesh and human waste. Emilia involuntarily clasped her hand over her nose and mouth as she walked towards the girl, trying to prevent the smell from penetrating her lungs.

"Great, now there's going to be two whores instead of just one," Emilia heard someone mutter as she was making her way towards the other end of the barrack.

"Birds of a feather flock together," another voice added.

This time Emilia stopped and glared at the bunk, on which three women lay on their stomachs, observing her with unmasked hostility.

"What are you staring at?" The biggest one of them, who was built more like a man rather than a woman, looked her up and down and motioned her head to the right. "Your new sister is waiting for you."

Emilia decided not to reply just yet and hurried to the redhead's bunk. The girl, who was about her age, outstretched her arms towards Emilia, helping her climb onto the third level. Emilia was careful to watch her feet as she did so; there was no need to make enemies on the first night there, considering that the way she was met by the barrack's habitants wasn't that welcoming to begin with.

"My name is Magdalena, but you can call me Magda." The redhead smiled, showing the most adorable dimples on her cheeks. Her curly, unruly hair was covered with a gray scarf, but even the worn clothes and scarf couldn't hide her natural beauty. Emilia sincerely hoped that they would become friends; so far the girl seemed to be very nice. "What is your name?"

"Emilia."

"Welcome to our little paradise, Emilia!" The girl laughed, a mischievous light playing in her amber eyes.

Emilia knitted her brow, not appreciating the jest.

"Oh, don't fret! It's not so bad here, and our bunk is right next to the stove, so we'll be warm, unlike the others, who sleep next to the doors." Magda moved, inviting Emilia to lay down next to her. "Sometimes they freeze to death there, so we're very lucky."

Only now did Emilia notice that Magda was probably the only girl who slept on her own bunk, with no neighbors, and she was right: the stove was right underneath them, by the wall, its meager light barely flickering.

"We get more wood when the temperature goes below thirty, but now it's more than enough to get by," Magda went on explaining. "And now I have you, so together it won't be too cold. You're new here, right?"

"Yes." Emilia paused for a while, wondering if she should tell her new bunkmate where she came from. "I was just released from the hospital today…"

"They did something to you?" The redhead widened her eyes.

"I was pregnant when I just arrived here… They…" Emilia was surprised that it was still so difficult to talk about it, but she made an effort to continue. "They aborted my baby and then… they injected some chemicals inside, to make me sterile. I can't have children anymore."

"You poor thing."

Magda reached out and started stroking Emilia's hair. This casual and almost childish gesture was so sincere, and so unexpected from a mere stranger, that Emilia burst into tears, telling her new friend her whole story, about the ghetto, Richter and how almost everyone in her family had been killed in front of her eyes. And now this.

"Don't worry your pretty little head about it." Magda was holding her like a child, rubbing her back slightly. "So many orphans are left out there with this war. When we come out of here, you'll just find yourself one. Or five, for that matter! You can have them all if you want, and they will love you just as much as your own children would have, or maybe even more. Now, you have to think of survival."

Hearing the same words that she had heard from Stefka before, Emilia looked up at the girl.

"Do you think we'll ever come out of here?"

"Of course, we will," Magda replied with such certainty, as if Emilia had asked her something that needed no discussion. "All this, it won't last forever. Nothing does. Now, sleep. The wake-up call is at four."

Emilia lay quiet for some time, listening to even snores coming from the rest of the bunks, before touching Magda's hand softly.

"Magda? Are you asleep?" she whispered.

"Not yet, why?"

"I just wanted to ask, why are those women so hostile? You remember, the ones that said things to me as I passed by?"

"Oh, that's Idit and her minions. Try to ignore them, and maybe they'll leave you alone soon. They're like dogs; they just bark a lot but almost never bite. But, still, watch your back when you're alone with them, and check your mattress before you go up to your bunk. They sometimes hide food under it and try to sell you to the capos, implying that you stole it. They did it to me a few times, but since I started reporting everything that I find under my mattress, they left me alone."

"Why would they do that?" Emilia was sincerely astonished.

"Well, the first reason is food: for each case they report they get an extra piece of bread, and that goes for the value of gold here. And the second reason is that they hate me."

"Why?" Emilia was never one to pry, but this time she wanted to know the reason.

"Because I can get food, and they can't. And it's not stale or moldy." Magda's eyes sparkled in the dark, like that of a cat. "I've been here for a year already, and look at me, still very much alive and healthy, aren't I?"

Before the lights went off Emilia had noticed that, indeed, Magda looked much healthier than the rest of the inmates in the barrack, even though she was probably as thin as Emilia.

"How do you do that?"

"How do you think I do that?" The redhead giggled. "I have a man, who feeds me and takes care of me. See my sleeping arrangements here? It's because he doesn't want me to bother anyone when I sneak out at night to see him."

"Is he a capo?" Emilia frowned, remembering Stefka's words.

"Have you gone off your head?" Magda made huge eyes at her. "Did you see them? They're not much better off than us. No, he's an SS man, one of the guards."

"I heard stories about them…"

"Well, yes, some of them are pigs. But not all. You just have to find yourself someone who will treat you right. That way it will be only one of them and not ten different men every night. If he really likes you, he'll tell them not to touch you. They have some sort of agreement amongst themselves, when it comes to women."

Emilia was afraid to ask, but then finally did. "Have they ever…"

"What? Raped me?" Magda rolled on her back and shrugged indifferently. "Yes, they did, when I just got here. They like it, 'the fresh meat' as they call it. So…you watch yourself tomorrow when at work. Try not to lift your head too much, and cover your hair, too. I'll give you my scarf if you want. You're a blonde, and that's a rarity here. They'll grab you in a second."

Emilia couldn't suppress a shudder. "But how did you survive? I mean…they didn't kill you afterwards…"

"No, they didn't. That's why I told you to find yourself a protector, and the sooner the better. I've learned the hard way. They dragged me out of my barrack on one of the first nights, and brought me to theirs. There was another girl there already, younger than me, but that wasn't enough for them I guess. There was fifteen of them. So…when they had just put me on top of the table, I was looking at that girl. I just couldn't look away for some reason…and she was screaming and crying so much, and they kept beating her for that, punching her right in the face, strangling her so she wouldn't yell. I figured that if I keep quiet, I wouldn't get beaten like her. I made myself smile at them and tell them how handsome they all were… They didn't hurt me… One of them even gave me a piece of bread. See, I told you they're not so bad," Magda concluded with a smirk, her last sentence full of sarcasm.

"That's horrible," Emilia whispered.

"Not really, if you think that I might have ended up like that girl – with a bloody face and a slashed neck, laying down on the ground right next to us as we stood on the roll call the next morning. At least I survived."

"I don't want to survive like this," Emilia whispered to herself, swallowing tears.

"Ach, you still don't get it, do you?" Magda chuckled softly. "Here you don't really have a choice."

The morning roll call lasted almost three hours, during which all inmates had to stand shoulder to shoulder despite the freezing morning cold. By the end of the roll call, Emilia thought her legs would give in. She almost couldn't feel her feet anymore, but thought with relief that she was still better off than some of the inmates, who only had rags wrapped around something that barely resembled footwear. She had at least been allowed to keep the half-boots that she had been wearing when she arrived.

Before they had left the barrack, Magda wrapped Emilia in the blanket which they had slept under, and tied it with a small rope making it look like an overcoat.

"This will keep you warm before I secure you something better today," Magda promised in her usual cheerful tone. "I work in a small sewing factory here, where we fix the clothes that later go to German families. I'll get you something warm today, don't worry. I wish they assigned you together with me, but...oh well."

"They won't punish you for that, will they?" Emilia asked with concern.

"No, they won't. I know the magic word." The redhead winked at Emilia.

"What magic word?"

"Hauptman Schneider." The girl giggled and pulled Emilia outside. "Let's go. Never be late for the line-up or you'll get it across the back from the Frau."

"Who's the Frau?"

"Our main supervisor. And you don't want to cross her."

Emilia was trying to remember and process as much information about the official and non-official, but just as important, rules of the camp: never be late anywhere, never get into arguments with the guards or ask them any questions, never leave any pieces of clothing on your bunk when you leave – they'll be long gone before you even step out of the barrack – and most necessary, never, ever, under any circumstances steal anyone's food, no matter how hungry you are. The last rule was considered the vilest of crimes, and anyone who committed it would get capital punishment.

"What do you mean, capital punishment?" Emilia whispered to Magda as they stood outside, waiting for their names to be called out.

"They will beat you to death at night, the whole barrack, and the capos won't even say anything. Food is precious here, that's why the ones who can't get it either end up dead in the morning, rolled up in a bloody bundle under blankets, or starve to death. Two-three months, and they're gone. That's how long people usually live here after they arrive." Magda turned her head to Emilia and looked at her seriously, for the first time. "That's why I'm telling you to find yourself a provider. Don't do it too obviously, but look around today while you're working. Check if any of the guards look at you with interest, and...just give them a little smile. If someone is interested, they'll get the hint, trust me."

Emilia kept thinking about Magda's words all the way to the pit, to which she was assigned. The work was hard and back-numbing after only a couple of hours, but at least it kept her warm. Emilia looked around several times, trying to find her mother among the workers. Magda had told her that she would eventually see her somewhere, but it seemed like today wasn't her lucky day.

At twelve, all the workers, following the loud sound of metal banging, stopped and looked at the guards, waiting for permission to go to lunch. Emilia pulled her bent aluminum dish out of the pocket of the dress she had been given after they had discharged her from the hospital, and waited in line for the meal. Only after the inmate behind the counter poured some liquid into it, liquid barely tinted yellow with one carrot swimming in it, did Emilia realize for the first time, with desperation, that Magda hadn't exaggerated when she said that people starved to death there. In the morning she was given only a small cup of ersatz coffee, and her stomach was already churning from hunger after several hours of exhausting work, and now...this?

The next woman in line rudely pushed Emilia in the back. "Move it, cow! There are people here besides you, you know!"

Emilia quickly moved out of the woman's way, sat by the long table on the furthest end from everybody else and started eating the watery soup, trying to stop the tears from dropping in it. How had all this happened to her so fast, and the main question was, why? What was she being punished for? She'd never hurt anyone in her life, she was just a regular girl, like everyone else around here, and all of a sudden her blood had turned out not to be pure enough for the new government, to which they had sent her to the only suitable place for her kind in their eyes – a labor camp.

What would have happened if she was born an Aryan, though? She would probably have suitors lining up at her door, who would shower her with affection, gifts and flowers – she saw those lucky German women with their gentlemen, when they had already moved to Poland and the Germans moved in after them. Those women always had curled hair, overcoats with fur, floral dresses in summer, and exhibited the sound of contagious laughter, floating out from the cafés where they loved to lounge with their dates. Emilia wasn't allowed in those cafés by that stage, because of her armband with a blue star. Nor was she allowed in the parks. Or in the stores. Basically anywhere near Germans. Yet the women's uniformed dates still eyed her. So, now she would have to try and entice one of them just to survive... Emilia wiped another bitter tear away. Earlier, back in the ghetto, she thought that her relationship with Richter was about survival; how mistaken she had been. Compared to this place, the ghetto was paradise.

By the end of the day Emilia started getting dizzy spells and could barely stand straight without slightly swaying from side to side during the evening roll call. Magda clasped her arm tightly and whispered, barely moving her lips, "Don't you dare fall! The Frau will have it with you!"

Emilia recognized the Frau now, a thin, blonde woman with a baton, which she didn't think twice about using. Emilia had seen her use it twice this evening already, when women had the misfortune to fall, not supported by their fellow inmates. Emilia thought once again how lucky she was to have Magda by her side, as the ones who didn't make any friends or acquaintances here didn't seem to last long on their own.

Seeing her sway slightly, the Frau shot Emilia a glare but didn't say anything, her thin lips pressed tightly in one line as her gloved hands twisted the baton. As soon as she looked away, Magda quickly pressed her hand towards Emilia's mouth, forcing her lips apart to stuff something inside. Emilia twisted her tongue around the small, grainy object in her mouth, tasting the long-forgotten sweetness: sugar.

"Suck on it," Magda whispered to her. "It'll give you some energy."

"Where did you get it?" Emilia whispered back.

"Schneider. I got you a coat, too." She slightly moved her own overcoat to show a second one hidden under it. "It's real wool. Very warm."

"You should keep it and give me yours instead."

"No. That's my sister's coat, I'm not taking it off, ever. She gave it to me before she…left."

"Where's your sister?"

"Dead, of course." Magda replied unemotionally, staring ahead blankly. "She was a very pretty girl, too. Prettier than me. They came for her the following night after me. She threw herself on the wire afterwards. Got killed instantly – the voltage there is very high. They didn't remove her body until the next morning. I could still see her during morning roll call."

Emilia followed Magda's gaze and fixed her eyes on the wire as well. Well, maybe Magda was wrong after all; maybe there was a choice.

Chapter 7

Almost a week passed without any incidents, and Emilia started hoping that no one would bother her. She had finally seen her mother, even though from afar, but at least she knew that Hannah was working in a nearby construction pit. Now Emilia was trying to come up with an excuse to go over to that pit to show her mother that she was alive and well.

It was Saturday, and Emilia knew that if she didn't get a chance to get close to Hannah till the end of the day, she'd have to wait till Monday to try her luck again, as on Sundays the inmates were granted a day off: not that it was a real "day off," because the inmates would have to busy themselves with cleaning the barrack and the territory nearby, but at least they could take a shower and just rest on their bunks for a few hours, some writing to their relatives, some just talking, and some trying to get as much sleep as possible before the new week.

Emilia kept craning her neck, observing both her own quarry and the pit where Hannah worked. Soon she noticed that one woman nearby loaded her wheelbarrow with sand, after making sure that there were no stones inside it, and that she took it to the construction pit, emptying it by the place where the inmates were making concrete. Throwing wary glances over to the female guards, who were strolling leisurely along the quarry, Emilia began slowly moving towards the woman with the wheelbarrow, until she stopped and pretended to dig barely five steps away from her.

"Frau." Emilia called out to her quietly and respectfully. The woman turned her head and frowned. "Frau, would you like to switch places with me for today? I can see that your barrow is very heavy. I can carry it for you if you take my shovel instead."

"Je ne comprends pas qu'est-ce que vous dites," the woman replied in French.

"I take your barrow." Emilia pointed at herself and then at the object. "And you take my spade. *S'il vous plait?"*

They were the only words she knew in French, and the addition of a small, begging smile seemed to do the trick as the woman gladly switched places with Emilia. The barrow turned out to be extremely heavy when Emilia filled it with sand, but just the thought of seeing her mother up close and talking to her if she got lucky gave her additional strength. Panting heavily, she made her way towards the pit, trying her best to navigate her way in between the rocks covering the path. She lowered the handles of the barrow to the ground next to the reservoir, in which two men were mixing concrete.

"Excuse me," Emilia addressed one of them, tall and thin as a rake. "Do you happen to know that woman over there?"

The man looked in the direction in which Emilia pointed, and squinted.

"We don't talk much here," he replied in a coarse voice. "But I do see her here every other day."

"Could you please, if it's not too much trouble, just pass her a little message?" Emilia tilted her head pleadingly to one side. "Her name is Hannah. Could you tell her that her daughter Emilia is alive and well, and that I'm working over there, not too far from her?"

The man nodded and handed her the barrow after emptying it. "Will do, girl."

"Thank you." Emilia quickly picked up the barrow and started heading back, from time to time throwing glances over her shoulder at her mother.

The man kept his word as it seemed, as the next time Emilia pushed the barrow towards the pit, she caught Hannah sending a huge smile at her, pressing her hands to the heart and wiping a few tears. Emilia beamed back and rushed to get to the construction site faster, however, in her rush, she didn't notice a small rock blocking the wheelbarrow's path, and she stumbled over it, watching with horror as her barrow overturned right next to an SS guard smoking nearby.

Emilia immediately froze on her hands and knees, lowering her head instinctually, expecting to be hit with a baton any second now. Far too many times she had seen it happen with her fellow inmates for reasons far less significant than this. She saw the black boots approach and, after several painfully long moments of dread, she finally dared to lift her head. The guard was eyeing her with amusement as it seemed, still enjoying his cigarette, with his baton still secured on his belt.

"Are you going to go back to work or are you planning on staying like that all day?" He chuckled.

Emilia got up at once, not wanting to run the risk of angering the guard, who seemed to be in a pretty good humor so far. She quickly made the almost impossible effort to bring the overturned barrow back upright, and hurried to fill it up with sand once again. As she walked past him for the second time, thoroughly looking at her feet, the guard only laughed kind-heartedly.

Emilia was feeling like her old self for the first time in a whole week, as she walked back from the showers, enjoying the long-forgotten feeling of being clean at last. She laughed with Magda as they almost ran back to the barrack, to dry out their hair with the one blanket that they shared, and which one of them always carried, so that no one would steal it. Turning around the corner, both stopped in their tracks, startled, as they almost crashed into one of the guards; the latter's mouth slowly stretched into a sneer as he leaned onto the wall of the barrack, looking the girls up and down.

"Sorry, sir," Magda said first. Emilia couldn't help but glance at her, not used to the girl's voice being so quiet and almost quivering. Her friend stood next to her, suddenly looking very pale and subdued, her eyes glued to the ground.

"You should watch where you're going, Magdalena." Even though he was addressing her friend, he was looking Emilia square in the eye. She decided to look down as well. "Who's your new friend?"

"This is Emilia. She's my bunkmate," Magda barely whispered in reply. Emilia shifted from one foot to another, feeling more and more uncomfortable. There was clearly some story between the two of them, and Emilia started praying to God that the story was not what she started to suspect it was.

"Emilia," the man pronounced slowly and lifted her chin with his baton, forcing her to look him in the eye again. Emilia swallowed involuntarily. "Are you new here, Emilia?"

"Yes, *mein herr,*" she replied quietly.

"Wonderful." He moved the blanket off her head and Emilia shivered more from his touch than from the frosty air biting into her wet hair. "Can you sew, Emilia?"

"I suppose…"

"That's very fortunate. I have a couple of loose buttons that need to be fixed. Do you mind sparing fifteen minutes of your day off to help out a man in need?"

"Certainly," Emilia replied, stealing a worried glance at her friend, who still stood next to her with her eyes downcast. Magda reached out to clasp the blanket in her hand.

"Just go," she whispered without looking at Emilia. "Go."

Emilia followed the guard, who clasped his hand around her wrist, as if preventing her from running away. Emilia looked back longingly and saw that Magda was still there, a small, bundled figure watching her being taken away. Emilia glanced at the guard, who gave her a sly wink and sneered once again.

"Don't worry, Emilia, we're going to have a wonderful time together. Do you like schnapps? My comrades and I, we have the best apple schnapps around." Emilia tried to jerk her hand away at those words, but he just yanked her forward more forcefully. "Oh no, you aren't going anywhere. Not until I tell you that you can go."

Already panicking, Emilia whimpered and rooted her feet to the ground, refusing to go further. The SS man, clearly in no mood for any resistance, grabbed her by the hair, wrapped it around his fist and kept walking, muttering under his breath. "We can do it the easy way or the hard way, Emilia. To me there is no difference whatsoever."

Grimacing from the pain and barely catching up with his long strides, Emilia realized the horror of her situation, but with some unhuman will stopped the tears as soon as they threatened to overflow from her eyes, which were wide open in terror. *I was smiling at them and they let me go after,* Magda's words kept replaying in her mind like a broken record. *Just smile and they will let you go. They will eventually let you go. It won't go on forever, they will let you go as long as you smile and don't aggravate them with tears and screams...*

The guard opened the door to the guards' barrack and pushed her inside, releasing her hair. The heat wave from an open stove near the entrance washed over Emilia's skin, while the overpowering smell of alcohol and tobacco, lingering in the air in thick clouds, immediately made her pull back only to bump into the SS man behind her back.

"Is this the one you were talking about, Bergmann?" The SS guard addressed one of the men sitting at the big table in the middle of the room, playing cards. Emilia begged her body not to give in and to not start shivering openly as all the men at the table began studying her with obvious interest.

"No, but this one is even better!" Bergmann, a tall blond man of probably her Ari's age, got up from the table and walked over to Emilia. "I've never seen you here before. Have you been hiding from us? Now, that's not good."

"I'm new here." Emilia hardly found her voice, holding her breath as Bergmann opened her coat nonchalantly and dropped it on the floor, leaving her only in a thin dress.

"Fancy a drink?" He winked at her, just like the one who brought her here, who was now busy removing his coat and belt with its holster.

"She hasn't earned her drink yet," someone shouted from the table.

Emilia swallowed and nodded slightly, without taking her begging eyes off Bergmann. When she saw him walk over the table and pour her a full mug, she breathed out in relief, thanking God silently in her mind that at least she wouldn't have to be sober through everything.

"Cheers." Bergmann theatrically toasted his mug with the one that he handed her, and Emilia started gulping from it without thinking twice, without paying any attention to her protesting mouth, throat and insides that started burning right away.

"Why would you give her vodka?" She heard the question, as she tried her best to keep the disgusting fiery liquid inside her empty stomach. The good thing was that she immediately felt its effect in her head. "She'll be too drunk to do anything."

"Well, maybe for once you should do something, Lenz? You wouldn't be so damn fat if you moved from time to time, you know," Bergmann replied much to the pleasure of his comrades, who met his words with laughter and cheers.

Emilia decided that he must be the leader amongst them and, even though her thoughts had started to drift off by now, one thought kept repeating like a most important mantra: *if I'm in his good graces, he'll tell them to let me go later. He'll tell them... I have to smile at him... Tell him that he's very handsome, like Ari was... So very handsome...*

"You're very handsome..." Emilia wasn't sure if she pronounced it out loud, but judging by the chuckles somewhere in the back of her mind and Bergmann's half smile as he sat her on his lap by the table, it suggested that she had.

"That's it. She's drunk. You ruined it," someone spoke again.

"Fuck off," Bergmann barked, as Emilia struggled to keep her eyes open, feeling the room spinning as she melted into the comfort of the warmth of the barrack and the human hands around her. He did look like Ari, Emilia thought when he turned his head towards her again. Emilia's smile didn't even feel forced now. Bergmann brushed the hair off her face. "You're very pretty too. Will you kiss me?"

Emilia nodded and obediently pressed her mouth to his, opening her lips to his. He smelled like vodka and tasted like it, but Emilia had already decided that she had to leave this place alive, so whatever he – or anyone else for that matter – was going to do to her, she'd take it as willingly as she could possibly make herself. She allowed him to pull the dress off her and didn't even bother to keep her eyes open anymore when she felt his hands on her shoulders, pushing her slightly backwards. She gave in and fell on top of the hardwood table, hitting the back of her head. She didn't fight their hands off when they started groping her small breasts, stomach and thighs. She didn't make a sound when Bergmann's belt scraped her skin painfully as he was moved fast and hard inside her; or maybe it wasn't Bergmann anymore, but someone else, because there were so many of them around her, panting heavily and digging their fingers into her soft skin. Only when one of them slapped her face hard and grabbed her by the neck, telling her to look at him, did Emilia force herself to open her eyes and look, and she smiled just like Magda told her to...

Emilia barely registered when someone dragged her off the table and started putting the dress back on her, cursing under his breath and breathing heavy cigarette smoke into her face. Soon, she was pulled upwards and someone shook her slightly.

"Wake up, Cinderella. The ball is over, time to go home." Bergmann chuckled at her half-opened eyes and put her arms through the sleeves of her coat. "Here, eat this. I need you to walk by yourself because I'm not carrying you back to your barrack. You understand?"

He took her hand and put something in her palm, closing her fingers around it. Emilia brought her hand to her mouth instinctively and smelled bread, the real kind that Richter used to give her in the ghetto. Emilia smiled at the taste as she bit into quite a thick slice, closing her eyes once again.

"Hey? What did I tell you?" Richter shook her again. No, it was Bergmann... Emilia was confused, and wanted them all to just leave her alone and let her sleep. "Walk, walk!"

The cold air woke her up a little as soon as they stepped through the doors and started making their way back to Emilia's barrack. Still chewing on her bread and concentrating on making her feet move, Emilia frowned slightly, noticing that it was already dark out. She wondered how much time she had spent there, but chased the thought away, as she started to sober up and feel sicker and sicker as her head started to clear out a little bit.

"Go to sleep. The roll call is over already. I'll tell Hilde that you were helping us with something, so don't worry about being absent." Bergmann let go of her arm at the entrance of her barrack, turned around and started making his way back to his. Emilia looked at the dark velvet sky, contemplating, shifted her eyes to the spot on the electric wire fence to which Magda had been looking at the other day, and licked her fingers, which still smelled of bread. Emilia frowned, made an uncertain step forward, but then stopped, shook her head defiantly and opened the door of the barrack to go inside.

"How are you?" Magda whispered when Emilia lay next to her.

"Alive," Emilia replied and finally closed her eyes.

Life settled down little by little. Emilia learned that if she kept the piece of bread from the evening meal and nibbled on it throughout the following day, instead of eating it all right away, the hunger pangs weren't so strong. She also learned that if she wrapped a cloth around her shovel, the barrow handles or whatever instrument she was using that day, then her hands wouldn't be covered in bleeding blisters by night. This also helped to keep her hands warm, especially with the barrow as the handles were made of metal and sometimes skin would freeze to them if it was particularly cold outside. The guards always kept warm by drinking hot coffee from their thermoses, cupping their gloved hands around the steaming containers, and Emilia always inhaled greedily when the whiff of hot drink reached her nostrils.

She also learned that seeing the Kommandant around, when he walked around with his adjutant inspecting the laborers, was a good thing. Magda explained to her that the guards wouldn't indulge in drinking bouts and look for a good time with the female inmates, unless he left for a couple of days on some business. Thereafter, Emilia always watched any vehicle leave with dread, hoping that it was just the Kommandant's adjutant leaving to run some errands and not the Kommandant himself. Only, as she soon found out, his presence in the camp didn't protect her in the slightest when it came to individual SS guards, and their quick deeds which were just as disgusting as what she had experienced in the guards' barrack.

At least then I was drunk and didn't comprehend most of what happened, Emilia thought, when she was grabbed for the first time after the incident in the guards' living quarters. The same guard who took her to the barrack caught her unawares behind the canteen for personnel, where one of the *Helferinnen* had sent her to fill a thermos with fresh coffee. Emilia named her assailant "The Bear," since she didn't know his real name; so, she named him after what he most resembled.

"I didn't have my fill with you," he breathed into her ear, grabbing her from behind with his paws and dragging her into the food storage section. She hardly fought back, gripping into the thermos and praying that he wouldn't break it accidentally. "I'll have you all to myself now. I hate sharing my things with the others!"

"Please, be careful," Emilia whispered, the grip of fear clenching at her throat immediately. She tried her best to keep the thermos above the floor, which was covered with a thin film of wheat powder, as he pushed her down on her hands and knees. "Please, don't break it…"

Concentrating obsessively on the silver thermos, which had an eagle engraved on it, somehow helped Emilia to take her mind off what "The Bear" was doing behind her. For some reason she remembered how, when she was little, she believed that all misfortunes would certainly escape her if she just didn't step on the cracks in the pavement, and that's why she always looked under her feet until she outgrew the habit at the age of nine. With the distanced curiosity of a scientist observing a patient with a mental illness, Emilia caught herself analyzing her own brain, which was trying to find escape from the man raping her, persuading herself that everything would most certainly be all right if she just held the thermos in her shaking hand and didn't let it break. She was more relieved that nothing happened to the thermos after "The Bear" was done with her, than from the fact that he finally wasn't moving inside her body anymore.

When she finally went back to her work post and handed the *SS Helferin* her refilled thermos, the guard frowned slightly.

"What took you so long?"

Emilia didn't reply and just lowered her eyes. She was thinking only of wiping between her thighs quickly when no one was looking, as the slippery residue was already freezing on her legs. *SS Helferin's* discontent was the last thing that troubled her.

"Did you have a smoke there or what?"

"I'm sorry, Frau." Emilia decided not to argue because she couldn't possibly tell the woman that it took her so long because one of her comrades had taken his time to force himself on her, and besides Emilia knew it too well by now that it would be fruitless to tell the truth.

"I'll forgive you for this time, but don't let it happen again."

"Yes, Frau. Thank you, Frau. I'm sorry."

"And they're saying we're not treating you humanely," Emilia heard her mutter after she had already turned away to leave.

Emilia watched her back closely after that day, but "The Bear" always seemed to come out of nowhere when she least expected it, to reopen the old sores that had just started to heal and leave her on the floor after yet another satisfied growl. Unlike Bergmann, "The Bear" did not once give her any food, not even a piece of stale bread. He even took the time to explain his position once, with a disgusting smirk, saying that she should thank him for granting her such an honor, to satisfy a German man. Food? She didn't deserve any food.

Emilia started staring at the barbed wire spot in which Gerda, Magda's sister died, more and more during each roll call. She wasn't sure how long she would be able to carry on like this. All the power to live was slowly draining out of her and the daily mind-numbing routine started making Magda's words about all this ending at some point a mere fantasy.

"This is never going to end," she slowly pronounced during one roll call, as she looked straight ahead once again. "We're all going to die here. What's the point in prolonging the suffering?"

Magdalena scowled but didn't say anything.

That day, Emilia and several more laborers were sent to the gravel pit almost at the outskirts of the camp. To her big surprise Emilia saw her beaming mother hurrying behind one of the *Helferinnen,* together with two other women from the other side of the camp.

"I volunteered," Hannah whispered to her daughter, catching her sleeve when the guards weren't looking. "I heard them calling out your name amongst the others, and I volunteered to go as well."

"You shouldn't have," Emilia whispered back as they made their way along the train rails. "The gravel pit is one of the worst assignments. We'll have to shovel all day; you won't be able to feel your arms later."

"I wanted to talk to you." Hannah seemed a little disappointed at her daughter's reaction, but tried to hide it behind a forced smile.

"It's not a picnic or café outing, where we can talk."

Emilia wouldn't stop scolding Hannah, even though she was glad to see her mother. But talking to her…talking was the last thing she wanted to do, especially with Hannah. Emilia still walked around with her head low and her gaze fixed on the ground, just because of some paranoid obsession that everyone would most certainly know what the guards did to her, and what they kept doing to her. Every whisper behind her back was most definitely about her, as if that shame was forever imprinted on her forehead for everyone to see.

"The guards don't take too kindly to talking," she added a little softer, feeling guilty for her harsh tone prior to that. "And you should preserve your strength more than anything."

Hannah nodded obediently, and decided not to argue with her daughter, seeing that she wasn't in the best disposition. After another twenty minutes of walking, she murmured quietly, "My feet hurt. Do they have to walk so fast?"

Emilia glared at the guards and pursed her lips. "They always walk fast, mother. I told you that you shouldn't have come."

"I wouldn't complain otherwise, but my soles are very thin, and we walk on gravel."

"My soles are as thin as yours, and I also walk on gravel. And that man in the front – he has rags wrapped around his feet, and he keeps quiet."

"Ach, Emmi, you just don't understand." Hannah allowed a soft whimper to escape her lips. "It's so hard for me here. We have the worst barrack guards! They beat us for nothing, I tell you, for nothing!"

"Everyone gets beaten here for nothing, mother."

Emilia sighed, feeling angry and ashamed at her own anger at the same time. She had to deal with her own issues daily, which were far worse that getting a couple of baton smacks, to which she was so used to by now that she didn't even notice them anymore. Now, Hannah had decided to make everything even worse by telling her daughter about her own abuse. Now, Emilia would have to worry about both of them, and not just herself; as if worrying would do any good.

Why would her mother even complain to her at all? She, herself, never complained about anything: not about Richter, not about the medical ward and the several weeks of agonizing suffering that she had to go through, and more than anything about more recent events that she preferred to erase from her memory forever. No, Emilia never complained, because she knew that everyone here was in more or less the same position, and complaining was just…impolite, disrespectful and disgraceful in her eyes. Even if the one who complained was her own mother.

"You're putting too much of a burden on me, mother." Emilia shook her head disdainfully. "Why did you come here at all? It's not our old ghetto, there's nothing I can help you with. Why would you tell me all this?"

"I'm just making conversation," Hannah replied, looking at a loss. "I didn't ask you for anything… I just wanted to talk to you."

Emilia tried to bring her emotions under control and whispered a little irritably, "I'm sorry."

The guard's command to stop interrupted their hushed conversation. After one of the capos handed the laborers their shovels and pointed to the two freight train cars, awaiting to be filled out before being transported to one of the factories in Germany, Emilia slowly worked her way closer to Hannah, who could barely keep up with the hard work after just one hour.

"Here, shovel small amounts of gravel, you won't get tired too fast," Emilia whispered, seeing beads of sweat on her mother's forehead, which creased with pain.

"But then we won't fill the quota for our sector," Hannah argued, breathing heavily.

"We will. I'll shovel for the two of us, and you just pretend to work. There's only three guards, and they chat all the time, so they never watch who works and who doesn't. Just mind the capo when he passes by."

"Thank you, *Süße*." Hannah quickly pressed her daughter's calloused hand with gratitude, to which the latter only nodded. Hannah volunteered with good intentions of course, but still she seemed to make everything worse; now Emilia would be dog-tired by the end of the day, and probably wouldn't even sleep at night, worrying over her mother, who would never survive here without her help. Only, Emilia couldn't even save herself from the constant abuse and hunger, so how on earth could she help Hannah?

Not sensing her daughter's anguish, Hannah stopped to take a break from shoveling and rested her chin on her shovel, watching Emilia with a small smile.

"You're so lucky that you're young, Emmi. If I was your age, it wouldn't be so hard on me. I get tired so fast... And they stand above us with batons and whips all the time, and if we take breaks, they beat us right away."

Emilia picked up another heavy shovel full of gravel, not replying.

"I saw men do it before in the ghetto, beat people up that is, but women... I never expected women to do such a thing! And here they do it even more than men, Emmi. Ach, our barrack *Helferin* is so vicious; sometimes she hits us just so we 'know our place,' so she says. No one ever beat me before, Emmi..."

"Me neither, mother. And if you don't want her to pick on you, you just have to work hard, and don't take so many breaks. Then they won't beat you as much." Emilia angrily shoveled into the gravel while her mother stood near, watching her. "I'm not being harsh on you, I'm just trying to help with the advice. That's the only thing I can help you with. I'm sorry. I know you hurt, I know you suffer, I know you're hungry. So am I. So is everybody else. There's nothing we can do, but only put ourselves together and work. Try to survive. Try not to pay attention to everything that hurts you. If you think about work and not your bruises, you'll forget about them."

"It's easy for you to say, Emmi. You're young and strong…" Hannah sighed and picked up her shovel again.

"You're looking for excuses again, mother. I don't have it any better than you, trust me."

"It's easy for you to say that I need to pull myself together, Emmi. I try my best, I really do, but it seems like our barrack *Helferin* just has it in for me… I slipped in mud one time and she kicked me right in the stomach, Emmi, can you imagine? Do you know how much it hurt?"

"Yes, I do!" Emilia straightened, losing her temper at last. "I could barely walk for weeks after what they did to me in the medical ward, mother! I couldn't go to the bathroom without crying! Do you know that they inject you with so many chemicals that they cause such severe inflammation in your fallopian tubes that they get permanently glued together?! How do you think that feels, huh?! You talk about a small kick that you probably forgot about the next day! Easy for me to say?! Easy for me to say that I will never have children?! Easy for me to say because I'm younger? I would give anything to be of your age, mother; at least no one rapes you daily, do they?!"

Having hissed her tirade into her startled mother's face, Emilia went back to shoveling, not even feeling any pain in her back or arms anymore, only anger, both at Hannah, who made her burst into a cross rant about things that she had hoped no one would ever learn about, and at herself for putting it in such a harsh way.

Hannah stood motionless for a few moments, tears collecting in her eyes while she tried to process her daughter's words.

"Emmi…" She outstretched her arm, trying to catch her daughter's sleeve, but Emilia only jerked her shoulder away irritably, not even looking at the crying woman. She needed pity even less than complaining. Feeling angry was better than trying to victimize herself; anger gave strength, while self-pity only took it away.

"Just keep shoveling. I'll try to get you bread from somewhere tomorrow. And don't volunteer for anything anymore, please. If I keep working for the two of us and I collapse, we'll both die."

Chapter 8

"He's looking at you."

"Magda, leave me alone, I'm begging you."

"He's positively looking at you. Smile at him, do something."

Emilia kept stubbornly looking in front of herself, refusing to acknowledge the guard, who, according to Magda, seemed to be interested in her. She was still sore and disgusted with herself after "The Bear" had had his way with her only yesterday, and, therefore, she couldn't even stand the thought of looking at another man. Eyes fixed on the barbed wire, she patiently waited for one of Frau's orderlies to call out her name and to go to work, away from them all.

Magda, as it seemed, sensed her tense mood and gave up her attempt at matchmaking. As they started making their way towards their respective working places, Emilia felt a rough shove in the back, which resulted in her landing right at the feet of the guard. Quickly getting up and apologizing profusely, Emilia stopped in the middle of the sentence as she saw the familiar face: it was the same guard at whose feet she had already landed once, together with her wheelbarrow. Only, this time he wasn't smiling.

"Who pushed you?" he inquired in a stern voice, gesturing to the inmates to stop where they were.

"No one did, *mein herr*. I stumbled. Please, forgive me," Emilia lied, quickly averting her eyes and rubbing her sore palms.

"That one pushed her!" one of the *Helferinnen* shouted, as she approached the crowd with a resolute step, baton in one hand. "I saw it!"

Emilia opened her mouth in meek protest, but the *SS Helferin* had already grabbed Magda by the elbow, thrown her on the ground and started whacking the girl across the back with her baton. Magda didn't make a sound throughout the whole punishment procedure, but only covered her head to prevent the infuriated woman from hitting her on the head accidentally.

"That will teach you to shove!" The *Helferin* said angrily as she finished her beating. "Get up!"

Magda got up obediently, all the while keeping her eyes on the ground.

"Why did you push her?" the male guard next to Emilia abruptly inquired in the same stern voice.

"I didn't mean to," Magda replied. "It was intended to be a joke."

"A joke? What kind of a joke is that, pushing people around?"

Magdalena only brushed the red hair off her face and kept quiet.

"I asked you a question! Answer me!"

"I don't want to say it in front of everyone." Magda averted her eyes, biting her lip nervously.

"Come up to me then and say it."

The male guard motioned to the rest of the inmates to get on with their business, and nodded to the *Helferin* who had taken charge of resolving the incident, indicating that she could leave as he would take over. Emilia eyed her friend incredulously, not understanding why she would have done such a thing.

"Well, you can speak now," the SS guard addressed Magdalena. "What was the reason behind it?"

"She told me this morning that you are very handsome and that she likes you. So, I told her that she should go up to you and make a formal introduction. She's very shy, so I kept teasing her and just wanted to shove her slightly in your direction, but I guess I pushed her harder than I should have. I really am sorry, *mein herr*. It was just a very stupid joke, and I apologize. It wasn't my place to make such jokes at all. Forgive me, please."

Emilia was looking at Magda with her mouth agape. She could not believe the acting talent of her bunkmate, or her audacity. To think of it, to say such a thing to an SS guard! Why would she even think to do that?

"Is that true?"

Emilia turned her head to the guard and noticed with relief that he was grinning, instead of getting angry as she had expected.

"Yes, *mein herr*." A thought flashed in her mind to deny everything, but then Magda would get into even more trouble for lying, and God knew where it all would end. If the guard just laughed at it and let them go, why not confess to it? So she did, even though she began blushing copiously. "Please, accept my apologies. I should not have made such an observation."

"Why, there's no need to apologize, you haven't insulted me in any way." The guard motioned his head to Magda that she could leave. "Go to work, and no shoving in the future, even as a joke."

"Yes, *mein herr*! Thank you!" Magda beamed and almost ran off, still smiling mischievously and leaving the two alone.

Emilia looked at the guard sheepishly. He eyed her for some time, took a cigarette out of his pack, lit it up and then asked, "Is that really what happened or is there another story?"

"It is." Emilia looked away nervously.

"I'm asking because I find it hard to believe. Usually inmates here don't take kindly to the guards."

Emilia swallowed a lump in her throat, feverishly thinking of a way out of the situation. It seemed that the guard had turned out to be smarter than the rest of their lot, or maybe it was because he was older and more observant. Emilia noticed the markings on his overcoat: he was an officer, too. A low rank officer, but, still, he was not just one of the regular guards. Emilia slowly started putting two and two together in her mind, eventually coming to the conclusion that her friend had done it on purpose, and that most likely it was the same officer who had been watching her during roll call, according to Magda. She decided to just say the truth and to hell with the consequences.

"You seem nicer than the rest of them. You didn't beat me when I fell for the first time. You seem kind."

"I seem kind?"

"They don't treat me too well, the others." Emilia suddenly felt tears welling up in her eyes. "I'm afraid to go anywhere alone. And even when I'm not alone, they don't care, they just come to the barrack sometimes with some stupid excuse, and the *Helferinnen* don't even say anything, even though they all certainly know…"

She suddenly found herself shaking from the stress which had accumulated throughout the previous weeks, and weeping openly in front of the first man who appeared to listen. Or maybe he didn't really care and only listened out of politeness; Emilia noticed that he was talking in that Prussian, refined dialect that indicated he was of good upbringing. She felt lightheaded from the emotions that had finally found an outlet and fell on her knees in front of the guard, lowering her head and not even thinking of what he would make of it. She had nothing to lose at this point.

"Please, help me, Herr Officer, protect me from them, I'm begging you, I'll do anything, I promise, I'll do anything for you, just please, don't let them hurt me anymore, please…"

"Get up, get up, you can't be sitting here crying." He pulled her upwards and Emilia clung to his overcoat with a feverish gleam in her eyes, like that of a condemned person.

"Shoot me then, Herr Officer, please, just shoot me then—"

"Stop it, stop!" The officer even shook her slightly, throwing a quick glance around, but Emilia didn't hear him anymore.

"Shoot me, Herr Officer!" She began falling again, supported only by his arms still holding her. Not finding any other option, the officer slapped her hard across the face. Startled, Emilia stopped crying at once and lifted her head to look at him.

"I'm sorry for hitting you, but you can't make scenes like this one here!" he told her sternly and once again pulled her upright. "Go to work, and don't worry, no one's going to hurt you anymore."

Emilia still stood in front of him, blinking and not moving.

"Go, I said." The officer nudged her slightly on her elbow. Seeing that she still didn't move, he added quietly, "I'll come get you in the evening."

Emilia nodded slowly at last, as if reassured by his promise and hurried to her construction pit.

He did come to get her after the working shift was over, after stealing occasional glances at her during the day. Emilia noticed and even managed to smile at him a couple of times. He smiled back at her.

As they were making their way to a small building which was occupied by the officers, Emilia kept throwing glances over her shoulder, worry furrowing her brow over her missed dinner. As if guessing her thoughts, the officer promised in the same polite, quiet tone, "Don't worry about the food, I have plenty of it in my room."

He did have a separate room, nice and clean, albeit small. As soon as they stepped through the doors, the officer offered Emilia a seat on his cot, apologizing that he only had one chair, and went to the cupboard to arrange some evening snacks. To Emilia, the cutting board that he put in front of her, with an opened can of sardines, bread, cheese sandwiches, bacon and even canned *sauerkraut,* all foods she hadn't seen for ages, looked like a feast.

"Please, help yourself." The officer pushed the cutting board closer to Emilia and offered her a reassuring smile.

Emilia indecisively stretched her hand towards the closest sandwich, but the officer said unexpectedly, "Would you like to wash your hands maybe? I'm sorry that I didn't ask you earlier."

Emilia only now noticed the difference between his hand, white and neatly manicured, and hers, grey from the construction dust, with dirt under the broken nails. She probably still had some dried blood on her palms, too, but she didn't want to look to see if she did. She felt even more miserable and dirty after noticing the contrast between the man in front of her, in his immaculately cleaned and pressed uniform and polished boots, and herself. She had no idea how she looked, but probably not better than her hands: filthy, disgusting and used.

"I didn't mean to offend you, I just don't want you to poison yourself." The officer obviously felt the need to explain that it was her health that he was concerned about, and not his personal disgust from observing her dirty hands. A sad smirk tugged the corner of Emilia's mouth; all the inmates ate with hands such as these every single day, and no one ever cared if someone might poison themselves. They died from everything else, but not food poisoning.

"I'm sorry, where is the bathroom?"

The officer pointed her in the direction of the only door, which led to the bathroom. It only had a toilet and a small basin, and for a moment Emilia hesitated, wondering if she could use his soap, a small white bar lying on a soap holder. Everything was so clean and immaculate that Emilia was afraid to touch anything.

"Please, feel free to use anything you need," the officer encouraged from behind the door, probably catching onto her hesitation when he didn't hear the faucets open for quite a while.

Emilia opened the water and took the soap bar, bringing it to her nose and inhaling greedily before lathering her hands thoroughly. She caught herself smiling when she lifted her head, only now noticing a small shelf with a narrow mirror above it. For the first time in God knows how long she was seeing her own reflection. She caught a gasp and froze for a moment, studying the person in the mirror. Whoever was staring at her was in no way herself, the old Emilia who she last saw in the ghetto in the small mirror that they had in their kitchen. This girl was not even a girl anymore; she had the eyes of a hundred year old woman, with a deep crease in between her brows, with cheeks so sunken that the contours of her skull were visible under her ashen, grey skin. Old streaks from hastily smeared tears were still there, just like the sores on her parched, greyish lips from her biting them relentlessly all the time. And the hair. Her beautiful, wheat-colored hair that her father was always so proud of, was all matted, greasy and hanged around her face in tangled knots. This new Emilia was repulsive, revolting and hideous. She wanted to cry and laugh at the same time, wondering what those idiot guards wanted with her. She wouldn't touch someone looking like her, even if there were no other women around whatsoever. Maybe she looked differently on other days of the weeks; today was Saturday and she hadn't washed in six days.

"Herr Officer," Emilia called him quietly, looking around the door. "Do you mind if I wash my face as well?"

"By all means, do whatever you please." The reply was refreshingly courteous. "And please, call me Manfred."

She didn't look half as bad after washing off all the layers of dirt that were stuck in the lines of her face. It even seemed to make her look years younger. After carefully wiping her face with his towel, Emilia noticed with relief that even though she was still very pale and scrawny, her eyes looked even bigger in her face and her former beauty wasn't all completely gone. However, she wasn't sure by now if that was a good or bad thing.

Five minutes later, Emilia was wolfing down the sandwiches under Manfred's amused stare. She didn't know his last name and was thinking of a way to ask, so she could protect herself in future if "The Bear" decided to continue his harassment, when Manfred gently placed his hands on her wrist, preventing her from taking another sandwich.

"I don't think it's a good idea to eat so much at once," he explained in a mild voice. "You can harm yourself. Your body isn't used to digesting big amounts of food anymore."

Emilia nodded, grateful that he had stopped her as she probably wouldn't be able to stop herself. She looked at the officer inquisitively. He got up to take away the cutting board and then sat next to her. Emilia was waiting for him to tell her to undress or use another instruction to let her know how she must repay him, but he started some general conversation instead, elaborating on subjects related to the war, bolshevism and national-socialism. It reminded her of terms and topics long forgotten. Here, all everyone spoke about was work and food mainly, and – in hushed whispers – about the transports leaving to take people "someplace else." Many of them said that "someplace else" was even worse than their own place, although there was no way to find out for sure, except to go on the transport itself.

Carefully, Emilia tried to probe her new acquaintance on the matter of the situation in the front. He shrugged uncomfortably and replied evasively that "the German forces were currently regrouping their armies to counterattack the Soviet army." It seemed like a euphemism for "retreating" in Emilia's mind, but she was too afraid to make any conclusions.

Manfred asked her about her family and if she was married or had children. Emilia told him everything like it was, not hiding the fact that she had underwent a forced sterilization as soon as she got into the camp. Manfred listened to her attentively and even pressed her hand slightly after her confession. Seeing her watch his hand on top of hers with caution, Manfred quickly took it off and started saying in a somewhat rushed manner that if she didn't like him touching her, she should just say so and he would never do it again. He went on to say that he could escort her back to her barrack and she would not hear a word of him anymore, because he would never pester her like the rest of their lot, on his honor as an officer…

Emilia interrupted him in that instant, reassuring him that she liked him very much and that he was indeed an honest officer and a gentleman, and that she was only afraid because the others treated her badly, and she was too used to being mistreated.

"I would never hurt you," he rushed to promise her and kissed her hand unexpectedly. Emilia still didn't know what to make of him, but at least he didn't drink like the rest of them, was polite and courteous and, what was most important, he fed her. To her, it was more than enough.

———————

Emilia shivered with pleasure as Magda scrubbed her back with a rough washcloth, generously lathered with a small bar of soap that each of the inmates received in the showers. The bars were common property and used by several other barracks before it was the girls' barrack's turn to shower, but Emilia couldn't be happier to hold a small, cracked bar in her hands.

"I'm sorry that I fell asleep last night before you could tell me everything," Magda said, handing Emilia the washcloth – also communal property – so that her bunkmate could scrub her back in return. "We had to sew buttons onto uniforms that were scheduled to go to the front right away, and we worked all day without even taking a break for lunch. I was exhausted."

"That's fine." Emilia smiled, soaping the washcloth. "There's nothing to tell, really. He just fed me and…we talked. That's all."

"You talked?" The redhead turned around, giving her friend an incredulous look. "And..?"

"And nothing, he let me go. It was almost roll call time."

Magda snickered and shrugged. "That's the first time I've heard that one of them prefers talking to…doing."

Emilia giggled too, more from her friend's ironic remark than from the very truthful fact that Magdalena had just stated, even though in a jesting manner. At the same time she caught Idit's hard glare, who stood merely steps away from the girls in the stuffed shower room.

"Are you seeing him again then?"

Emilia wished that her bunkmate would speak a little quieter at least, but it seemed that Magda didn't care too much about being discreet in front of Idit and her friends, and the more accusing and disdainful glares the latter threw her way, the louder the girl spoke, just out of spite.

"I suppose," Emilia replied quietly, trying to concentrate on Magda's shoulders with their adorable, just visible freckles, instead of Idit and her scornful grumbling that she exchanged with her minions, most certainly on their account. "He seems nice enough."

"If I were you, I'd take advantage of him being so nice and secure my position the sooner the better. Don't expect that talking is all he's after; he's a man after all, even though a relatively refined one. If you don't take note he'll find someone… more willing."

"I know." Emilia muttered, taking the soap out of Magda's hands to wash her hair. "I'm not… being 'unwilling' with him, it's just… he didn't ask for anything, so I didn't do anything either. As soon as he does, I'll…"

Emilia went quiet, and Idit immediately used the pause to snort with contempt. "Aren't you afraid that your other boyfriend will get jealous?"

Emilia just glared at the woman, but decided not to reply.

"Oh, you know who I'm talking about. That big guy who always takes you behind the barrack at every chance. What happened, he can't satisfy you anymore? Or this new one pays better? Does he give you more food, huh?"

"The first one never gave me any food," Emilia barked back.

"Really? Was he so good that you didn't charge him?"

Magda's wet washcloth, thrown with remarkable precision, landed on Idit's face, making her stop talking. "Go to hell, Idit!"

Infuriated, Idit yanked the cloth off her head and threw it back at Magda, who caught it in her hands and laughed intentionally loudly. "What are you going to do, Idit, huh?! Beat me up? Go ahead, just try to touch me – I'll tell Schneider and you'll end up in a solitary cell faster than you can say 'apple strudel.' Guess what, Idit? I had it yesterday for dinner. It was delicious! My mouth is watering just thinking about it!"

Emilia and Idit's friends stepped between the two women at the same time so the confrontation wouldn't end up in violence. The rest of the inmates preferred to turn their backs on the small group of shouting women, pretending not to see anything. No one needed to get it across the back from the capos for being involved.

"Idit, don't." One of the women, Irene Nemkoff, a short Polish brunette with piercing black eyes, pressed her hand into Idit's chest, preventing her from stepping closer to Magda. "This whore isn't worth the trouble."

"Let me smack her, just for my pleasure!"

"Not here and not now." Emilia heard Nemkoff reply quietly, but with unmasked menace in her voice.

Later that day, when they were busy braiding each other's hair on their bunk, Emilia chastised her friend for almost provoking a fight. "What's gotten into you? She's caused you trouble already, you said it yourself. Why would you irritate her even more?"

"Oh, don't fret, she won't do anything." Magda waved off Emilia's concerns. "I've been here longer than you and I know her. She wouldn't hit me. And even if she did, it wouldn't end too well for her. And besides, I've had it up to here with her constant remarks. She always starts calling us names, not the other way round."

"Well, maybe she has the right—"

"No, she doesn't! I know how we pretend all the time that everything is fine, and how we laugh it all off and even joke about it, but – Emilia! Both you and me, we got raped by the whole barrack for several hours as soon as we arrived; we got raped almost daily afterwards, and whatever our situation is now, well…it's not so peachy either. Not as horrid as it was in the beginning, but believe me, if I wasn't afraid they would all be after me again if I ended it with Schneider, I would never, ever in my life go with him willingly. My sister died, for God's sake, because of them! So no, Emmi, she has no right to accuse us of anything. She has no idea what we've been – and keep going – through."

———————————

Emilia kept eyeing the bread and cheese that was left on the cutting board after she had eaten exactly as much as Manfred allowed her to. He was deliberating on the subjects of bolshevism and national-socialism again, not even suspecting that his guest was barely listening, and instead wondering if he would allow her to take some bread to her mother. She had managed to pass Hannah her piece of bread left over from dinner the day before, but how wonderful would it be to give her a cheese sandwich tomorrow!

"You do agree with me, don't you?" Manfred's question made her shift her eyes towards him. Emilia froze for a second, afraid that he'd get angry with her for not listening and throw her out once and for all; luckily he had enough tact to repeat his question. "About private property? Everyone is entitled to have private property, aren't they?"

"Yes, most certainly," Emilia agreed readily and offered him a small smile.

Manfred beamed back. "You see? If everyone thought like you, how much easier would it be to eliminate a gap between our people; the Germans and the Israelites that is."

Emilia's brow furrowed slightly, wondering how he got onto that subject and what point he was trying to make, and why he even bothered… She just wanted her bread and to go to sleep. Hunger didn't encourage much of political musings, but her host obviously never thought about that in his desire to impress his guest with his education, or whatever reason he had for starting this monologue, which Emilia wasn't in the slightest interested in.

"I made an offer to the camp Kommandant that we should have political re-education classes for the inmates," Manfred continued, oblivious to Emilia's indifferent gaze. "If everyone here understood what they are here for, and how they can work their way out, imagine how it would benefit all of us!"

"You're suggesting that we can make our way out of here?" Emilia asked her first question, amused by his latest idea.

"Well, yes, most certainly!" Manfred got up from his chair and started pacing the room, animated more than ever. "Your people, the Israelites, are here because you were infected with wrong ideas, which in turn created hostility between us. How long have ethnic Germans and Jews lived together side by side? Since the fourteenth century! The Great German Empire took Jewish refugees from the kingdom of Poland as recent as the nineteenth century, after the state persecutions started; and not only the Polish kingdom, but also from the Russian Empire as well! So why, if all this time we have coexisted in perfect balance, do you think the Führer felt the need to separate us – now?"

Because he's a deluded maniac, with a greed for world domination, who is not right in his head, Emilia thought but she kept silent, knowing perfectly well that it was most definitely not the answer her host had in mind.

"It's because of two men." Manfred smiled with a gleam in his eyes. "Two men only, who managed to infect the whole Jewish world population with their absolutely utopian ideas: Karl Marx and Friedrich Engels. It was 'The Communist Manifesto' that planted the first seeds of anarchy in the minds of vulnerable men, which developed into a truly devastating catastrophe, the impacts of which we still have to face – and fight – today. Those highly dangerous, utopian ideas create nothing but chaos, destruction of private and intellectual property, submit the masses to the will of the few in charge, and need to be eradicated before this disease – bolshevism – spreads to the point when no one can contain it within one state only. Just look what the Bolsheviks did to their Tsar, Nicholas II! To think of it, they shot him together with his family – his wife and children – now tell me if it's not true savagery! They ransacked and destroyed everything that the great Russian traditional culture had built for centuries; to replace it with what? Collective farms? Factories and five year plans? A cultureless society?"

Manfred paused and waited for Emilia to argue with him or ask more questions, but she remained silent.

"I personally always resent saying it," he continued, his tone softening a little after his rather agitated speech. "But it's the Jewish people that carry that Bolshevik threat more than anyone. I'm not talking about the Jews living in the Soviet Union, where almost every *politruk* is of Jewish descent, but of the situation in our country as well. All the works that we had to burn during the purges were written by Jewish authors. All the dangerous ideas, taught by the highly respectable university professors, sympathetic to Bolshevism, to their vulnerable students, are taught by the Jews. The Führer's only fault was that he tried to stop that Bolshevik plague from spreading by starting this war; he didn't wish our fatherland to experience a repetition of the year 1917 in the former Russian Empire. Do you see now? The measures are harsh, yes, but in a situation like this there is no other choice. I, myself, vehemently disagree with the treatment of the inmates incarcerated here, but I understand the big picture, and the reason why some have to suffer to save the many. It's a necessary evil, unfortunately, even though it is still evil."

Emilia caught herself smiling crookedly. Manfred watched her attentively as she pondered something.

"It's interesting that you say that," she said at last, her eyes slightly squinted as if she was reminiscing about something. "That we carry the Bolshevik threat."

Manfred tilted his head to one side slightly, inviting her to explain her point further. Emilia smirked and murmured after a pause, "My father voted for Hitler in 1933."

Manfred seemed to be at a loss at first after her words, but then a beaming smile went back on his face. "That only proves my first point, don't you see? That you can all be saved through re-education, so that later you can return back to society and everything will be as it used to be years, centuries, ago! Perfect harmony between us."

"And you're trying to save me?" Emilia almost felt sorry for her host; so highly educated and maybe kind inside, but so deeply lacking touch with reality.

"Why, yes, I am." Manfred blushed slightly and took her hands in his indecisively, sitting on the edge of the cot. "If you allow me."

If you want to save me, just give me more bread. Emilia smirked inwardly, and after a moment's thought pressed his hands.

"Thank you for your generosity, Manfred."

He blushed even more, leaned forward and planted a light kiss on Emilia's cheek, then waited a few moments for her reaction before kissing her on the corner of her mouth.

Savior. Emilia shook her head slightly at the hand he had placed softly on her lap, and lay on her back, her thoughts trailing back to the cheese sandwich. That evening she walked away with it hidden in the folds of her dress. Manfred didn't mind at all giving it to her after she "admitted" that her mother was an ardent supporter of national-socialism, and needed "saving" as well.

Chapter 9

Today had been the first day that Emilia could celebrate a small victory. One of the guards had asked her to bring lunch to one of his comrades, who was supervising the laborers from a watchtower. It was usual practice for the guards to ask the workers to take lunch to their comrades, as the guards couldn't leave their post. Often, the inmates were sent up to the watchtowers with provisions, only this time, when Emilia climbed the steep stairs, making sure not to drop or spill anything, to her utmost horror she saw her abuser – "The Bear" – inside. She froze in her tracks at once, her whole body tensing under his hard glare. Seconds passed, filled with a pregnant pause, until Emilia finally placed the food items on a small ledge inside, slowly turned around and left, leaving "The Bear" standing still and motionless. Only after she had made it safely back to her working place did she breathe out in relief: it seemed that Magda wasn't mistaken after all, saying that the guards did have some sort of an arrangement when it came to women in the camp. And her new protector was an officer on top of it, so maybe the worst was indeed over.

Emilia didn't want to think of what her life would be like after they left the camp (if they ever would). Lately all her emotions, thoughts and musings returned to one thought only – one of survival. It was easier that way, living day by day, thinking only of work and food and nothing else, because she would have most certainly lost her mind if she started overthinking and analyzing everything that she had been through, and was still going through. For now, she was at least happy that "The Bear" and the rest of them left her alone. Manfred on his own she could handle.

Emilia wasn't getting lightheaded too often anymore. Her new… she stumbled over the words, thinking about what she should call Manfred…rapist?… He wasn't raping her in a sense, no more than Richter had been, as she willingly submitted to his needs, although in other circumstances she would never consent to any of their advances. Who was Manfred then? A lover? Most definitely not, just because of the very meaning of the word: there was nothing resembling love from her side that was for certain. There was gratitude for keeping her safe and fed, yes. An owner then? A benefactor? Yes. They were probably the closest terms to use. Her new benefactor made sure that she always left his quarters full, and even though the dinners that he generously shared with her were the only rich meal of the day for her, it was more than enough for her to preserve enough energy so as to not be left swaying during roll call, or to stop working for a moment just because her vision would go completely dark from hunger. Once she had been bashed on her shoulder and back a couple of times for "stalling" as *Helferinnen* called it, demanding that she go back to work at once or spend the night in a solitary cell in a basement. Now, there would be no more beatings because she could work efficiently without the threat of being thrown into the basement.

One new girl who had just arrived several days ago asked Emilia warily on her first night, after she was explained the rules of the camp, if there were rats in that basement. Emilia recalled how hard she and Magda had laughed: there were no rats or mice in this place – if one had the misfortune to wander inside one of the barracks or a canteen it would get caught in a split second and eaten as a great delicacy.

"Why do you think there are no roaches around as well, even though we live in such filth?" Magda asked the girl, and lifted her eyebrows at her disgusted look. "Yes, people ate them all. And grass, that too, that's why the ground outside and everything around is covered with dirt. Everything's been eaten. People chew on wood sometimes."

"I used to." Emilia nodded knowingly. "If you're lucky enough to find a good stick, not a dry one that is, you can suck its juice out. And wood itself, if it's soft and chewable, it fills your stomach too. Here, everything is edible."

Emilia and Magda decided to take the newcomer under their wing as soon as they saw her tiny frail frame in the entrance of the barrack on the first day of her arrival. In Emilia's mind, her own fear of the unknown in the new and quite unfriendly place was still fresh, and she had no idea how she would have managed if it wasn't for Magda. However, catching Idit and her bunkmates' hard glares and hostile grumbling at the sight of the small brunette with black eyes wide open with terror, Emilia suggested to her friend that they should help the girl discretely and try not to associate with her too much in front of everyone.

"Let's not talk to her, unless we're alone," Emilia whispered to Magda as they lay on their bunk that night. "Idit has already branded her a new 'field whore,' and I bet the girl is barely sixteen and has most likely never seen a naked man before."

"She keeps asking where her grandmother is." Magda sighed in reply. "I told her that she is probably in the other barrack and she'll see her someday."

"Is she?"

"No. They were sent two different ways after the selection. But I just couldn't bring myself to tell her that."

"She'll learn very soon what the other side means. Someone will tell her."

"Well, that someone won't be me. She's terrified as it is; who am I to tell her that the only relative she had left, is dead?"

Both went silent for a few minutes.

"The poor thing is so naïve, too," Magda said suddenly, letting out a soft giggle. "A guard offered her a cigarette, and she thanked him and replied that she didn't smoke."

Emilia smiled. "Did you explain to her that it's the local currency, and that she can buy two pieces of bread with one cigarette?"

"I did. As a matter of fact I told her to go back, apologize and ask for that cigarette."

"Did she go?"

"No, of course not. She's new, she's too young and she's terrified of the guards. She'd never ask them for anything."

"Lucky girl, being offered a cigarette on her first day."

"Yes... That's what got Idit so mad, too; that the guard noticed her."

"It's not good to get that sort of attention, from the guards, that is."

"No, it's not."

"Shall we tell her..?"

Emilia heard Magda chew on her lip in the dark.

"No, I don't think we should. We'll just scare her even more."

"But shouldn't we warn her at least... of how to behave with them?"

"No, I'm telling you, there's no point. It's better to come as an unexpected shock for her; besides, she won't fight them. She's afraid to even talk, leave alone scream or fight anyone. No, let's not tell her anything. They won't harm her...well... They won't kill her, I mean."

Magda turned out to be right, as she always was. Helene, the "new girl," was absent from the roll call, and Emilia and Magda climbed onto their bunk in silence and agreed not to go to sleep before she came back. Helene walked through the doors long after the lights had gone off, found her way in the darkness to the furthest wall, next to which the girls' bunk stood, obviously trying not to disturb the sleeping bunkmates, and curled into a ball next to the stove.

Emilia and Magda climbed down as quietly as they could, shifted Helene to an upright position and wrapped her in their own blanket.

"Here, have some," Magda whispered, touching Helene's mouth with a piece of bread, saved especially for her.

The girl's unblinking stare didn't even register that someone was talking to her, nor did she make a move to take the bread from Magda. Emilia brushed Helene's hair gently, also coaxing her to eat in a hushed voice. After several more minutes Magda gave Emilia a knowing look and shook her head slightly, sighing at their fruitless attempts to get Helene to respond, or to at least eat something. After leaving the bread in her limp hand, Magda and Emilia went back to their bunk.

Despite the exhaustion, they couldn't really sleep that night and spoke in hushed whispers instead.

"To think of it, we're relatively lucky," Emilia observed, toying with the end of her braid. "At least we didn't lose our innocence that way. I lost mine in a way that was not much better, but at least it was just one man, and not fifteen of them."

81

Magda sniffled quietly.

"I lost mine to my first love. He was my best friend, too."

Emilia caught herself smiling. At least one of them had good memories of the event.

"Where is he now?"

"I don't know. His family immigrated to Switzerland in 1939. We moved to the Protectorate. We lost touch."

"How was it?" Emilia smiled wider, nudging her friend with her elbow slightly.

Magda was silent for some time, and then admitted, smiling dreamily, "It was wonderful. It always is, with the right person."

"Too bad I'll never know that feeling." Emilia closed her eyes, sighing.

"Of course you will. When we get out of here, you'll find your right person, and you'll see for yourself, how wonderful it will be."

"I'm not planning to look for the right person. If men leave me alone and don't give me their attention, I'd be more than happy to spend my life in solitude."

"You can say all you want, but when the time is right, he'll come and find you himself."

"You're such a hopeless romantic."

"No, I'm not. I just honestly believe that we deserve a little bit of happiness after all this, that's all."

"And Helene? Do you think she'll ever be the same?"

"I don't know. For now I'll just look after her, share my bread with her and make sure she doesn't do anything stupid."

Helene didn't talk to anyone for the next few days, only nodded slowly with a vacant look on her face when Emilia or Magda sneaked a piece of bread into her tiny hand. Emilia suspected that 'The Bear' had replaced her with the new girl as his victim, and it was only when Helene collapsed during one of the roll calls and was taken to the medical ward, that she was saved for at least a few days; or so Emilia and Magda thought. When the Frau asked one of the *Helferinnen* the following morning why Helene Rubenstein hadn't been discharged yet, the uniformed woman only shrugged indifferently and reported that Rubenstein had an inflammation of the ovaries and the doctor would keep her under observation for some time. Emilia exchanged glances with Magda; she knew all too well how that observation would most likely end for the girl.

———————

Emilia and Magda were chatting on their way to work, both in very high spirits. Manfred had hinted the night before that the following day Emilia would get a very nice surprise, but she never expected that the Frau would call her name together with a few others, subscribing them to work in the sewing factory, where Magda worked. As soon as the roll call was over, Magda almost squealed with delight and gave her bunkmate a quick hug, but quickly stepped away under the Frau's stern look. Emilia caught a glimpse of Manfred on the way to the factory, where he gave her a quick wink like that of a conspirator. Emilia beamed back, almost sincerely this time, and listened to her friend who kept repeating in a hushed voice about how lucky she was to secure a man like that.

"You hold onto him tight," Magda kept whispering, clinging close to her bunkmate. "He seems like a very nice man, you can't afford to lose his interest."

"I'm trying to be as nice to him as possible," Emilia whispered back, throwing another glance in her benefactor's direction, to then continue after a pause. "But, don't you think we're prostituting ourselves for food?"

"Rubbish!" Magda snorted with contempt. "Who told you that, Idit? Don't listen to her, she's just a mean hag. We would be prostituting if we had a choice. We're not prostituting, we're surviving. It's not our fault that we have a little bit of an advantage over the others with our looks, and anyway, we've also paid for these looks in full, in ways they haven't even seen in their worst nightmares. They have no right to judge us for what we're doing."

Emilia didn't reply and only envied her spirited friend's confidence. She wasn't so sure what to think of herself and Idit's poisonous remarks thrown her way whenever their ways crossed only added to her own broodings. Now that hunger wasn't the only thing that occupied her mind, her musings had started coming back and Emilia wasn't so certain that it was a welcome change. Living like an animal in constant fear and abuse like she did in the past few weeks seemed like hell, but that hell didn't just disappear now that things had changed somewhat for the better; the fear and abuse still haunted her now and would haunt her for the rest of her life, she knew it. And yet, she didn't contemplate suicide anymore. Together with food and relative safety, the desire to live had also come back, to survive against all odds. She didn't know why she even wanted to survive after everything she'd been through, but somehow it just appeared unfair to die now, to die after such misery and suffering.

"The circle always completes itself," Magda had said once in a thoughtful manner, and, for some reason, that phrase stuck in Emilia's mind. "We'll come out of here and we'll be happy again. And the victors will be the defeated, and the defeated will be the victors. We'll be happy again, you'll see. God can't stay with his eyes closed forever."

The small sewing factor was like night compared to day in regards to the construction pit, in which Emilia had previously worked. As soon as she was assigned to her sewing machine, the one close to Magda by pure luck, Emilia kept smiling in a silly way, not able to believe that she would be working with an actual roof above her head, in a heated room and sitting down and not standing for twelve hours in a row.

A female capo dropped a pile of clothes next to her and nodded at the sewing machine that Emilia kept inspecting with reverence. "Do you know how to operate it?"

Emilia shook her head embarrassingly, fearing that she'd get kicked out from the factory that instant. However, judging by the capo's rolled eyes, her desperate grunt and the way she motioned one of the women to join Emilia at the table, the capo knew that she was here to stay.

"Another one. The field wife," the capo muttered under her breath and turned to the inmate she had called over. "Show her how to sew."

"Let her friend show her," Idit chimed in with her low, hoarse voice, addressing the capo and motioning her head towards Magdalena. "She's a good teacher, showed her how to open her legs in no time."

Emilia only lowered her head over the sewing machine, feeling the heat burning her cheeks. Idit worked as a seamstress because she was one before she had been sent here. She obviously didn't appreciate the two girls taking much desired positions even with a lack of qualification. Magda, meanwhile, turned to their neighbor from the barrack and, after eyeing her up and down contemptuously, snorted with a grin. "Why, are you jealous that no one pays attention to you?"

"I don't want that kind of attention."

"You're not getting any! As a matter of fact, I don't think you would get any even if you were the only woman in the camp!"

All the women snickered at the insult and Idit's face, which was turning red with anger. Idit had just opened her mouth to reply, but the capo smashed her baton on one of the sewing tables, bringing order to the inmates she supervised.

"Quiet, all of you! The *Helferinnen* will hear you laugh and you'll all be left without a lunch break *and* dinner today! Now, go back to work!"

After the capo turned away, Emilia turned her head to Magda and mouthed a silent "thank you." The redhead only shrugged with a smile and mouthed back, "my pleasure." For the rest of the day, Emilia felt Idit's eyes boring into her back, but even that didn't ruin her mood. For the first time in God knew how long she felt rested after a full day of work.

―――――――――

Emilia soon noticed that her body was changing a little as she'd put a little meat on her bones. Going to Manfred's room two or three times a week didn't seem that much of a price to pay for all the food he kept sneaking out for her every day, leave alone feeding her properly each time she came by. She went to his room under the guise that she was supposedly cleaning Manfred's place. Emilia was very fearful of such arrangements and wondered if the two of them would eventually get into trouble for *Rassenschande*, only, as it seemed, even the supervisors looked the other way despite their knowledge of the situation, not only regarding Emilia and Manfred, but many other "benefactors" and their "field wives". "Field wives" was the term used by the guards and officers' comrades; "field whores" was the term used by fellow inmates, but Emilia gradually taught herself how to turn a deaf ear to those insults. After a while, she wasn't even embarrassed by the whispers behind her back. She only wondered why those women could be so hateful of them, when the only reason they allowed such things to happen was for no other reason than to attempt to survive the best they could.

"Maybe we should share bread with them?" Emilia suggested once to Magdalena, when they lay on their bunk nibbling on their benefactors' offerings as quietly as they could.

"With the whole barrack?"

"No. With Idit at least. Maybe she'll stop then."

"She'll never stop. And why would I even share my bread with her? I earned it. Let her go and get her own bread."

"Maybe we should... just to help the others to survive, too."

"We can't feed the whole camp. And besides, do you think someone like Idit would be grateful to you for what you did for them? Don't count on her gratitude. She'll eat your hard earned bread while she can, but as soon as you fall out of your protector's grace, she won't share a crumb with you." Magda turned away from her and muttered under her breath, "You're still too nice for this place. People here are evil, all of them. We should just hold onto each other, and forget about the others."

Emilia didn't think that they were evil; it was the camp life that made them like that, slowly stripping them down from everything human to pure animalistic instincts: food and survival. Compassion was a rarity here, the sole privilege of those who had just arrived with the new transport or who had been lucky enough to secure themselves a protector. After days and days of seeing people die in front of you, and watching your own neighbors from the same barrack stripping a corpse of all of its meager clothing before the morning roll call, to when you didn't even notice hanged bodies in the front plaza because you pass them daily on your way to work and back, that was how Emilia knew that the camp numbed you down to the point of not caring for human life anymore, to become just like those who ran the camp.

Maybe it was their plan from the very beginning, to make us not care for each other and to not stand up for each other anymore, so it becomes easier to get rid of us all, Emilia pondered sometimes. When she questioned Manfred about such things he simply shook his head and patiently tried to persuade her that it was merely "a war time necessity," and that as soon as Germany won the war, life would get back to normal.

"And what will happen to us?" Emilia inquired. "The Jews, I mean."

Manfred flushed a little and lowered his eyes before answering. Emilia guessed that he was probably disappointed that she meant her people as "us," and not him and herself. To her that question needed no answer, war or no war. For now, Emilia found no shame in eating from his hand – she paid him for it in full – but deep inside, behind her clenched teeth and stubbornly closed mouth she knew that she would make a run for it the first chance she got, and she would not look back once. She dreamed about making a run for it, where she would have the chance to forget it all, like it had never happened, where she could cross out the memories and pretend that certain things had never happened to her. She would go as far as she could where no one knew her and she would pretend that she was a different person; a lucky refugee who had waited out the purges somewhere in hiding, lucky enough to never see firsthand the atrocious accounts of what was done to the unfortunate victims of the regime.

She had already decided that if she did happen to survive all this, to leave this place like Magda promised so many times that they would, she would never tell her story to a one living soul. She would guard her memories and keep all the darkness inside, to herself only, and let others see only the other, old, good Emilia. That Emilia had already died, but her new twin sister practiced performing her smile from time to time in front of Manfred's mirror to later offer it to him, like the most precious gift, wrapped in the sincerest gratitude and adoration. Emilia almost applauded herself for mastering the fakeness to the point of him really believing that she liked him and cared for him. Only, little slips of the tongue would give her away sometimes and furrow his brow with doubt, but Emilia would brush her hand on his as if unintentionally, smile again in the most genuine way, and he'd start beaming back at once, promising her that he'd certainly not leave her uncared for after everything was over and that he would find a way, as he always put it, "to save her."

"I suppose you'll all be released after the war is over and probably be sent to farm the land in Russia. The territory is so vast, it's impossible for only Germans to work on it... Yes, I think that was the Führer's plan from the very beginning."

Emilia seriously doubted this last statement, as she and her family, most members of which were dead, were living proof of the contrary. No one wanted them alive, not the Führer, not anyone, they were spared for now only because they could work, and as soon as this ability to work was gone there was only way out of the current hell – "disinfection." "The Bear" had once sneered and asked her why she thought it was called "disinfection." When Emilia didn't answer – not that he ever needed her to answer, preferring her to be terrified and mute, just the way he liked it – he cackled and replied with a typical SS jest: the Reich is disinfecting itself of all the Jewish vermin. Then he laughed loudly, spat in her face and got off of her, leaving her to lay on the filthy floor with his filth inside.

Emilia involuntarily shuddered at the memory and hurried to put her clothes back in order. They never risked taking their clothes off, even though Manfred's fellow officers had a pretty good idea that Emilia didn't come to his room just to clean it, even though she really did. Manfred was exceptionally clean and it only took her ten minutes to take care of the room; the other twenty were his.

"I have to go back." She gave the man on the bed an apologizing smile.

He nodded sadly and handed her several pieces of bread and dried meat wrapped in newspaper, which lay prepared on his nightstand, next to the picture of his family: his strict looking father, his mother, beautiful even in her forties, who he obviously took after, himself and two brothers – all of them were wearing black uniforms.

"Emilia." Manfred caught her hand as she was getting ready to leave, and kissed it unexpectedly. "I don't care…"

Emilia tilted her head to one side with the same half smile that she always manufactured for him, indicating that she didn't understand what he meant.

"I… I don't care that you're Jewish." He finally finished his thought, almost in a whisper, lowering his eyes as if confessing to something very, very shameful.

Emilia almost felt sorry for him and barely contained a chuckle for some reason. She outstretched her hand, brushed his blushing cheek softly, took her meal from his hand and hid it in her pocket.

"I know you don't. Goodbye, Manfred."

He nodded and whispered a quiet "goodbye" as well.

I hate you though, Emilia thought sulkily, making her way back to her barrack. *I hate you all, with your uniforms. I hate every single one of you. Jewish. I never thought of myself as Jewish before all of you suddenly started pointing it out. I was a German, just like you. What made me so distinctive from you all of a sudden? The red J in my papers? The armband? Because if I had taken it off, I could have easily passed for one of your highly praised BDM girls. You'd never know the difference once you saw me next to them. You never knew the difference before, and now all of a sudden we're Jewish? Now, we're different from you and you have to kill us, why? Just because? Why us? What did we do to you? Nothing at all. Why do I have to listen to your condescending 'I don't care that you're Jewish' remark? Why should you care?! I'm a human being, just like you are, and my heart is on the same side as yours, and my blood is also red, and it hurts me to hear that we are vermin, just as much as it would hurt you if someone told you the same thing.*

"Why do they hate us so?" Emilia asked Magda later that night. "I just don't understand why?"

"They at least have a reason for it: their policies and their Führer with all his propaganda." Her friend sighed and rubbed her eyes tiredly. "It's when your own kin starts hating you as well, that's when it becomes frightening."

Emilia herself never understood the hatred and resentment that was directed at her and Magda. While most of the inmates went on with their lives, too exhausted or too indifferent to those around them, trying to survive the best they could, Idit, Irene Nemkoff and their friends just didn't seem to let go of the fact that someone "had a better life" than they did. However, they couldn't see or acknowledge that this "better life" came at a price; a life that Emilia wouldn't wish for her worst enemy.

The only confrontation that Emilia had with Idit happened when the latter caught her unawares behind the barrack one Sunday, when Emilia was cleaning her assigned territory.

"You could share some of your delicacies with the others, you know."

Emilia turned to the hoarse voice, which always hissed curses and degrading comments her way, and found herself face to face with the tall Idit, her square, angular face emanating contempt.

"'The others' meaning you, Nemkoff and your friends?" Emilia asked tiredly, resting her hands on her broom.

Idit didn't reply at first, and only sneered. "We're all in the same boat here. We should be helping each other."

"I'm helping who I can. I can't feed the whole barrack."

Emilia and Magda still supported Helene discreetly, after she had returned to the barrack recently. She still wouldn't talk, however she soon started trading cigarettes for extra bread. Magda had shared a sad smile with Emilia; well, at least the guard, who had noticed Helene on the day of her arrival, seemed to claim the girl as his own and she was thus spared from constant harassment from "The Bear" and his drunken buddies. Between the little Helene, her mother Hannah, and the elderly woman who was also a newcomer and soon replaced Helene's late grandmother, Emilia didn't have much food left for herself.

"One day tables will turn," Idit said with a shadow of menace in her voice. "And the ones who you refused to help will remember your greediness and selfishness. We're ready to close our eyes regarding your amoral behavior, and only ask to share what you have. But you won't do even that."

"I refuse to help?" Emilia snorted at the irony that Idit didn't see in her own words. "How about you, Idit? Do you want to help me earn the bread? Well, why don't you answer? Do you, or don't you?"

Idit cast a despising look Emilia's way, turned around and left, without saying a word.

Chapter 10

On a Wednesday in June 1944, the day started like any other day. Emilia and Magdalena laughed about something on the way to work, and at the entrance Emilia waved at her mother who was coming from the other side. A couple of months ago Emilia had mustered up enough courage to ask Manfred if it was possible to transfer Hannah to the sewing factory as well. Emilia had been sneaking food to her mother at any opportunity she could, but the work at the construction pit was taking its toll on the fragile former housewife, who had never worked a day in her life before the Germans marked them as vermin. Watching her mother's health deteriorate and her figure getting more and more frail had finally encouraged Emilia to coax her benefactor to help her out. Reluctantly at first, he still agreed, stressing that he wasn't promising anything. When, one day shortly after, Emilia saw her mother walk towards the sewing factory from her side of the camp, she could barely contain herself from running up to her and hugging her; she was very *grateful* to Manfred later that evening, leaving him in his room with a beaming smile.

"I think it's going to storm today," Magda observed while working on her sewing, nodding at the window as soon as Emilia lifted her head up from her work. "Look at the sky. And it's humid, like by a swamp."

Emilia nodded and sighed, thinking that if that happened then they'd have to stand soaking under the rain for the evening roll call. But the rain itself in June wasn't such a terrible thing; what was worse was that after a few hours their feet would be buried in mud, washed out with water. It had happened on several occasions before and the inmates had even invented their own way of washing their feet prior to going to bed: they'd stick their shoes through an open window, and hold them in the rain, wash them down first and then hose off their feet with the water which collected inside the shoe. The line was always long when this happened, as no one wanted to get onto their bunk with muddy feet, and yet some (to Emilia's big surprise) weren't too bothered about that and preferred sleep to staying clean. She didn't judge them though; maybe they were so tired that cleaning off some mud that would just fall off by itself the next day wasn't on their list of priorities.

Heavy, pregnant clouds gathered all evening and the feel of electricity lingered in the air, but it seemed that this time they were spared and the girls both breathed out a sigh of relief when the roll call was over and they were dismissed. They ran towards their barrack, giggling about being able to leave unscathed this time.

Thunder rolled menacingly somewhere in the distance, and the girls lay on their bunk, not ready to go to sleep yet.

"I wish we could hear artillery someday," Magda suddenly said dreamily. "Can you imagine, what a wonderful sound it would be! We would lay like this and think that it's just thunder, and not pay any attention to it, but then a Russian soldier would open the door to our barrack and say in heavily accented German: "You're free, all of you! We liberated you! All the guards are dead! You all can leave this place!" And we would all cry and laugh at the same time and hug and kiss each other, and kiss the Russian Ivan too – we would hug and kiss him and tell him how long we had waited for them to come and save us! Wouldn't it be wonderful, Emmi? To walk through the gates of this camp together, holding hands – to freedom?"

"Sounds a little too good to be true." Emilia chuckled kindheartedly.

"No! Doesn't your Manfred tell you anything?" Magda started whispering excitedly, her eyes sparkling in the dark. "The front is getting closer to us, Emmi! Germany is losing the war! They opened the second western front and now Adolf will have to fight on two fronts – East and West! It's impossible for him to win now! It's only a matter of time when they come here to save us all."

"How do you know all this?"

"From Schneider, of course, how else? He tells me about the Eastern front a lot – his father is fighting there, so he gives me a firsthand account, and not what Goebbels writes in his little *Beobachter* filled with propaganda. They're fighting in Belorussia already, pushing closer and closer to Eastern Poland. If you think of it, the frontline isn't too far from us!"

"Well… yes, but then…" Emilia wrinkled her brow, digesting the news. "Do you think the SS will just hand us over to them, together with the land when they come?"

"What choice do they have?" Magda shrugged. "They'll have to retreat. They can't take us with them, too many trains and too little time. No, they'll just leave us here. When the Russians come, we'll be the least of their troubles."

"What if they decide to just kill us all?" Emilia barely whispered in response.

"Why would they do that?"

"Because that's what they've been doing this whole time and because they want us all dead?"

Magda went quiet for a moment, but then shook her read head defiantly.

"No, they won't do that. They won't be able to send us all to disinfection, and if they just start lining us up and shooting us, everyone will just scatter and run away. There aren't enough of them to overpower us all."

"They've been doing quite well so far."

Magda sniffled quietly and started studying the wooden ceiling.

"No, I still don't think they would do something like that. Besides, both my Schneider and your Manfred will surely warn us of any of such actions, and would hide us someplace safe."

"Do you think?"

"Oh yes. I'm more than positive." Magda turned to Emilia and pressed her hand, smiling at her in the dark. "I just want to come out of here alive, Emmi. Together with you. And then we'll start such a life, a new life, a very happy life that we'll forget all about this horror. You'll see we will. They'll come for us soon. We just have to wait."

With those words she let out a contented sigh and tried to relax her muscles. Emilia rarely prayed, but this time she closed her eyes and begged God for Magda's words to be true. She lay there looking into the darkness, allowing her mind to wander where it wanted, until she could feel her eyes becoming heavier. This was the one time in the entire day that silence prevailed, and she felt a brief moment of peace lying there next to Magda, as she let her body sink into the small bunk. Her mind dropped into a state of disconnection without her even realising, in that moment before the body drops into true sleep, and she felt so light and at ease that, at first, her mind didn't completely register a sound next to her. With a sudden jolt back into reality, she felt rough hands, yanking her down and dropping her on the hard ground from the height of the third level bunk. Emilia landed with a loud thud and judging by the sharp pain in her side she might have cracked a rib or even a few.

She opened her eyes to the darkness, only to see several faces above her, all twisted with hatred, before a folded blanket, stinking with sweat and human waste, was pressed to her face, closing her frantic intake of air and muffling any possible screams. Then the blows came. Someone was holding her hands apart so she wouldn't be able to protect herself from the violent attack that came out of nowhere, and a shower of painful kicks and merciless strikes poured on her side, chest, legs, and, worst of all, her stomach, kicking the small amount of remaining air out of her lungs. She would have most certainly suffocated if someone hadn't decided to hit her in the face, too, and the blanket was lifted for the first punch to break her nose.

With searing pain, panic kicked in and Emilia realized that she would get beaten to death if she didn't do something that very instant. Another fist broke her lips but she was already screaming, screaming at the top of her lungs. Her screams were filled with agonizing pain, and she shrieked as loudly as she could, not even noticing another two blows that tried to make her stop. The blanket landed on her face again, and the approaching barking of the dogs and shouts outside were the last thing she remembered before slipping into unconsciousness.

Emilia woke up when someone splashed a bucketful of water onto her, and she immediately jolted to a sitting position, coughing and gasping for air. The searing pain returned at once and it seemed that there wasn't a hair on her whole body that wasn't hurting. The light in the barrack was on and Emilia saw several *Helferinnen*, together with a few regular SS guards, standing in a circle around her and shouting orders at the capos. The Frau, who pushed her way through her subordinates, had clearly just woken up from her sleep as she hadn't even buttoned her uniform jacket. She stopped in front of Emilia and ordered her to get up.

"Who did this to you?" she demanded in her harsh commanding voice.

"I don't know," Emilia replied hoarsely, wiping the blood running down her face from her broken nose and lips. "It was dark, I didn't see them."

"Order the whole barrack to line up outside," the leader of the *Helferinnen* barked at her orderlies and lifted her head up to the bunks. Emilia followed her gaze and realized with shock that Magda must have been beaten too. Everything went cold inside her as she saw two SS men stand on the second bunk to inspect the bunk where Emilia and Magda slept. "What's with the other one?"

"Nothing." Both guards jumped down, while Emilia held her breath. "Dead. They strangled her it seems."

"You got lucky today." The Frau snorted after a pause, looking Emilia up and down. "You could've been dead too if it wasn't for your remarkable pair of lungs. Out."

"Are you sure that she can't be helped?" Emilia whispered to no one in particular, as the guards got busy with herding everyone outside. None of them paid attention to her, as she stood swaying slightly on her feet and looking helplessly at the bunk, from which two capos were lifting the lifeless body of her murdered friend.

Emilia followed them outside, hardly suppressing her tears, and tried to catch Magda's dainty hand before they could lay her down on the ground.

"Please, be careful with her," she kept repeating, stepping outside under the blinding light of the projectors, all illuminating the small space in front of the barrack where the inmates were lining up. Rain began pouring down, soaking Emilia to the skin as soon as she left the barrack.

"No, not in the dirt, please," she begged the capos, and clenched Magdalena's clothes when they tried to put her down on the muddy ground beside the inmates. "Here, on the planks, here's good…"

She took a piece of wet bread from her pocket in a feverish gesture and quickly put it into one of the capo's pockets. The woman, who was still holding Magda by the legs, motioned to the other one to put the girl where Emilia showed them, on the wooden planks left from the recent re-roofing of their barrack.

"Honey, they're not going to hold a formal burial with flowers for her, you know," the capo muttered quietly, lowering Magda's body onto the wood. "They'll just burn her together with the others. Why do you bother?"

"She was my friend," Emilia whispered, sobbing and petting Magdalena's wet hair, stuck to her still beautiful face. "My only friend in the whole world…"

"Come, come." The capo, who seemed to suddenly warm up to the her either because of the meager bribe or because she did indeed feel sorry for her, took Emilia firmly by the shoulders and turned her away from the body. "The Frau will get mad if you aren't standing with the others in a minute."

Emilia didn't even try to suppress her sobbing, feeling such an incredibly intense sense of loss as if another member of her family died, and not just some vivacious redhead who she'd come to know barely a year ago. Magda was more than a friend to her; she was her rock, and an understanding and never-judging shoulder to cry her heart out to, her sister, her soulmate in some sense, who took her in from day one and who refused to give up on her when Emilia was ready to give up on herself. If it wasn't for Magda, she would've been dead by now, most certainly dead, either starved to death, killed by "The Bear" and his friends during one of their drunken orgies, or she would have thrown herself onto the electric wire to end it all. Magda had just said mere minutes ago how she dreamed of walking out of this camp holding Emilia's hand. And now she was dead, killed for...

For what? Emilia had a vague guess about the reasons of the attackers, only she still couldn't believe that they could go as far as murder. Human hatred just couldn't go this far in her eyes, and yet she stood next to the people who had potentially tried to murder her and who had succeeded in taking her friend's life.

The Frau was yelling something at the inmates in front of her, but Emilia couldn't even make out her words. Only when the leader *Helferin* took her gun out and stated in a loud stern voice that she would start shooting every second person if someone doesn't come forward with names did a young girl step forward and point a shaking hand at Idit and several women standing next to her. Emilia recognized the girl as Helene, who began stuttering and explaining that she had heard them plan the attack over the last few days, but that she had been too afraid to say anything to the capos or *Helferinnen* fearing Idit's retaliation.

Emilia turned her head to Idit and the others, who were forced to step forward under the Frau's hard stare.

"Why did you do this?"

When Idit didn't reply, the Frau took a baton out of one of her orderlies' hands and hit Idit on the shoulder. The woman yelped and lowered her head, instinctively expecting another blow. The Frau's hand clasping the weapon froze above Idit's head.

"I asked you a question. Why did you do this?"

"They stole my bread," Idit mumbled defensively, throwing a hostile glance at Emilia.

Emilia couldn't believe her ears.

"We never stole anything from her," she replied, feeling the anger slowly growing inside her. "We had our own bread."

The two eyed each other like two sworn enemies, which they had now become since one of them had decided to kill the other. Idit had nothing to lose at this point and had obviously decided to try and drown her opponent as well, thinking that if she got hanged for the assault, that Emilia could dangle on her own rope with her perhaps.

"Of course you had bread," Idit stated quietly, slowly raising her voice as her fists started clenching once again. "You two were the lowliest whores, prostituting yourself to the SS!!! Hang her too, Frau, for *Rassenschande.* Everybody here knows it, she's a dirty whore and nothing else, just like her whore friend was—"

The Frau's baton smashed into the woman's mouth and made her stop shouting at once as Idit clenched her bleeding lips with a shaking hand.

"How dare you badmouth the Führer's elite SS, you filthy Jew?!" The Frau almost shook with anger herself now, raising her hand for another violent blow. "No one here would commit a crime against his race, that much I can tell you with certainty, you liar!"

The SS guards watched the unfolding scene with blank expressions on their faces, only tensing for a second right after Idit's accusation, but visibly relaxing after the heated defense of their honor from their female colleague. Emilia wondered if the Frau herself believed the guards' innocence. The others weren't so delusional and yet no one said a word in confirmation of Idit's accusation.

"Hang her," the Frau ordered after she had finished beating up her victim. Idit, who lay in the mud in a heap of rags and dirt, didn't utter a single protesting sound. Emilia wondered if she was still alive. Not that she cared for a second about her assailant's well-being; she only hoped that she wouldn't die too quickly and easily and that she suffered for a while. Magda had been right after all: people were evil here, and Emilia felt the same evil engulfing her from the inside. Any good that had been in her died together with Magdalena that night.

Chapter 11

Emilia lined up together with the rest of the inmates on the platform, ready to board the train. Her ribs still hurt with every breath she took, but the rest of the bruises were unexpectedly healing quickly and didn't bother her too much. She had had enough time to rest in the basement solitary cell, in which the Kommandant ordered her to be put the following morning after the assault. After both the Frau and Emilia couldn't provide him with a sound reason for the attack, he decided to transfer Emilia, together with the rest of the inmates who didn't pass the SS medical staff inspection to another camp in order to free up space for the fresh working force in their case and to "not cause the staff any more trouble" in Emilia's. Now they were heading to the dreadful "someplace else" which everyone here feared so much.

A very nervous Manfred had snuck into the solitary cell in which Emilia was restricted to while awaiting transfer, handed her some food and couldn't stop gasping at Emilia's bruised face, pressing her hands, promising that he would certainly find her after "everything was over" and "keep taking care of her." Emilia smiled out of politeness, quickly wolfed the sandwiches and only nodded in agreement to everything he was saying just to pacify him.

After several hours locked in the heat of the cattle car, with her unseeing eyes looking through the bleak mass of emaciated people in front of her, Emilia wondered when was the last time she had her mother next to her, and what would happen to her now that Emilia was gone? She could only hope that Manfred would have enough decency to keep watching over her mother, unless he found himself a new girl from a new train and forget all about Emilia.

"Who did this to you?" An old woman's voice interrupted her thoughts. Emilia turned her head to see a fragile, hunched figure looking sympathetically at her battered face. "The capos?"

Emilia lowered her eyes and shook her head with a small smile. "No. Barrack mates."

Shock reflected in the kind woman's eyes. "Why on earth would they do that to you?"

Emilia only shrugged uncomfortably with one shoulder and smiled again. What could she possibly reply to such a question?

The ride wasn't long, but Emilia still breathed in relief after the door to their car was opened and capos, just like the ones they had had in their camp, marched them outside to form a line on the platform. This time, people around Emilia shifted nervously, as they already knew that the line meant selection. Two SS officers stood at the end of the platform, and one with a whip started pointing the newly arrived inmates to his right or to his left.

"What do you think, is it the same like it was in our camp?" a voice whispered behind her back. "The right is good and the left is…"

"How would I know?" another girl barked back irritably.

"Ach, what's the difference? It's all the same. We'll all end up dead," someone else joined in.

"Stop being so morbid. Maybe this place is better than the other was. It looks bigger at least…"

"Why would they send us here then, if we're such valuable workers? No, I tell you, this one could be worse, like the dead end for all the ones who aren't fit to be in any of the other camps anymore. After this one – there's no other way to go."

Emilia tried to concentrate on the movement of the line and the shining black boots of the two SS officers, getting closer and closer to her. She wished that all of the inmates would just stop talking. As if talking could save them in any way.

"You." The whip suddenly landed on her shoulder, not painfully, but enough for her to jerk her head upwards, to look at the man who stood against the sun. "I remember you. Emilia Brettenheimer, isn't it?"

Emilia squinted, and even raised her hand to her brow, trying to make out the features of the SS man talking to her. He slowly moved her hand away with his whip and touched her mouth with its tip while Emilia froze in her place. There was something very familiar about him and something very menacing. It was as if all her senses, sharpened by the animalistic survival instincts that were necessary in recent times, started screaming "danger" immediately; not that she had anywhere to run or hide.

"Come with me," the officer ordered, and effortlessly jumped off the small podium he stood on. He motioned one of his aides to replace him and finally turned to Emilia. That second she instantly recognized him – the SS man with a whip in Krakow, who had ordered the execution of her father and brother in front of her eyes. His lips slowly moved into a smile as he saw the recognition in her eyes. "Come right this way, fraulein Brettenheimer. What an unexpected meeting, huh?"

He led her away to some sort of small administrative building next to the platform and closed the door behind himself, walking around her and looking her up and down with curiosity.

"What happened to your face?" he finally asked, stopping in front of her, much too close. Emilia fought the desire to step back, but only swallowed and lowered her eyes instead.

"Women from my barrack beat me, Herr Officer."

"Why?"

"I don't know."

"Oh, but I think you do." He made another circle around her, like a shark circling its prey. Emilia began to feel more and more uneasy. "You must have done something to anger them."

"No, Herr Officer."

"People don't beat other people up for no apparent reason." He made another circle, his whip moving behind him, its tip slightly brushing her feet. "When I beat someone up, I always have a good reason for it. I either punish them or teach them a lesson. So which one was it?"

"I don't know, Herr Officer." She prayed for him to leave her the hell alone and just sort her out to the right or left like the rest of them. Naturally, God didn't really listen to prayers in places like this.

The man stopped in front of her, boring into Emilia with his cold blue eyes. With intention he slowly took the whip from behind his back and twisted it in his hands. "See, now I'll have to hit you because you're lying to me. And as I have already said, I have a good reason for taking such action: I have to punish you for lying so you won't do it again in the future."

"They beat me because I had bread," Emilia blurted out, covering her face instinctively as he raised his hand to strike her. Several agonizing seconds passed but the strike didn't follow. Emilia slowly took her hands off her face. The SS officer stood in front of her with his hands crossed over his chest, almost beaming.

"See how easy that was?" He slightly tilted his head to one side. "The rules are simple here, fraulein Brettenheimer: if you listen to what I tell you and obey me, we'll get along just fine. But if you do things that I don't like or approve of, then we can have a certain problem, which will probably end badly for you. I don't want that, and you most definitely don't want that. Now, where did you get that bread that they didn't have? Did you steal it?"

"No, Herr Officer. I never stole anything."

"Where then?"

Emilia paused for a moment, thinking of the best words to choose. "A man kept giving it to me."

"What man?"

Emilia was silent for too long and the officer impatiently jerked his wrist, his whip slightly biting the skin on Emilia's legs.

"An SS man," she quickly replied, already accepting her fate. She would have to tell him the truth and he would order her to the left if he didn't decide to shoot her right where she stood.

"An SS man? Now, this is getting interesting!" He chuckled slightly, clearly amused by her words. Emilia frowned slightly, not understanding what was really happening. So far his reactions were as chaotic and unpredictable as a flock of birds, scared away by a thrown rock.

"And why would a mysterious SS man give you bread?"

Emilia shrugged slightly. "I guess he liked me."

"You guess? You weren't sure? Didn't he say anything to you when giving you bread?"

Emilia kept quiet as her interrogator started yet another circle around her, still smiling mysteriously. There was something in his eyes that Emilia couldn't quite place and that scared her more than his whip. *Insanity.* The word suddenly came to her mind. His hand fell on her shoulder from behind her, making her jolt once again.

"Well, did he?" He slowly moved his fingers onto her neck and then suddenly twisted her face towards his roughly, still holding her by the neck and chin. "Wasn't he saying pretty words to you? What beautiful eyes you have? How sweet your lips must taste? How he wanted to kiss you again and again?"

Emilia froze and didn't even dare blink as he leaned so close towards her that his mouth almost touched hers.

"How he wanted to make love to you?" Emilia tried not to shiver when he whispered the last words to her, looking at her intently with his unblinking eyes.

He released her as unexpectedly as he had grabbed her, and burst out laughing. Emilia observed him with her eyes wide open, thinking that she was right. He was definitely insane.

He became serious once again. His constant demeanor changes caused Emilia even more uncertainty about what to expect from this madman.

"We don't go for that here. Not after we hanged Romeo and Juliette after catching them in a warehouse with Romeo's pants down. We have a special house for the SS men to attend, with women of approved racial status. You would be a nice addition to it, but alas, you're a Jew. No handsome Germans for you anymore, fraulein Brettenheimer, I regret to inform you. However, I could still use you. Can you cook and clean?"

"I can do everything, Herr Officer," she quietly replied, wondering what he had in store for her.

"Splendid. The old Kommandant's maid died quite unexpectedly of an unfortunate accident just two days ago, and I, being his first adjutant, have had no time to replace her. I think you'll fit the necessary criteria nicely."

Emilia glanced at him inquisitively, still not trusting the possibility of getting such a position, which was considered most desirable around the female population of camp. A position in the Kommandant's premise was saved for Jehovah witnesses or political prisoners. Most Kommandants, from what Emilia had heard, didn't like Jews making their food or living with them under one roof.

Meanwhile, the Kommandant's adjutant had already opened the door and mockingly invited her out with his hand outstretched gallantly. It seemed a little too good to be true, following the uniformed man out of the territory of the camp and closer to a big house. She wondered if her interrogator lived in the house as well. For some reason she hoped that he didn't.

Emilia finished up scrubbing herself off in a small aluminum wash tub, which she would share with the Kommandant's second maid, Friede, a tall woman well into her forties. Her new uniform, which consisted of a simple black dress and a white apron, lay on her new bed – a small cot with a thin mattress and even a real pillow. Emilia found that she could not stop smiling from the moment that she stepped through the doors of the small, closet-size room that was going to become her new living quarters together with the second maid. After the filthy barrack and a wooden bunk this small but clean room with an actual bed, and even a basin, seemed like the most luxurious palace apartment to her.

Emilia giggled, washing the soap off her hair, not believing that she would actually be able to wash herself every day, fix her hair in front of the small mirror, and brush her teeth with a real toothbrush – even if it was one that was left from the dead maid, but the camp had taught Emilia not to be picky a long time ago.

When she first saw herself in the small cloudy mirror right after she stepped out of the wash tub, she sighed softly, observing her nose, which was still a bit swollen, with a small bump on its bridge now – definitely evidence that it had been broken. The cut right below her left brow was healing nicely and was barely visible, while her lips would look just fine in a day or so. *I am lucky they didn't break my teeth at least,* Emilia thought and went on to brush her hair – also with a late maid's hairbrush.

"You better stay in the kitchen today," Friede said, as soon as they were left alone, nodding at Emilia's face. "I'll serve food to Herr Kommandant alone today, so there is no risk of him asking you unnecessary questions."

"Is he… a strict man?" Emilia asked tentatively.

"Who? Herr Kommandant?" Friede raised her brow. "No, not at all. He's a very nice man, well… for a camp Kommandant, that is. It's his aide, that's who… Oh, well, you'll see for yourself in time."

"Is it that man who brought me here?" Emilia caught Friede's arm before she could leave. Life had taught her to be constantly on guard and she preferred to have as much information as possible on her hands. "He's Herr Kommandant's first adjutant, isn't he?"

"Yes, he is. Untersturmführer Engel. I couldn't think of a least fitting name for him than that," Friede muttered quietly, alluding to his name – 'angel' – and left Emilia alone.

For the rest of day she didn't have much time to be immersed in her brooding. Since Friede needed to do all the chores around the house, in order to shelter Emilia from the Kommandant's eyes until her bruises had completely healed, Emilia was kept busy in the kitchen, cooking, washing the dishes and scrubbing the floors.

"Always mind the floors," Friede had instructed her. "The Kommandant never comes in here, but his children might run in, and if they get any dirt on their feet their mother will have a fit, and you don't want to make that woman angry. Edda and I used to wash the floors early in the morning, but you'll have to scrub them during the day too because people from the camp come with food that they sort out when it's delivered from the town nearby, and they always bring dirt on their feet, so you'll have to wash the floors every time after they leave. Also, make sure that the wine glasses are always sparkling clean. The Frau checks them thoroughly herself."

Emilia made a little note to herself to adjust to the new 'Frau' – the Kommandant's wife. The old one, with the baton, had become a distant memory now, even though just a few days had passed since she last saw her.

"I'm not too good with cooking," Emilia confessed when Friede handed her the menu for dinner and showed her where to find the ingredients.

"Use this cook book for now, and I'll come and check every thirty minutes to see how it goes. Oh, and one more thing: never, under any circumstance, should you taste the food."

"But how am I going to…"

"I'll come here and taste it. You're Jewish from what Engel told me?"

Emilia nodded, lowering her eyes instinctively. It was as if she had almost been taught to be ashamed of it by now.

"Fine by me, but if the Frau finds out that you're tasting their food, she'll stage such a scene and will most likely demand that Herr Kommandant send you to the camp, or worse," Friede explained. "I'm political, so I guess a communist slurping some soup from their pot doesn't bother them too much. And another rule, but quite an obvious one: never eat any leftovers. Our meals are quite decent, you'll see for yourself, so if they catch you finishing off whatever they didn't finish during dinner, that won't end up too well for you also. And there's really no need to steal anything. Look at me, do I look like I'm starving?"

Emilia glanced over at Friede, who wasn't large by any standard, but she at least seemed *normal* and healthy, and for any inmate it was more than enough to appear normal. A hopeful smile touched the corners of Emilia's mouth. Maybe she'd be able to survive all this after all. For herself, and in poor Magda's memory, Emilia decided that she would be a most obedient servant, that she would do anything to please the Kommandant and his wife, and obey all the rules that Friede set for her. She stopped from time to time when stirring the broth in the pot, to stand smiling silently for a few moments, not believing that she had miraculously found herself in such a favorable position.

Emilia met the Kommandant quite unexpectedly. She was hanging sheets and several shirts that she had just finished washing and bleaching outside in the small backyard to dry in the sun, when an unfamiliar voice behind her back startled her.

"You must be the new maid that Engel brought?"

Emilia turned around swiftly, pressing her hand to her heart instinctively, which made the uniformed man in front of her smile.

"Did I frighten you? I apologize, it was never my intention," he said in a mild voice, still smiling.

"I'm sorry, I didn't hear your steps," Emilia apologized in return. "Yes, I'm the new maid… Herr Kommandant?"

She finished her introduction with an inquisitive intonation, not wanting to offend the man with a direct question.

"Yes, I'm the Kommandant of this place." He gave her an encouraging nod. "And your name is?"

"I'm sorry, Herr Kommandant. Emilia. My name is Emilia Brettenheimer."

"Engel said you were Jewish?"

"Yes, Herr Kommandant."

Emilia bit her lip nervously, fearing that he might decide to throw her out; but the man only nodded and smiled again.

"Welcome, Emilia. And don't hide from me anymore, I don't bite. Start helping Friede around the house; she's managing it all by herself since Edda died, God rest her soul."

"Yes, Herr Kommandant." Emilia nodded enthusiastically and smiled back at him.

"Nice work with the shirts," he stated, after observing the laundry that she had almost finished hanging. He gave Emilia another smile, turned around and left. Emilia breathed out in relief.

"You were right, he is very nice," Emilia whispered to Friede later that day in the kitchen, after telling her about her encounter with the Kommandant. "He told me to start helping you around the house."

"Really? Good. Did he ask you anything about your nose?"

Emilia's bruises had all healed during the few days that she spent in the kitchen; all but a small one on the bridge of her nose, but even that one was barely noticeable.

"No, he didn't. But if he does, I'll just tell him that I fell on the platform when I was boarding the train."

"Yes, that's probably a good idea."

After some time spent in the Kommandant's villa it started to seem to Emilia that she didn't even live in the camp. Neither she, nor Friede were allowed to leave the territory surrounding the villa, but it was actually a positive restriction. Emilia didn't want to see what was going on inside the gates, after getting out of the same type of place just a few weeks ago.

The Kommandant's wife proved to be a difficulty though, clearly not wanting Emilia anywhere near her children or husband. On the very first day when Emilia had just started the housework with Friede, the Frau entered the bedroom that she occupied together with her husband, where Emilia was making the bed, and ordered her out.

"I don't want you touching my sheets. Please, tell Friede to do it. You can do the rest of the work around the house, but not in our room or our children's room."

Emilia only nodded silently and walked past the mistress of the house, who stood in the doors with her lips pursed and her brown eyes sparkling with disdain. Several minutes later, she heard the husband and wife argue about the unmade bed, and hurried to the kitchen to fetch Friede before matters got worse. Later, when Emilia served him coffee in his office, the Kommandant thanked her and before dismissing her, he added with a wink, "Don't pay attention to Gretl. She's jealous, that's all."

Emilia hid an embarrassed smile and went back to the kitchen, grateful for the little joke that surprisingly made her feel better.

The Kommandant and his wife received many guests in their villa, especially on Fridays and Saturdays, but Emilia quickly understood that she had to keep her mouth shut concerning her ethnicity. Fortunately, the Kommandant came to her rescue as soon as one of his guests, having drank a little over his limit, started asking her difficult questions.

"What is such a pretty girl as yourself doing here?" a man asked, while Emilia was refilling his glass with wine. "Don't answer, let me guess. You're either a liberal or probably ended up here for something anti-governmental. Am I right? Did you seduce someone unfortunate in order to get some information out of him, but the Gestapo got you both?"

He laughed and Emilia chuckled politely as well, under Frau Gretl's hard stare.

"Well, which one is it?" The officer refused to let the matter go.

Emilia threw a quick glance at the Kommandant, who immediately replied instead of her. "Emilia's a communist. She was sent here for re-education."

"Ach, a communist girl." The drunken officer gave her a sly smile. "Your people are not too far from here, you know. You might meet your comrades soon, if you're lucky."

The rest of the guests shifted uncomfortably in their seats, and the Kommandant intentionally cleared his throat loudly. The officer spread his arms out in a helpless gesture, laughing.

"It's a joke! Why is everyone so serious all the time? Just a joke. I know what Goebbels says, we'll regroup our armies and attack… They just stand barely within two hundred kilometers from us, that's why… Uh, never mind."

"Gustav, I think it's time for bed," the Kommandant addressed him sternly.

"*Jawohl,* Herr Kommandant." The Kommandant's friend got up and playfully saluted him, bowing to the women present at the table. "Ladies, good night."

"Emilia, would you be so kind as to show Sturmbannführer his room?" the Kommandant asked.

"Of course, Herr Kommandant."

Emilia had nothing else to do but escort the drunken officer to one of the guest bedrooms. As soon as she turned on the light and went to take the shams off his bed, she heard the door close behind her and quickly turned around to see the smiling officer walk towards her.

"Come here, my little comrade." Despite Emilia's half-hearted protests and meek pleading to leave her alone, he grabbed her by the waist and pushed her onto the bed, quickly laying on top of her. "Re-education is always a good thing, if you do it right."

Emilia tried to stop him from pulling up her skirt, but he didn't even seem to notice her thin hands pushing him away. He opened her legs with his knee, straddling her so he could straighten for a moment to undo his holster and take off his military jacket. Emilia watched him without blinking, numbly giving in to her fate, when, much to her relief, the door opened, and the Kommandant walked in, muttering a curse under his breath as soon as he saw his friend on top of his maid.

"Gustav! I knew I shouldn't have let you go off alone with her! Get off of her, now!"

"Why? She likes me." Gustav laughed with the gaiety of a drunkard.

"No, she doesn't." The Kommandant firmly pulled him by the arm, making his friend get off the bed.

Emilia quickly jumped to her feet as well, readjusting her clothes and hoping that her superior didn't think that any of this was through her taking the initiative.

"Oh, don't be like that, leave her to me just for tonight."

"No. You're drunk, Gustav, go to sleep."

"But I want the communist girl." His eyes drifted back to Emilia, who was cautiously hiding behind the Kommandant's back.

"You can't have her. Go to sleep." The Kommandant helped his friend with his holster and even took his boots off.

"Why not?"

The Kommandant straightened up before his friend, who was sitting on the bed. He folded his arms over his chest, frowning. "Because I said so. Go to sleep."

Gustav gasped and pressed both hands to his chest.

"Is she... She's yours, isn't she? Oh, no, what an idiot I am! I'm sorry... You know you're like a brother to me... I would never do something like this on purpose... I respect you too much... Do you forgive me?"

He outstretched his arm towards his friend and got up, swaying slightly on his feet. The Kommandant looked at his hand and reluctantly took it in his, after which both men hugged, slapping each other on the back.

"I'm sorry."

"It's really nothing. Don't apologize."

"I would never touch anything that's yours."

"I know."

"She's just very pretty... I wasn't thinking."

"That's fine. We're good. Now go to sleep, will you?"

"Yes. I love you, brother."

"I love you too. Good night."

After he closed the door to the guest bedroom, the Kommandant turned to Emilia. "Are you all right?"

"Yes, I'm fine," she replied quietly and then added quickly, "I didn't do anything at all, Herr Kommandant, I was only taking the pillows off the bed to get it ready for him and then he started—"

"I know, I know, you don't have to explain yourself." The Kommandant chuckled slightly. "He's always been... that sort of the man, if you know what I mean. When he sees a pretty face, his brain stops working."

"Thank you, Herr Kommandant."

"Let's go back to the living room, shall we?"

Emilia nodded, but before she could leave he caught her by the arm and said quietly, "Don't tell anyone here that you're Jewish, do you understand?"

"Yes, Herr Kommandant."

He nodded, scowling for some reason as he motioned her to go in front of him. Whether it was Gustav's big mouth or just pure luck, Emilia was spared any further drunken harassment both from Gustav and all the other guests from that point, whenever they frequented the Kommandant's villa.

For quite some time after the incident, Emilia wondered if her superior had solely helped her with good intentions in mind, or if he had some other plan for her, just like Gustav had assumed. But after another couple of weeks had passed, her relations with the Kommandant remained purely professional, with only one exception – some harmless occasional flirting from his side. Emilia constantly breathed out in relief that maybe she'd soon meet her "comrades" and her ordeal of being someone's bed toy had finally come to an end. She prayed every day for that to be true.

Chapter 12

The first day when fall made itself known with gusty winds and the first September chill in the air, Emilia shivered while helping Frau Gretl bring the rest of her things into the car, while the Kommandant arranged the seating for their two children in the back seat. They wanted to ride in the front with their father and the driver, but he told them sternly that they would ride in the back with their mother, or it was no ice cream for them in the city. Emilia smiled softly, wondering at how easily fathers always put things in order, where mothers usually didn't succeed.

She watched the car leave for the weekend to visit the Kommandant's relatives, and couldn't contain a sad sigh, feeling an unexpected pang of jealousy over someone having relatives to visit and a family of their own. Emilia had no idea where her relatives might be; she didn't even know what might have happened to her own mother and if she was alive at all. She could only hope that they'd see each other in the future.

As for a family of her own... That was surely out of question for her. Emilia rubbed her forehead irritably, wondering why she even had such a longing after something that was so contradictory to her other desires, because having a family meant having a husband and children; she couldn't have children anymore, and a husband... Well, she just hoped that no man would ever touch her for the rest of her days. If she ever got away from here, she would find herself a house somewhere far, far away from people and live quite happily as a hermit.

Immersed in her brooding, Emilia arranged lunch for Untersturmführer Engel, whom the Kommandant had left as his substitute during the time of his absence. So far all their interactions were restricted to simple greetings and orders to bring him coffee or more paper when he was working on some documentation for the Kommandant. Emilia began to gradually feel more comfortable in his presence, and she was relieved that the Kommandant's first adjutant mostly ignored her, despite frightening her so much on the first day she had arrived here.

She didn't notice how tense Friede had become since the departure of the Kommandant's family and she paid little attention to her offer to serve lunch to Engel herself instead of Emilia. Emilia just shrugged and thanked Friede, going back to washing the dishes and her unhappy thoughts. She didn't hear when Friede came back to the kitchen barely a minute later, still holding a tray in her hands.

"He doesn't want me to serve him. He says he wants you to do it."

Emilia turned to her fellow maid's voice and wiped her hands on the towel. "Why, what's the difference?"

"There is a difference to him." Friede seemed distressed for some reason, and Emilia started feeling uneasy again. Friede put the tray of food back on the table and almost yanked the towel out of the Emilia's hands, taking her position by the sink. "Go, before the soup gets cold."

Emilia picked up the tray obediently and heard Friede mutter under her breath as she was exiting the kitchen, "Just don't fight with him. You'll only get it worse."

"What?" Emilia turned on her heels, frowning.

Friede kept her head lowered over the sink, refusing to meet her eyes. "I tried to help you. There's nothing I can do. Just go."

Emilia swallowed nervously, but started to make her way to Untersturmführer to give him his meal. He was sitting in the Kommandant's chair, a deep scowl creasing his brow. Emilia placed the items from the tray on the table in front of him. All of a sudden he grabbed her by the wrist, making her drop the fork that she was laying out for him.

"It's not nice of you, what you're doing," he said in a calm voice, although it was interlaced with so much ice that Emilia felt the coldness crawling under her skin, spreading up from his iron grip on her hand. "I bring you here, I give you the best position in the camp, and how do you repay me? Whore around with another man?"

"What?" Emilia watched him with wide eyes, utterly terrified of the pure hatred radiating from his blue eyes. Her wrist started hurting. "I didn't do anything, Herr Untersturmführer—"

"Shut up!" he shouted loudly, and yanked her hand down, making her fall on her knees in front of him. "Didn't I warn you on the very first day when you just got here that your old Jew-whore ways won't fly here?! Didn't I tell you to stop spreading your venom everywhere?!"

"I don't understand what you're saying, Herr—"

He hit her so hard across the face that she would have fallen backwards if he didn't still hold her wrist in his hand. Engel grabbed her by the hair, making her look him in the eye. Through the stinging tears that blurred her vision, she saw the vicious scowl on his face as he lowered his face to hers and asked in a menacing whisper, "Did I warn you or did I not?"

Emilia quickly remembered Friede's warning not to fight him and recalled her thoughts on how she suspected that Engel was not too stable mentally.

"Yes, you did," she quickly replied, fearing another blow.

"Why do you walk around the Kommandant then, trying to get his attention all the time?!"

"I don't..." Emilia whispered, wondering which other delusions he had on her account. "I would never... I'm just doing my job..."

"Liar."

"I swear, Herr Untersturmführer, I really don't," she repeated pleadingly, wincing as his fingers entangled themselves more forcefully in her hair. Her cheek throbbed painfully as well.

Engel suddenly released her hair and stroked the place where he'd hit her.

"It's not your fault." His fingertips caressing her cheek worried her more than whatever he had done prior to that. Emilia froze on her knees, hoping that he would release her. Instead, he put a finger in between her lips, forcing them apart.

"Open your mouth," he ordered in the same cold tone as before. His constant changes of mood were getting more and more unnerving, but Emilia just kept repeating Friede's words in her mind, just like she did with Magda's words, from when she had warned her of the SS guards and their drunken rampages: *Don't fight him, you'll only get it worse.* A disgusting cold chill traveled down Emilia's spine at the sudden thought of what had happened to the late maid Edda, whose place she had taken up; Emilia decided not to anger Engel further, and opened her mouth like he told her to.

He ginned crookedly, and slowly traced his thumb around her both lips, examining her teeth. All of a sudden, he spit in her mouth and pushed her roughly to the floor.

"Dirty fucking whore. I'll teach you how to make eyes at the other men."

He got up and yanked Emilia by the scruff of her neck, dragged her back onto her feet, to then just throw her face down on the table. She quickly understood what his intentions were as he pulled her skirt over her hips, undoing his pants with one hand afterwards. She didn't make a sound when he started raping her, but simply fixed her clouded gaze on the white embroidered tablecloth, thinking that it would never end. They would never leave her alone, none of them. She pressed her tongue against her teeth, thinking with defiance that she had seen too much of this already in her life and that at least she wouldn't give him the pleasure of hearing her cry or the satisfaction of having her beg for him to stop.

Her silence angered him, though; she could tell, because he started moving with intentional roughness, clearly desiring to hurt her as much as he could. He grabbed her breast with one hand and twisted her nipple painfully, but even then Emilia stubbornly kept quiet.

"You're one obstinate little bitch, aren't you?" he hissed in her ear, pressing her down even more with the weight of his body. "You wait, I'm not done with you yet."

What else can you possibly do to me, Emilia wanted to ask, barely containing a cynical smirk. *Your comrades have taught me too well. I'm not afraid of your lot anymore, you just disgust me, that's all.*

She figured that he'd leave her alone after he took his pleasure with her, but Engel it seemed had other plans in mind. Emilia tried to get up and rearrange her dress as soon as he got off her, but his hand pushed her back onto the table, to unbutton her dress and pull it off her shoulders all the way to her waist, restraining her all the while from moving her hands. Already sensing danger, Emilia's body tensed and she tried to release herself from his grip, but to no avail.

"Not so fast." His voice had the same ice cold determination she now knew was a part of him, and she heard his belt buckle hit the redwood table. "I told you I wasn't done teaching you a lesson. I don't have my whip with me, but the belt will do nicely instead."

Emilia screamed instinctively as soon as the metal buckle landed on her bare back, spreading searing pain all over her body. Her skin split with the first violent blow. The second one followed before she could even contemplate escape, not that he would allow her such a possibility. Soon all she could do was to take in short sharp breaths in between the screams, although she didn't even realize that it was her screaming at first. What Idit and her accomplices did to her seemed to be just a child's game compared to Engel's steady hand. Each strike was given with calculated, heartless force, purposefully laying one hit on top of the other, just to make the pain even more agonizing. It continued for what seemed like an eternity in hell.

"Oh, so you can scream if you want to?" He stopped for a moment, breathing heavily. "I guess I'll always just have to beat you from now on, since that makes you scream? Just having me is not enough I guess, is it?!"

"No, please," Emilia managed to beg, in between hysterical whimpers. "Please, no more…"

"Will you be so obstinate again in the future?"

"No, no, I won't, just please stop…"

Emilia heard him snort behind her back and with the side of her eye saw Engel wipe his buckle with his handkerchief, getting her blood off it before putting it back on his waist. After that, he left his victim at last, circled the table and sat back on the Kommandant's chair, placing a napkin on his lap.

"You see, you might think that I did it to you." He started talking calmly as Emilia tried to get up. Her knees gave in and she fell on the floor, steadying herself with her shaking arms. She noticed that Engel had started to nonchalantly cut the steak that she had brought him. "But, in reality, you did it to yourself. If you had listened to me in the beginning and didn't try to show me your nasty, obstinate side, you wouldn't have been hurt. Do you understand what I'm telling you?"

Emilia slowly pulled the sleeves of her dress back onto her shoulders, noticing little droplets of blood on the hardwood floor.

"Emilia!"

His shout made her jerk her head up to him and she hurriedly nodded, even though she could barely make out what he was saying.

"Good. It means that next time you won't make the same mistake, will you?" he asked, tilting his head to one side and holding a piece of red meat out on his fork.

Emilia felt nauseous and lightheaded, but still managed to reply. "No, I won't, Herr Untersturmführer."

He eyed her for some time as she desperately held onto the last of her power, telling herself not to collapse on the floor from the shock and scorching pain that her body had to endure. Engel placed the piece of steak in his mouth, chewed a couple of times, and then spit it out back onto the plate.

"*Scheiße,* it's cold."

With those words he got up, threw the napkin on the table and barked over his shoulder as he was leaving the room, "Go tell Friede to make me a new one. And tell her to hurry up. I'm hungry."

As soon as she couldn't hear his steps anymore, Emilia fell on the floor and allowed herself to close her eyes at last. She hoped that she'd just die, to end it all.

Life in the villa after that day was like walking on eggshells for Emilia. Trivial things, like the way she served coffee to the Kommandant or any of his guests when Engel was in the room, became a duty of watching her every move, making sure that her tormentor didn't interpret a polite smile from one of the guests for something different.

Her back started to heal, thanks to Friede's applications of vinegar to draw away the heat and any infection, and her generous supplies of Vaseline that she rubbed onto the girl's back in the morning and at night. Emilia didn't know what she would do without Friede's help, as she once again sent her away to the kitchen, not necessarily to work but just to be away from everybody's eyes. Friede didn't complain about the double amount of work that she had to do all by herself, because she knew that Emilia couldn't even move her arms freely without tears forming in her eyes. For the first few days after the assault, even wearing a uniformed dress felt like torture itself.

"What a pig," Friede muttered under her breath, trying to soak the scabs off Emilia's back as gently as possible, to make it at least easier for her to move more freely. "He did the same with Edda. Nasty wounds. You'll have scars, I'm afraid."

"It doesn't matter," Emilia replied, speaking into the pillow she lay on. All this time she had had to sleep on her stomach only, wincing each time the blanket rubbed against raw skin whenever she moved. "I'm not planning to undress in front of anyone in the future."

"That's up to you, but just don't do anything stupid; we'll all come out of here soon."

"Stupid, like Edda?" Emilia already had her suspicions about the real circumstance of the former maid's death. "She did something to herself, didn't she? Or was it him who killed her?"

Friede was quiet for some time, then she sighed and answered quietly, "Supposedly she hanged herself on the belt she tore off her uniform dress. I found her body. But I can't tell you whether it was her who did it or him. It could've been him. He's capable of anything, as you know by now."

"Why is he doing this?"

"Why are any of them doing things like this?"

"Not like this…"

"Ach, it means you haven't seen anything yet. I was interned in Mauthausen, it's in Austria, before they transferred me here. I'm Austrian, if you hadn't guessed that yet."

"I did." A small smile touched the corners of Emilia's lips. "We speak alike."

"Yes, only you have that Bavarian brawl that we don't like," Friede teased her, seeing her grin.

"You started saying?"

"Ach, that… Yes. Well, Mauthausen is the camp that enemies of the state or prisoners of war, the Soviet ones for the most part, are sent. And what the guards amuse themselves with there is tormenting POWs to the point that they turn into animals. I was there in winter, and do you know what game they invented? They would pour the soup on the snow, wait until it froze and then let out the Soviet commissars from their barrack, who were so starved by then that they would actually start fighting each other to get to the frozen soup. Another one of their amusements was to tie an inmate – also a commissar most likely, they seemed to have some special hatred towards them – to a pole in the middle of January, absolutely naked, and they would start pouring water over him until he looked like an ice figure. The next morning they would shoot at the frozen corpse and laugh, watching the pieces of ice break off. And you're saying 'not like that.' No, girl, you've been lucky so far. Even with that back of yours. It'll hurt for a while, but in the end you'll walk out of here alive. Many people are already dead, and they died a horrible death."

Lucky, Emilia pondered. Somehow, in the course of just a few short years, luck had become such a relative notion. *Lucky to be alive. Lucky they just raped you, but didn't slit your throat. Lucky they beat your friend to death and almost did the same to you, but you still survived. Lucky that you are still here after a madman belted your back for several minutes without stopping, but at least he didn't hang you with your own belt yet. Yes, after consideration, she was a very lucky girl.*

"Maybe Edda did it herself," Emilia said thoughtfully.

Friede frowned slightly, but then shook her head dismissively. "Whatever it was, there's no need for you to concern yourself with that. The Russians will be here soon. It will all be over, you'll see."

"I'm afraid to think about that."

"Why on earth would you be afraid?"

"My friend, Magda, used to say the same thing, about everything being over soon." Emilia went silent for a moment. "And she died before she could get out. They killed her."

Friede knew the story, so she only sighed again and pinched Emilia's cheek lightly. "Don't fret. Life goes on. It always does."

Yes, it did. Soon after, Emilia went back to fulfilling her duties around the house, the easy ones, but at least she wasn't locked all by herself in the kitchen, alone with her depressing thoughts. She would still start to instinctively shake every time Engel entered the room, even though he seemed to go back to completely ignoring her like he used to before, once the Kommandant returned home. However, Emilia knew how deceitful his appearance was; it was just a mask of indifference that he wore before others. He became like a dark shadow, following her every move, like a predator ready to pounce at its prey at the first opportunity. He enjoyed reminding her of his presence when no one else could see; scratching her leg with his nails when she served him dinner, when the Kommandant was looking the other way; catching her alone in the hallway to block her way, just standing there and staring at her with his shining eyes, sharp and cold, like the blade of a knife.

The next time the Kommandant left with his family to move them back to German territory, after another offensive by the Soviet army, Emilia dreaded staying alone with that madman in the house. She tried to hide from him and did it successfully for the first few hours by staying in the basement under the pretense of shelving preserves, while he was busy inspecting the territory of the camp and giving orders to the guards. When he came back he searched and found her, of course he did, and dragged her out of the basement where she hid. For some time, he silently towered over her shivering body, smiling in an almost kind manner, but twisting his whip in his gloved hand.

"Did you miss me, Emilia?"

His leather coat brushed her shoulder as he stepped closer. He started slowly removing his belt and holster without taking his eyes off Emilia. He raped her, right there on the floor and then whipped her, accusing her indignantly that she was "the dirty Jew-whore," that made him do it. The following two days passed in the same manner, all becoming one never-ending nightmare with his cold hands digging into her soft skin right above her hipbones, more whip bruises raising on her barely healed back, and disgusting hisses in her ear, speaking whatever strange things came into Engel's disturbed mind. He would grab her hair painfully and lick her face, all the way from her mouth to her ear, hitting her immediately after with horror in his eyes. He would kiss her, but spit in her face seconds after, claw into her soft flesh, to then just bury his face in her neck, almost purring something indistinctive directly afterwards.

"We need to kill you all," he whispered softly, after dragging Emilia's stiff body onto his lap and stroking her hair after yet another one of his fits.

Long before she had decided to lay still, so as to not provoke him even more, because in his case only God knew what would set him off next time. He leaned against the wall, looking at the ceiling, his face looking frighteningly angelic now that he finally had his prey in his arms. For some reason he reminded Emilia of one boy, who had lived on the same street as her as a child. The boy would chase a kitten all day, just to snuggle its wriggling body tight against his chest and force his petting on the poor animal, with or without its consent. The more the kitten tried to claw, the tighter the boy would squeeze it, until he strangled him completely. The last time Emilia saw him, he had grown up to be a very handsome teenager, dressed in the black *Hitlerjugend* uniform. That boy had had the same eyes as Engel: sharp, blue and insane.

"Yes, we do. It can't go on like this. It's true what they say, you're all witches. You have the power to entice us, and the only way we can protect ourselves from you is to kill you all." More absent-minded strokes followed on her hair and shoulder, while his unblinking gaze remained fixed on the ceiling. "You're all vermin, you can't keep poisoning our blood with yours. And it's hard, you know, even for me, because it's very difficult to carry out my task, because I'm a human being and I have feelings too, and I don't want you all to suffer, but why do you keep following me everywhere, all of you. I don't understand what you want from me."

All of a sudden he lowered his gaze and looked Emilia straight in the eye.

"What do you want from me, Emilia?" After Emilia didn't answer, as she was too afraid to even utter a word, but more than that she didn't even know what to say in response to his insane ramblings, he smiled kindly and offered his own reply. "You love me, don't you? Are you in love with me, Emilia?"

She stared at him with her eyes wide open for some time, too appalled to form a suitable reply, but as soon as she saw his frown form again, she nodded readily a few times, hoping that it was what he wanted to hear. He smiled again and sighed contentedly.

"But you can't be in love with me. I'm German, you understand? And you're Jewish. It's unnatural." His eyes went back to the ceiling and the soft stroking resumed. "But, don't you worry, even though you're a Jew, I still won't leave you to those Asian hordes. Yes, don't be afraid, I'll kill you before they come. I'll protect you from them, because nobody deserves that, even you."

Emilia allowed her thoughts to trail off, since he most likely wouldn't move in the next hour or so – that much she knew already, having witnessed several fits like this before. He'd just sit and stare into space, trying to analyze what was wrong with the world and with himself personally. He spoke of ridding himself and his Führer of their worst enemies, and yet he found himself catching and holding in his forceful embrace yet another one of those enemies. This gave him much to think about obviously.

They shouldn't have prohibited our entire race, Emilia mused, following Engel's glazed-over gaze towards the ceiling. *Prohibition only creates temptation and counter-action, and that's exactly what seems to have happened to all of these men. They hate us as they were taught to, just like children who are taught what sin is and how one mustn't commit it, and yet they go and commit it just because they were told not to.*

The same story had started with Adam and Eve; after all if God hadn't told them not to touch the fruit of that particular tree, they likely would never have even noticed it in the garden. But, it became the forbidden fruit, which has always been considered the sweetest. Just like Jewish women – they were sinful and forbidden, and that is why the SS men would lower their eyes shamefully in front of their *Helferinnen* colleagues, smile at them respectfully, but almost shiver in anticipation of the night to come, when they could snatch yet another terrified victim from her nest, drag her into their smoke-filled quarters and attack her with almost unhuman greed.

And now Engel? Why had he chosen her? Why Edda before her? He could easily get any woman from within the camp staff, or any girl from the town nearby with his looks. He was even married, as Emilia had seen both his ring and the picture on his table, of his smiling wife next to him. Most certainly he didn't belt her each time he made love to her, but Emilia got beaten, because in his eyes the only explanation of his unhealthy obsession with her was that it was her own fault, and it was she who had been following him all the time. She had purposefully tried to awake his jealousy by "flirting with another man," and it was supposedly she who wanted him. It had nothing to do with him, no, he tried to resist her, according to his deluded mind. He was the victim. He would never look at a Jewish girl, the Führer told him that he couldn't…

With surprising clarity, Emilia understood him and his twisted mind that had been driven to insanity between his own desires and what was asked of him. If that madman Hitler didn't announce their whole race as the outlawed one, this would have never happened, and Engel would probably be quite normal, and 'The Bear' would sit somewhere in jail as a simple rapist and wouldn't be able to torment one victim after another, going unpunished all these years. Richter would have married his Heini and be just a regular family man, most likely with five or six children and with a very happy, round face. None of this would have happened, but it did, and it had wrecked all of these men, so they were pushed to go and wreck her as punishment, because she happened to be one of the defenseless ones.

Engel's hand resumed its thoughtless stroking. Emilia sighed quietly and hoped with doomed indifference that he would keep his promise and kill her in the end. After all, understanding these men didn't mean she could ever forgive or forget.

———————

The mood in the camp grew more and more agitated as winter approached. The Kommandant spent every day locked in his study, with the phone ringing almost ceaselessly. Engel was busy maintaining order in the camp territory, even though the distant roar of the artillery could be heard if the wind gusts blew from the East.

One morning, Emilia and Friede were summoned to the Kommandant's study, where he and Engel were throwing files and files of paperwork into carbon boxes.

"Go take some gasoline from the basement, and some wood and make a bonfire in the backyard," the Kommandant ordered both maids, without even looking up.

Both women exchanged worried glances, but went to the basement, only there exchanging quiet remarks.

"What do you think is going on?"

"The Ivans are standing a few hundred meters from us, that's what I think is going on," Friede replied, grabbing firewood that they normally used for the Kommandant's fireplace.

"What do you think they're going to burn? What's in those papers?"

"I don't know. Probably something camp related."

"I figured as much. There's a little too much of the paperwork though, don't you think?"

"What do I care? The sooner they burn it, the sooner they leave, and the sooner we'll be free."

In the garden, the women lit a fire, and the Kommandant and Engel immediately proceeded to carry out the boxes filled with papers, to throw file after file into the fire, pressing the papers down with a fireplace rod that Engel had brought with him, to make sure that none of the papers could fly away.

"Go grab a box each and bring them here," the Kommandant told the maids, for the first time not adding 'please' or 'thank you' like he normally did. His agitation made the women move faster, and soon both of them were almost running from the Kommandant's study to the backyard, while the men were busy burning the papers outside.

Emilia couldn't just let go of the matter and stopped for a moment in the middle of the hallway, carefully opening one of the files. It consisted of papers filled with the same type-printed lists, with a date on top of each, with names and serial numbers listed below. Each list was underlined meticulously, with a total number written on the bottom. March 28, 1943: two hundred forty-five. March 30, 1943: one hundred seventy-one. April 1, 1943: three hundred eighteen.

Emilia flipped the pages to the end of the file, to the very last page. There were no names on this one, only what seemed to be a quarterly statistic: twenty-one thousand eight hundred thirty-two. The Kommandant's name and signature were underneath.

"What are you doing here stalling? They're waiting!" Friede ran into the hallway from outside, catching her breath. She stopped, seeing Emilia's deep scowl. "Why are you reading that?"

"Do you know what this is?" Emilia lifted the file in her hand for Friede to see. "People they killed. Day by day, year by year. It's all here, their names, serial numbers, classification. Gas chamber production. Cremation. Everything is documented. They're burning the very proof of what they did."

Friede stood silently for a moment, but then took the box out of Emilia's hands. "Let's go. We can't help those people now."

"We can help to punish the guilty though," Emilia muttered quietly, catching Friede by the sleeve. "Let's hide several files. They won't notice anyway."

"Have you gone off your head?! They'll kill us if they find out that something's amiss!" Friede hissed at her, getting ready to leave.

"How do you know they won't kill us anyway? Just like all the inmates inside these files?"

Friede just shook her head and rushed back to the door. Emilia stood, pondering, then turned around and went back to the Kommandant's study, her resolute steps resounding in the empty house. She grabbed a few files, hid them under her dress and ran to the basement, where she placed the stolen papers strategically in a safe place where she knew the men wouldn't go – where Friede and she kept all the cleaning products, like chloric acid and lye. Afterwards, she ran back to the study, grabbed another box and ran outside, apologizing to the stern looking men, explaining that she had to use the bathroom. They were too busy getting rid of the evidence to question her further.

The Kommandant and Untersturmführer Engel spent the rest of the day locked in the emptied out study, from time to time summoning the heads of the guards into their makeshift headquarters. Emilia and Friede watched the uniformed men run in and out the house. The Kommandant even ordered dinner to be served in his study, and when Emilia and Friede walked inside with two trays of food – one for their boss and another for his adjutant – they were overwhelmed by the smoke that stood inside the room from all the cigarettes they must have smoked. An opened bottle of cognac stood on the desk with two empty shot glasses next to it.

"You are now free for the night. Don't bother cleaning after us," the Kommandant said quietly, nodding at the maids still standing in the doors. "And thank you for your service. I appreciate it."

"Thank you, Herr Kommandant," both women replied in unison and left the room, after which they exchanged yet another concerned glance, silently asking each other, what next?

Their superior's words almost sounded like a farewell, only who knew if it meant that he was getting ready to run back to Germany that night, leaving the camp to the approaching troops, or whether it would be the last night of their lives, when they would be murdered in the next few hours, and their bodies burnt together with the rest of the evidence they had already gotten rid of.

Chapter 13

The next morning, Emilia woke up at the same time as usual, only to find Friede sitting silently on her bed, frowning at something with her head tilted to one side. Her eyes were slightly squinted, as if she was trying to overhear something, but unsuccessfully.

"Friede?" Emilia called out to her quietly. They had both barely slept, partly due to the fear that the Kommandant would send Engel to finish them off, and partly due to the constant shouts and vicious barking outside, which had only died out into the distance at three in the morning. It was six now.

"Do you hear it?" Friede asked in a mere whisper, shifting her gaze to Emilia.

"What?" Emilia tried her best to concentrate, but couldn't possibly make out what her friend was listening to so attentively. "No, I can't hear anything. What are you talking about?"

"Exactly," Friede said pointedly. "There's not a sound outside. The roll call is from four till seven. Can you hear a single voice calling people out? Dogs? Guards? Anything?"

Only now it dawned on Emilia, that there was an overwhelming silence that she hadn't noticed before. Friede was right; it was deadly quiet outside.

"Do you want to go see what's going on?" Emilia suggested warily.

"I don't know. I'm afraid," Friede confessed, toying with the blanket in her nervous fingers. "What if they killed them all and by the lucky chance forgot about us?"

"I don't think so." Emilia pricked her ears once again but the house and the camp outside remained as quiet as a cemetery. "I heard shots being fired last night, but not enough by any means to kill all of the inmates inside."

They sat in silence for a few more minutes, until Emilia couldn't take the oppressive muteness anymore. It was as if the whole outside world had just died out and there was only the two of them left on the whole planet. Emilia got off her bed and started putting on her dress on top of her shift.

"Come, let's go see what's happening."

The house met them with only the sound of their steps echoing on the hardwood floors. No water was running in the shower as it usually was in the morning when the Kommandant started getting ready for the day and Engel's voice could not be heard on the phone as it usually was at this hour. Emilia and Friede stood in the hallway shifting from one foot to another indecisively, until Emilia finally mustered enough courage to call out to the room in front of them. "Herr Kommandant?"

Silence.

"What would you like for breakfast today?"

Again, no answer followed.

"I think he's gone," Friede whispered.

Chewing on her lip nervously, Emilia outstretched her arm wearily and pushed the door open to the Kommandant's bedroom. The room stood empty and silent, with the bed still made and the wardrobe completely emptied out, with only bare hangers still left inside.

The women proceeded to check Untersturmführer Engel's room to find it in the same state of bareness. After an inspection of the entire deserted house, the maids put on their coats and ventured outside the villa, still throwing cautious gazes over their shoulders.

"Look!" Friede grabbed Emilia's sleeve, pointing to the guard's tower, the one that stood before the front gates. "There's no one there! And the gates! The gates aren't locked!"

Indeed, the front gates with *"Arbeit Macht Frei"* – the signature "welcome" sign of every concentration camp – were half-opened. They, also, were without their usual uniformed SS men and dogs guarding them.

"Do you want to look inside?" Emilia made the first uncertain step towards the gates.

"I don't know if we should..."

"There's no one here to stop us." Emilia shrugged and proceeded to the gates, Friede trailing behind her.

The same dead silence lingered in the air as the two women made their way in between the first few barracks that also stood with their doors open. There was no one inside. There was no one in any of them.

"Where are all the people?" Friede whispered, because even a regular voice sounded too loud in this unnatural quietness.

Emilia shrugged. Besides a few corpses that were outside where the guards had shot them, the camp seemed to be completely devoid of any trace of its former population.

"I think they took them all...somewhere," Emilia suggested, pointing to multiple footsteps in the frozen mud, leading towards the gates.

Rustling behind their backs made both women turn around quickly. A lonely, frowning face with wary eyes showed from behind the door of the closest barrack.

"Hello?" Emilia called to the stranger, who finally showed her frail body, bundled in multiple wraps and blankets. The figure approached them slowly, with caution.

"Who are you?" the woman asked in a raspy voice, looking them up and down.

"We are inmates. We're maids in the Kommandant's villa," Friede replied.

"Is he gone?" the stranger asked.

"We think so. The house is empty."

"They took them all away, the ones that could walk that is." The woman nodded at the gates, fixing the grimy blanket on her head. "Some of us hid."

All three went quiet for a few moments, until the stranger broke the silence again. "Do you think the Soviet army is near?"

They got their answer barely an hour later when Emilia and Friede brought what food they had in the kitchen to share with the few remaining inmates, who had decided to take a chance and stay in the camp instead of being marched somewhere by their former guards. Emilia invited them to come inside the house, but the inmates just shook their heads vigorously in unison, still too afraid to wander away from their barracks.

A man on a horse trotted through the gates with a rifle across his lap. Noticing the inmates, who came out to the sound of the hooves, he nodded and said something in Russian, smiling and trying to sound encouraging.

"Is the army near then?" someone whispered behind Emilia's back.

"What is he saying?" someone else asked.

"Is he from the Soviet army or the allied forces?"

"Soviet of course, look at his uniform! See the stars?"

"The *Amis* have stars too!"

Noticing the two uniformed maids in opened overcoats, the soldier obviously assumed they were in charge and addressed them in broken German mixed with Russian, telling them not to be afraid and that they were now free.

"Frei, frei, sie sind frei! Vy vse svobodny, armiya uje tut, skoro budet eda y odejda. Ne boytes'! Hicht haben angst!"

Despite his thick accent, the people understood what he was telling them and slowly started turning to each other, as if looking for confirmation of the Soviet soldier's words in the eyes of each other. Tears came, flowing freely down their emaciated, dirty faces, awkward hugs were given with shaking hands, and words of relief and prayers were spoken, as they began to understand the full meaning of it; words that they had waited to say for so long, and were almost too afraid to believe: *"You're free. You're all free now."*

Emilia and Friede stared at each other for a long moment, before Friede grabbed Emilia's coat and buried her face in it, repeating the same words over and over, just like the rest of them. "We're free, Emmi. It's all over! We're free!"

It was still too hard to comprehend: the Soviet troops arriving two hours later (the horseback riding soldier turned out to be just a part of an avant-garde force), the absence of the grey uniforms and shouts in German, the smell of the horses that the soldiers brought with them and their strange language, in which they tried to communicate with the former habitants of the camp. After several years of persecution and a certain regime that they all had gotten used to, this new freedom was overwhelming – they didn't really know what to do with it. Luckily, a Polish woman was among them and she kept directing their questions to their new commanders: *What do we do now? Where do we go? Where are we to get food? Where are we going to live? Who's going to sort us all out?*

The commander patiently answered every question, smiling at the eyes filled with both hope and concern, reassuring them that they would never be left to fend for themselves, that they would be delivered by red-cross trucks which would follow the advancing army to several hospitals on liberated Polish territory, where they would be taken care of till the war was over.

"You're winning then?" Emilia asked the commander with the help of the Polish woman.

"We are," the woman translated. "We're closing on Germany from both fronts. It'll all be over very soon, in mere months."

Emilia nodded and handed the commander several files that she held in her hands after fetching them from the basement. "Tell him that these papers are very important. They tried to burn them all, but I saved some of them. He'll find numbers in them about the camp operation. The Kommandant destroyed the rest of the papers before they left us here."

The Russian nodded and took the papers from her hands, his scowl growing deeper as he flipped through the pages.

"So they killed people here too?" The Polish woman translated his words once again.

"I think they did it in every camp," Emilia replied and lowered her eyes.

Long hours of interrogation followed, during which she and Friede were placed in two different rooms in the former Kommandant's villa. They were bombarded with questions, given that they were familiar with the Kommandant's routine, and were considered to be most valuable witnesses. Too bad that they didn't have too much to say, no matter how insistent the Soviet interrogators got.

The trucks with red crosses arrived at last and took everyone who was still left in the camp to a small hospital in a liberated town nearby. The international Red Cross workers had extensive lists of names and former internment places, to which they meticulously added all the details of newly arrived people. Emilia, nor Friede, didn't need any medical attention since they had been fed quite well at the villa, but the Red Cross workers still dusted them with some powder before processing them into the hospital, explaining that the powder killed all the lice causing typhus, and no one needed yet another outbreak here.

The women offered their help to the short-staffed nurses in the few days after their arrival, and each day Emilia checked the new lists to see if her mother's name was in one of them. However, her former place of interment didn't seem to have been liberated yet, and therefore there was no news of her mother's fate.

Little by little, Emilia got used to hearing mostly Polish and Russian speech, and she even started picking up certain lines and terms that helped her better communicate with the new owners of the place. For the first time she saw the German prisoners of war, who were locked up in a former hospital garage right across the street from them. Every morning, they lined up for their scarce meal. They were grimy, disheveled and subjected to constant humiliating comments from both the Russian troops and Polish civilians. The first time she saw them, lining up in the snow mixed with mud, Emilia couldn't look away for some reason, that's how odd it was – finding the former masters of the world in such a pitiful state. What was even more unexpected was that she didn't feel the sense of gloating that the rest of her kin openly expressed. Strangely, she felt sorry for them, and looked away each time someone from her side threw a mud ball at one of the Germans. They wouldn't even react for the most part, and just brushed off the dirt and keep looking under their feet, as if silently agreeing with the treatment.

More and more posters with photographs of masses and masses of corpses started appearing on the newspaper stands. They depicted the atrocities committed in the camps, camps liberated by the Soviet army. *"These crimes: Our common fault"* it read in German. Clearly, they were meant for the eyes of the German-speaking civil population.

Once, one of the Poles mistook Emilia for a German civilian who had been resettled to Poland according to the Führer's wish to expand the Reich's *lebensraum*.

"Look, look what your Führer did!" a man shouted, pointing at Emilia, who stood perplexed in front of the newspaper stand looking at a poster which revealed the heinous crimes of the Nazi government. "It's your fault as well! Their blood is on your hands!"

Emilia looked around, thinking that he was addressing someone else.

"I'm Jewish," she replied quietly, frowning. "I was in one of these camps."

"Jewish, all right." The man snorted with contempt, attracting more and more spectators and unwanted attention, which Emilia was desperate to escape. "You don't look too Jewish to me!"

"I looked Jewish enough for them to put me there!" Emilia barked back, feeling unexperienced anger rising inside her, inflaming every pore of her body. Her fists clasped without her even noticing it and she stepped forward, openly confronting the man. "I looked Jewish enough for them to do all sorts of unimaginable things to me and tell me that it was my fault! There is not an unmarked spot on my back because of how Jewish I was for them, so God will curse the day when I start listening to something like this from some lowly little worm like you. Where have you been during the war, huh? I bet not in the camp. I bet not in the army. I bet you just sat out the whole five years in some warm kitchen, hiding behind some skirt and bitching about the German invasion! You probably weren't even in the Polish resistance, and do you know how I know that? Because people like you are cowards. People like you never have enough courage to stand up for the ones that suffer, but after the abusers leave, you all crawl out of your little nests and start pitying the poor victims and barking at the fallen beasts, killed for you by someone else! So stop throwing mud at the ones who have given themselves up and have no means to stand up for themselves. You should have thrown mud at them when they were marching on your streets, then we would have seen what you could do! If all of you had stood up to them back then, there wouldn't be any stands like this one now, and no pictures with corpses. So, get lost before I report you to the Russians as a former collaborator!"

The man shifted from one foot to another, sniffled, looked around, backed down and left. The small crowd that Emilia's shouting had attracted also followed suit and dispersed. Emilia turned back to the poster and stood in front of it stubbornly, still shaking with nerves. A small smile appeared on her face after a while; somehow, someway, she had managed to find her voice and stand up for herself. She wiped her sweaty palms on her overcoat and gave herself a promise that since that day no one would ever offend her without her biting back at them. Enough was enough. She's been through hell and back and managed to survive. They tried all they could to break her, but she still stood here, marked for life, but stronger than ever. The old Emilia would never have dared raise her voice at anyone, but the new Emilia refused to be muted. Friede was right when she said "Life goes on." It did.

Part Two – Liberation

Chapter 1

Poland, Red Cross hospital, April 1945

Emilia rubbed her eyes, which were red and stinging mercilessly from the several hours it had taken to process the newly arrived people from the recently liberated territories. The Russians had decided, as they always did, that their work finished once they had helped the emaciated, struggling people from the train onto the trucks and from the trucks to the hands of the nurses. Where the nurses were to place them and what they were to feed them, that the Russians didn't care about, and they pretended to not understand not only the indignant exclamations in Polish and German (which many of the soldiers spoke at least on some level), but those in their own Russian as well, when one of the Polish nurses tried to address them in their mother tongue.

"We have our own wounded soldiers to take care of. Those are your people, you take care of them." That was their usual reply. It was true that at least their own former prisoners of war, recently liberated from the camps, were taken care of, and for that, at least, Emilia was grateful to these mysterious people, who seemed to be completely unorganized with constantly absent commanding officers, but somehow they always managed to get things done.

"Name, last name, date of birth, place of birth and the place of internment/internments? And your internment number please?" Emilia raised her eyes to an elderly woman in front of her.

"Karina Lifshitz, August 19, 1875. I was born in the former Austro-Hungarian Empire, arrested and transported in 1938 from Vienna to Dachau, then Ravensbrück. My last place of internment was Buchenwald, my number was 15498," the woman replied, and Emilia couldn't help but smile at her sharp memory, and at what was more incredulous: the very fact that the woman was still alive.

"You were in different camps for seven years?" Emilia didn't care for the line behind Karina, and kept staring at the frail lady as if she were a walking miracle.

"Oh, you're exaggerating, *schatzi*. They only arrested us at the end of 1938, and it's only April of 1945. Five years and a bunny's tail," the elderly woman replied with a mischievous smile, her dark brown eyes sparkling vividly on her face, which was creased with wrinkles.

Emilia smiled at the familiar but long forgotten expression her grandmother used to use, and put down the newcomer's information onto one of the multiple sheets that were constantly copied, updated and sent to all of the Red Cross centers around Poland and the liberated parts of Germany, Hungary, Austria and France. So far, these sheets were the only way for relatives to find out about the fate of their loved ones and their current addresses.

When she had time, Emilia checked the sheets to find her mother's name, but they weren't in alphabetical order and it turned out to be an almost impossible task when her free time was so pressed; Emilia worked sixteen, and sometimes eighteen hours a day, hardly ever asking the Polish head nurse, Edwina, for a day off, and only then when she felt like she was about to collapse in the middle of her shift. Edwina never refused her, thanking Emilia immensely for offering her help to the short-staffed hospital after only a couple of days after her arrival; just like Friede, who had decided to postpone her return to Austria as well and help their fellow former inmates instead.

"We don't have enough cots unfortunately, but you go ahead and find yourself a free mattress; there should be some by the windows, we discharged a few people yesterday and today."

Emilia pointed Karina in the right direction, but before she could motion the next person in line to approach, the elderly woman suddenly spoke again. "Wait, *schatzi*. I've been a mid-wife and a nurse my whole life. I see that you could use some help around here."

"You better rest and regain your strength first," Emilia replied politely, stealing a glance at the frail woman's frame, which barely weighed eighty pounds. "I appreciate your generous offer, but we can manage."

"It's the rest that will be the death of me, *schatzi*. My father, god rest his soul, he was a farmer, he worked till the very last day of his life and lived to be nighty-eight! It's idleness that kills you, not work. Work kept me alive all these years, and I don't intend on lounging around when so many people could use my help. If it's my age that you worry about, then don't – I have all my wits."

"No, no, I didn't mean to insult you in any way, I just don't want you to work yourself to death," Emilia clarified quickly, smiling.

"*Schatzi*, if they couldn't work me to death – no one will," Karina replied resolutely, and straightened her shoulders proudly.

"Well, go ahead to the head nurse's office, it's at the end of that long corridor, and tell her that Nurse Emilia Brettenheimer sent you. She'll tell you what needs to be done."

"Thank you, Emilia!" The woman beamed at her.

"No, thank you, Frau Lifshitz."

Later, Emilia blessed her decision to allow the elderly woman to work next to her, as she proved to be not only a highly experienced and efficient nurse, but an amazing friend and an example to everyone around with her will-power to not only live, but to live without looking back by not carrying the weight of her past on her feeble shoulders.

"Don't you feel any anger towards them at all? Resentment at least?" Emilia asked her once, when the two were helping the Russians unload the trucks with medicaments, which the Germans, interned just across the street from them, were eyeing longingly through the barbed wire separating their makeshift camp from the civilians. The Russians refused to spare even simple aspirins for the sick and wounded prisoners of war, leave alone any bandages or morphine.

Her question was overheard by a Russian standing close by. "Them?" the Russian said, spitting on the ground next to the barbed wire, glaring at the Germans who huddled together meekly. His face showed unveiled loathing when Emilia turned to him and reminded him that someone inside likely needed medical attention. "They can all die like dogs, what do I care? Do you think they cared for our prisoners of war? Do you think they fed them or changed their dressings? No, they only beat them more when they complained or begged for relief from their sufferings. Let them suffer now."

He added a few curses in Russian and flung an unfinished cigarette into the group of German prisoners of war, sitting on the ground nearby. One of them jerked slightly as the cigarette butt hit his sleeve, before picking it up from the ground to take a greedy drag on it.

"Told you they're like animals." The Russian snorted, throwing another despising glance at the Germans, who were now sharing what remained of the cigarette.

For some reason Emilia remembered Friede's story about Mauthausen and how the guards there treated the Soviet commissars.

"You're no better," she muttered under her breath so that the Russian wouldn't hear her. She turned back to Karina and repeated her question.

"Anger or resentment?" Karina raised her white eyebrows as if in surprise. "No, I don't. What good will anger do?"

Emilia opened another box with medicaments and started sorting them out. "I don't know. I'm just certain that some things can't be forgotten. Or forgiven."

"Not everything can be forgotten, but everything can be forgiven, *schatzi*. And the more that evil was done to you, the more you need to forgive the ones who did it."

"No, never. Never will I forgive them." Emilia grimaced crookedly, her eyes sparkling with defiance.

In reply she saw yet another kind, toothless smile and a world of wisdom in the old woman's deep brown eyes.

"And a lot of good it does to you, your hatred?" Karina asked softly, cautiously taking several bottles of morphine out of the box.

"No," Emilia admitted at last. "But it's just there."

"You need to get rid of it then." Karina shrugged as if stating the obvious. "Harboring hatred towards your offenders is the same thing as twisting the knife in your own stomach and hoping for them to die from the wound. It damages you more and more, not them. It drains you, and leaves you empty and hollow, like a used eggshell. Do you want to remain an empty eggshell for the rest of your life? You're far too young to hold onto your anger, and your life will be miserable if you don't let go of it."

"It was my anger and hatred that helped me survive all these years." Emilia glowered.

"And why now do you keep clinging onto such emotions?"

Emilia pondered her response, making a mark of each of the boxes with pills and dressings mechanically, before answering quietly, "I have nothing else left."

"Oh, but you do! Your kindness." Karina caught her sleeve, making Emilia look her in the eyes. "You could turn your back on all these people, but you chose not to. You work relentlessly when you could play the victim and not do a thing for them. What is that, if not kindness?"

"It's not. It just takes my mind off things. The more I work, the less I think."

"It would help you to think, believe it or not. Or better, look in the face of your enemies and say, 'I forgive you.'"

"They don't deserve to be forgiven."

"God will decide that. You do it for yourself, not for them. You'll see how much better you'll feel. How *free*. Unfortunately, so many of us were liberated, but many choose not to liberate themselves."

"You're a philosopher, Karina, not a nurse." Emilia grinned, trying to change the uncomfortable subject. So far she had only spoken about her internment days with a local American psychiatrist, who the allies had sent to their hospital to help the victims. The problem was that he was a young man, and on top of it Emilia had to turn to the help of an interpreter, since she spoke no English. She was too reluctant to talk in depth about the most traumatic experiences of her life with the man. Such 'therapeutic sessions' only made her blush to the roots of her hair and mumble something in response to his questions about *how it made her feel?*

Just like it does now – exposed and disgusted with myself, Emilia wanted to bark back, getting angry for no obvious reason. It wasn't his fault that he was a man and hadn't suffered like she had suffered, so he couldn't truly understand her, and therefore help her. The young American gave up his attempts to get anything out of her and suggested she write everything down in a journal instead. Emilia was just glad to be left alone.

Good, old Karina with her radiant, kind eyes, was right about everything, as Emilia learned later. Two recent events made Emilia come to terms with the old woman's perplexing philosophy, which she didn't understand at first but which soon started making so much sense.

Emilia noticed a particular German soldier again as she walked across the street to the Soviet guard, who had asked her for aspirin earlier that morning.

"You're the world's strongest army and you don't have aspirin?" Emilia had raised her brow in amusement, teasing the young soldier.

"No." He lowered his head in embarrassment, grinning. "We have a lot of alcohol and bandages, but no aspirin. Our commanders think that if the injury isn't life threatening, you have to just 'tough it out.' If someone complains about having a headache, he'd be the laughing stock of the whole division for weeks."

"Interesting," Emilia murmured, chortling.

While they were talking, the German soldier had outstretched his arms through the barbed wire to a passer-by, and in a pleading tone asked the man if he spoke German. No one would react to his meek voice, and Emilia had been watching him do the same routine for two days now.

"What does he want?" Emilia asked the Soviet guard, motioning her head to the prisoner of war.

"Who the hell knows, those fascist rats?" He shrugged indifferently. "To socialize probably."

Emilia didn't laugh with the guard at the crude joke, and called out to the German instead.

"Hey! What do you want?"

"Oh, Frau, God bless you!" He rushed to the side of the enclosure, where Emilia stood. "You speak German, don't you? You're the nurse from the Red Cross, aren't you?"

"Yes, I am. Why?"

"They wouldn't allow us to seek any medical help—"

"Don't you start badmouthing us, *suka ty fashistskaya*." The Russian interrupted him rather rudely, adding a curse in his mother tongue. "You have medics among you, let them treat you!"

"But they don't have any bandages, any alcohol, nothing at all!" The German clung onto the barbed wire as carefully as possible so as not to cut himself, but seeking Emilia's gaze insistently. "Frau, please, take a look at one of our comrades.

He's been injured badly, and no one changed his dressing since we arrived here, two weeks ago! His wound is badly infected, and he's in a great deal of pain. Please, Frau, just take a look at him… He's dying, and we all know that you'll most likely not be able to save him, but at least try to relieve his sufferings and give him a shot of something, so he can die in peace…We can't stand seeing him suffer like this, it really is inhumane. And these so-called liberators won't even shoot him out of mercy."

"You don't deserve any mercy," the Russian replied coldly.

"Please, Frau." The German outstretched his arm through the wire, as if to touch Emilia's hand, but only brushed her sleeve slightly, ignoring the Soviet guard's hard glare.

Emilia looked at her sleeve where his fingers had touched her, and turned her head to the Russian.

"Let me in, I'll take a look at him." Noticing hesitation in the Soviet guard's face, Emilia leaned towards him and whispered, mustering her best persuasive look. "You never know what kind of infection it could be. It could be tuberculosis or typhus, not a wound. And you're the one in constant contact with them; what if it spreads around the whole camp and then onto you as well?"

The Russian threw a wary glance at the German, and then at Emilia.

"Well… all right, I guess. But just take a look at him and make sure it's nothing contagious. If it's not, let him die on his own."

Emilia nodded and followed the guard to the gates, with the German in tow trailing on the other side of the enclosure. As she walked inside, Emilia couldn't help but hold her breath at the overpowering stench, reminding her of her own days of incarceration. Only, here there were no barracks, nor bunks, and there were no showers for the prisoners of war to take at least once a week; just an old, one level former garage for the ambulances, in which the lucky ones could at least hide from the rain and the wind, and open territory around it with several layers of barbed wire, where the rest of the Germans huddled together in their begrimed uniforms, on which all the military insignia had been torn off after their capture.

"Please, this way." The prisoner of war turned around every two steps he took, almost stepping on his comrades, who were sleeping on the ground, to make sure that Emilia continued to follow him. Only a few men paid attention to their unexpected guest, the others mostly staring blankly into space or sliding their glance over Emilia and back to the ground, with doomed and distant expressions on their faces.

As they made their way inside the former garage, which now served as a temporary place of confinement to the prisoners of war before the Russians could send trains to transport them to Siberia, Emilia noticed that even here her compatriots, who loved order more than anything, had organized some sort of makeshift hospital in the corner, separating the wounded and sick ones from the rest.

"There he is." Her guide pointed Emilia to one of the men laying on the floor and breathing with obvious difficulty. Unlike most of the men who were dressed in *Wehrmacht* uniforms, he was wearing an SS one, with the insignia torn off as well, but Emilia had seen such uniforms far too often in recent years not to recognize it immediately.

"Jochen." The German squatted next to his comrade and shook his shoulder gently, waking him from his fever induced sleep. "The nurse is here. She'll take a look at your eye."

Lowering herself next to the wounded soldier, Emilia already knew by the rancid smell coming from the bandages, covering part of his face and soaked with yellowish colored blood, that the wound was indeed badly infected.

"You should have taken the bandages off." Emilia shook her head, carefully unwrapping the dirty dressing. "They aren't helping at all. All they do is let the flesh rot under them."

The wounded soldier moaned, as the last layers of bandages were stuck to his skin. He looked at the nurse tending him with his only good eye. As his eye met hers, Emilia's gaze was torn from her concentration on the ugly shrapnel wound which cut through the upper left half of his forehead and down to his jaw. They both stiffened for a moment as recognition came to them at the same time.

The soldier swallowed hard. She knew all too well who he was, but out of some twisted desire to prove herself right, Emilia slowly picked up the military jacket that he was covered with and looked at the name on the collar.

"Joachim Bergmann," she read quietly and with such ice in her voice that the wounded former SS guard, the one who had given her schnapps before he had raped her together with his friends in their barrack, held his breath for a moment.

She shifted her eyes towards him again and could swear that she saw tears clouding his eye. He tried to move his hand closer to her, but Emilia pulled away at once.

"I'm sorry," he whispered in a barely audible, hoarse voice.

Emilia shook her head resolutely.

"Frau?" She had almost forgotten about the young German who had brought her here, until he addressed her in his polite manner. "Do you think you can help him?"

"He's dying," Emilia replied, looking Bergmann in the eye instead of the soldier who had asked her the question.

"Yes, we know," the voice spoke behind her back again. "Our medic told us that already. Do you think you can help him…die sooner? Give him a shot of something? Some poison? Something?"

Emilia kept looking at her former tormentor in his pitiful state, as if waiting for him to start begging her to relieve his sufferings. He remained strangely quiet; a single tear only rolled from the corner of his eye, and he whispered hoarsely once again. "I'm sorry. Please, forgive me."

"No." Emilia pursed her lips defiantly, feeling that her own throat was starting to scratch from unexpected tears. "Die without forgiveness."

Having hissed that to the dying man, she got up from her knees and said over her shoulder to his comrades, as she stumbled back to the gates, "Sorry, there's nothing I can do for him."

The next day, one of the Russians walked inside the hospital and announced in a cheerful tone that the allies had agreed to hang certain camp commandants in their former camps, together with their closest accomplices. It was the end of May, after the unconditional surrender had been signed, and most of the wanted war criminals had been caught. From his rather joyous speech and his generous offer to drive the ones who were in the closest camp to watch the first execution, Emilia recognized her Kommandant's name as he read out those sentenced to hang.

"Is his adjutant with him as well?" she asked, her voice quivering slightly.

The Russian shrugged and said that it was likely.

"I want to go," she said right away and gave the Soviet soldier her name, which he put in a small notepad.

"I can't take too many people, twenty at the most," he explained and then he smiled at her. "But, you can ride with me in the front. I'll get you the best spot, too. You'll see everything from the first row!"

With that remark, accompanied with laughter, he went on to ask the patients if they wanted to come watch the execution.

"You shouldn't be going." Karina, who was stirring bandages in a pot next to her to sterilize them, shook her head with a sigh. "There's nothing for you to see there."

"You don't know that," Emilia replied rather harshly.

"Do as you must." Karina slightly patted her hand, using that soothing, soft tone with her that always reminded Emilia of her own grandmother. "Only, it won't do you any good. Just like your refusal to help that soldier yesterday."

"I refused him for a reason," Emilia replied, already regretting that she had told Karina about her encounter with the former guard. Maybe she should have told the old woman exactly what he had done to her, maybe then she would understand...

"Whatever you say." Karina went on with her business, walking away from the argument as she always did. The woman had lived a life far too long to know how useless such arguments were. Her new young friend would understand it all in her own time, when the time was right. Karina knew she could only push her in the right direction, but Emilia would have to make the rest of the way on her own.

Two days later the Soviet soldier, with his fair hair brushed back neatly and with his black boots freshly polished for the occasion, opened the door to his truck and helped Emilia to climb inside. His commanding officer stood waiting behind her – or perhaps it was just a comrade; it was always difficult to tell with them because, unlike the strictly regimented Germans, they acted the same way with their superiors as with orderlies, and Emilia still hadn't had time to learn all of the insignia on their uniforms in order to differentiate their ranks. Whoever he was, he squeezed next to Emilia once she had climbed into the truck. The driver chatted away in his broken German all the way to the former camp territory, although Emilia barely replied, immersed in her moping.

After over two hours of driving Emilia was glad to get outside to stretch her aching legs and to take a breath of fresh air after breathing in the tobacco smoke from the strong Russian cigarettes that the two Soviet soldiers had smoked. However, as they started approaching the former gates of the camp, with American GIs chatting near the entrance leisurely, Emilia started getting more and more nervous.

"Excited?" her Soviet escort asked her, perhaps mistranslating and using the wrong word for 'nervous.' Or perhaps he had chosen it on purpose, for him and his comrade, who was busy organizing the rest of the people, did indeed look *excited.*

Emilia only smiled without replying. Their group made their way inside the camp, towards the small plaza near a former administrative building, where a flag with swastika used to fly and SS runes had been set in gravel in the center of it. Now both symbols were gone, replaced by small wooden gallows with more soldiers in American uniforms around it. Her guide explained to her that the American military police were in charge of the executions, and that the Russians were only here to supervise the procedure as "invited guests." Emilia once again frowned slightly at his rather odd choice of words.

They didn't have to wait long: barely ten minutes later a general commotion started as the allied press got their cameras ready, while occupying the first "row," right in front of the military police that stood on guard around the gallows. The voices behind Emilia's back rose just a bit before the silence overtook them all, as two handcuffed men were led out of the former administrative building by the same allied MPs.

The former Kommandant hadn't changed a bit since Emilia had seen him last, several months ago; only now the insignia had been taken off his uniform. He walked steadily with his head high, his face devoid of any emotion, although it was unnaturally pale either from his recent confinement or from fear. But it was Engel who Emilia couldn't take her eyes away from, from the moment he appeared in the doors. He was marched out after the Kommandant, and dressed in civilian clothes, and clearly devoid of his former powerful stride that used to petrify all the inmates during inspections. He was looking at the ground under his feet, with that same peaceful and dreamy expression that he had when he was holding Emilia in his arms after beating her to the point where she was barely conscious.

She heard a collective gasp from behind her back as the former inmates also recognized their tormentor, although he was without his uniform and the whip that had landed on their backs far too many times to forget it. They all held their breaths at once, just like they did when he was still in power. Emilia started trembling herself, even without realizing it, and didn't even notice as the Russian next to her put his arm around her shoulders and asked her something. With an overpowering hatred for Engel and even more for herself, Emilia admitted that Engel still had power over her, over all of them, even though it was him who was about to get hanged this time, and not one of his former victims.

He was to be executed first; Emilia guessed that the Americans had decided to leave the Kommandant for the main act and hang his orderly first, as it was him who they were leading on the gallows under Emilia's fixed, unblinking stare. Engel wore a serene, distant look as the MPs put a belt around his ankles to tie them, and answered something softly to the priest, who stood next to him. The latter nodded, made a sign of a cross in the air in front of Engel's impassionate face and stepped aside, allowing the executioner to throw a rope over the top.

Only when the noose was placed on his neck did Engel slowly shift his gaze towards the reporters in front and then the crowd behind them. His brow furrowed slightly, either with annoyance at the reporters or at the presence of his former inmates. Emilia stopped breathing at once, not able to take her eyes away from her former tormentor and at the same time praying that he wouldn't notice her; but he did. He always did. Their eyes locked, and Emilia thought she would have most certainly fainted if it wasn't for some incredible willpower that made her hold his gaze and not look away. He tilted his head slightly as if in surprise that she was still alive, that she had come to see him, and his lips slowly moved into a smile. A split second later the executioner pulled the handle, the trap door snapped open and Engel fell through it.

Emilia turned around and rushed out of there, feverishly pushing people out of her way and gasping for air that suddenly felt lacking.

"Hey!" She heard the Russian call her, but didn't even turn around, almost running back to the entrance. "Hey! Wait!"

He finally caught her by the arm and laughed. "What happened to you? You've never seen someone get hanged?"

"I have. Many times," Emilia replied, still feeling lightheaded. "Just…not like that."

"Not like what?" The soldier guffawed. "Hanging is hanging. It's always the same."

"No. It's not the same." Emilia shook her head stubbornly. "Everything is not the same, not the way it's supposed to be. Why did he have to look at me?"

"He looked at me, too." The Russian shrugged dismissively.

Emilia just shook her head again. No, he didn't understand, the Ivan. Engel wasn't supposed to look at her, and more than anything he wasn't supposed to smile at her! He was getting hanged, he was supposed to be defeated and somber, frightened and meek, and not the way he was… And she, she was supposed to be gloating, even if he did look at her. She was supposed to laugh in his face and enjoy watching him squirm on the rope, just as he had always watched her squirm when he twisted her arms or wrapped her hair on his fist. But she wasn't gloating; she was terrified of him again, and didn't feel a tiny bit of that celebratory triumphing that she'd expected to feel.

"Karina was right. She was right all along," Emilia whispered, forgetting all about the Russian once again. "I shouldn't have come here at all."

Staring ahead, she recalled a story that Karina had told her not that long ago, about the liberation of her camp.

"The Americans liberated us, not the Russians. The SS tried to evacuate the camp, but most of us were left inside just because there was nowhere else to go, so we were locked inside the camp, together with the administration, the guards, everyone. They gave themselves up of course, because the war was everything but lost at that point, and handed us to the *Amis* relatively unharmed. And the Americans, after seeing the condition we were all in, decided that it would be fair to allow the inmates to punish the guards, and so they did. The men, who were at least somewhat strong, attacked several guards, the especially vicious ones, and beat them to death. I stood and watched, together with the others… But there was one very young guard, he was always far too quiet and had never touched a hair on anyone's head. He was still a guard of course, and that was already his guilt, just being a part of that camp, but you know, I couldn't stand and watch when they started beating him. I tried to explain it to the Americans so they would intervene, but they said that it was none of their business if the inmates decided to kill him as well. And so I, the old woman, had to physically stand between two men and that young boy, who was my youngest grandson's age, God rest his soul. 'Leave him alone,' I told them. 'He didn't harm anyone. What are you beating him for?' 'Because he wears a uniform,' they replied. 'So? Shall we kill anyone who wears a uniform now, good and bad?' I asked them again. 'They're all bad,' they replied. 'They all need to be killed.' And do you know what I told them then? I said, 'My friends, we were in this camp together. We suffered together, and I went through the same daily misery like you did. I should be on your side, but why do you think I'm standing by this young boy in this situation? Because dooming the whole nation to be 'bad' and claiming that all of them need to be killed doesn't make us any different from them. Don't you hear yourselves? You sound just like them, when they said that all the minorities, the Jews, the homosexuals, the Gypsies, the Poles, the Slavs were 'bad' and 'needed to be killed.' No, my friends, this can't go on like this, or we'll just end up destroying the Earth itself. Someone has to stop first. Someone who has every reason not to, who has every reason to avenge themselves, needs to put a stop to it. Leave the boy alone. Killing him won't bring your loved ones back, just like it won't bring mine. But if you let him live, he'll carry your forgiveness in his heart till the end of his days, as forgiveness is much stronger a weapon that the severest punishment, and he'll raise his children, teaching them the same compassion and forgiveness, and a good nation will be reborn, from former enemies, who we forgave."

As the Russian hurried back inside to watch the second execution, Emilia sat on the ground by the truck, looking at the bright blue sky above her head. *No, I'm not ready to forgive him yet,* she thought, *but I understand Karina now. It's a good thing that I didn't gloat over his death then; it means that they didn't teach me how to be as evil as they are, even after everything they have done to me.*

Emilia filled the syringe with morphine, closed the needle with a glass cap and hid it in her sleeve. She walked across the street to the German detention camp and smiled at the familiar Soviet guard, handing him a bottle of aspirin.

"I thought you might want to share it with your less fortunate comrades," she said as he shook her hand with gratitude, thanking her profusely, promising to bring her stockings the next day.

What was with the Russians and stockings and where exactly they got them from all the time was an utmost mystery to Emilia, but it was the universal currency in the Soviet occupied ("liberated," Emilia mentally corrected herself) Poland. The officer who took her to watch the executions also offered her stockings, together with an invitation to go to the dance later that day. Emilia declined both offers, politely explaining that she was still too shaken up after what she had seen in the camp.

"Is the wounded soldier that I saw three days ago still alive?" Emilia asked as nonchalantly as possible.

"I suppose. At least they didn't report any deaths," the guard replied, shrugging. "Why?"

"Do you think I can go inside just for a moment and see him?"

"Why?" This time he frowned.

Emilia met his apprehensive gaze and slowly stretched her lips into a grim grin.

"He was a guard in my camp. Just want to laugh in his face once again and kick him under the ribs maybe."

"That's always a good idea!" The Russian smiled brightly and went to open the gates for her.

Emilia nodded at him as she passed him by and reassured him that she didn't need an escort. She made her way into the garage, carefully stepping over the sleeping Germans, and saw Bergmann right away, together with the soldier who had asked her to take a look at his wound. Unlike Bergmann, the young soldier wasn't sleeping and got up from the floor as soon as he noticed Emilia.

"How is he?" she asked instead of a greeting.

The German glanced at his comrade, who was barely alive judging by his shallow breathing and the wound, which they had left open and which looked even worse than when Emilia had first inspected it, and gave her an awkward one shoulder shrug.

"May I?" she asked again, motioning to the soldier so he could move aside. He did, and Emilia kneeled in front of the unconscious Bergmann. She sat silently for some time, and then warily placed his arm on her lap and started to roll his sleeve up. Bergmann moaned and tried to pull his arm away; Emilia guessed that his fever had climbed so high that even a slight touch was hurting him now.

"Could you hold his arm in place, please?" she asked the young soldier, who readily dropped to his knees next to her and took hold of the former SS guard's arm, smiling, as he noticed the syringe that she had produced out of her sleeve.

Emilia took the cap off the needle and allowed several tiny drops to run from it, making sure that there was no air left inside the syringe.

"Squeeze his forearm as hard as you can, please," she instructed the soldier, and waited for several seconds for a blue vein to appear from under the sweaty, burning skin.

Bergmann jerked once again, but this time opened his only eye, fixing his gaze on Emilia, who froze at once with the syringe over his arm. He slowly shifted his gaze to her hands and back to her face, a small smile touching the corners of his lips. Emilia decided not to hesitate any longer and inserted the needle into his vein, releasing the lethal dosage of morphine into his blood stream.

"Forgive me?" he barely whispered with the last of his power, catching her fingers with his. Emilia nodded several times and pressed his hand in return.

"I forgive you. Go in peace."

Bergman's strained smile transformed into a most serene one, as the morphine gradually relaxed the muscles on his face, replacing his permanent mask of pain and suffering. He sighed contentedly, for the very last time, before falling asleep, to never wake up again. Emilia carefully placed his arm on his chest, and picked up the empty syringe from the floor.

"Thank you." The young soldier nodded at her.

"I did it for myself, not for him," Emilia replied coolly, getting up.

"Whatever your reasons for it were..." The soldier caught her wrist and smiled, repeating insistently, "Thank you."

"I ask you not to report his death for a few hours if it's possible," Emilia replied, changing the subject. "Otherwise we'll both have problems."

"Of course," the soldier reassured her.

After she returned to the hospital, Emilia spent the rest of the day in a strangely tranquil state, immersed in her memories and barely noticing when anyone addressed her.

"It's a nice thing you did," Karina murmured quietly, when they were eating their dinner alone in the staff room later that evening.

"What thing?" Emilia blew on her soup, feigning ignorance.

"With that soldier who you knew and who was dying."

Emilia glanced at the old woman sharply, but the latter only lowered her head over her plate, hiding a smile. "Don't worry, I covered for you and for the missing bottle of morphine when the head nurse asked about it. I said that I broke it this morning."

Emilia couldn't help but smile herself. She faltered for a moment and then got up from her chair and hugged Karina tightly.

Chapter 2

Emilia helped the cook to count exactly ten dumplings each for every patient, when a nurse walked into the kitchen and motioned her to come outside.

"Some woman is asking for you in the front. She says her name is Hannah Brettenheimer and that she's your mother." The nurse finished with an inquisitive intonation, hoping that the woman with the same last name as Emilia was indeed her mother. Many times people came to the hospital claiming to be someone's relative, only to find out that they shared a common name with the patient, or that there was a mix-up in the lists again.

Emilia wiped her hands on her apron anxiously, also persuading herself not to put too many hopes in the woman claiming to be her mother. Still she couldn't help walking faster and faster towards the front of the hospital, where the small reception hall was. She stopped in the doors indecisively, craning her neck to take a better look at the woman with completely gray hair, who was talking animatedly to one of the nurses. When the woman turned her head to Emilia, and gasped loudly, holding her mouth with one hand, Emilia ran forward.

"Emmi!"

"Mama!"

Both women rushed to embrace each other, and then stood for a few moments just looking into each other's eyes, not able to believe their luck to be reunited at last.

"How did you find me?" Emilia asked, stroking Hannah's shoulders.

"Through the lists of course!" Hannah wiped away yet another happy tear from her face and beamed at her daughter. "I looked through them every day. I was such a nuisance for the nurses, but they understood. I even learned some English while I was in the hospital. I was in the American occupation zone, so they fed us quite well, too."

"Where were you?"

"Near Munich, believe it or not! Our old house is destroyed by the way; I went to take a look at it after they discharged me."

"It wasn't our house anyway. We sold it before the move."

"Yes, I know, I know. I was just nostalgic... I wanted to take a look at it before I went to see you."

Emilia hugged her again, pressing her mother close to her heart.

"I'm so glad to see you, Mama!"

"Oh, how am I glad to see you, *schatzi*! I didn't know what to think after they transferred you then... See this?" She pointed at her head. "I went completely white in a matter of weeks. But a mother always knows; deep in my heart I always knew that you were alive, and it gave me strength to go on and survive to find you. My little girl... Not so little anymore, huh?"

"Do I look old?" Emilia smiled.

"No, of course you don't, kitten. Just tired. In your eyes."

"I am. It'll pass, Mama, don't concern yourself about me. Everything is over, and we have to look into the future now, don't we?"

Hannah put her hand on Emilia's cheek and brushed it affectionately. "I'm just happy to see you, *herz*. Just happy to see you."

"Me too, Mama. Come, I'll fix you something to eat."

Later that night, after Emilia had finished her shift, she lay with her mother on the small cot they had to share and spoke of the liberation, of the Americans, the Russians and their plans for the future. Hannah tried to inquire only once about Emilia's life in the camp to which she had been transferred, especially after noticing the ugly raised scars on her daughter's shoulders, visible under her shift, but Emilia stopped her at once, shaking her head and raising her hand in a somewhat defensive manner.

"It's all in the past, and I don't want to *ever* talk about it. In fact, I don't want to talk about camps at all. Let's just bury all that, shall we?"

Hannah nodded silently and decided not to pry, for the sake of her daughter's sanity. It was obvious that even the very memory of recent events put Emilia in a state of anger and panic at the same time, and the less she was reminded of them, the better it would be for the both of them. As they were falling asleep, Emilia squeezed her mother's hand in gratitude, for her silence and understanding.

It turned out that Hannah wasn't eligible to live in the hospital together with the rest of the patients because she had already been given her discharge papers and was therefore announced healthy and not in need of any further medical attention. After some hesitation, Emilia asked her mother if she wanted to go to Danzig to try and re-claim their old house that had been taken from them by the Aryanization Office.

"You can't stay here unless you work here, and I don't have any money to rent a room for you," Emilia said the next day. "Shall we try our luck and go to Danzig? They discharge more and more people nowadays, so they can handle the patients without me here."

"Whatever you think is best, Emmi." Hannah just smiled, letting Emilia know that she was in charge of the decision. Since their days in the ghetto Emilia had become used to being the head of the family. Even when her father and brothers were still alive it was her who had managed to keep them all alive for as long as she could, sacrificing herself for the sake of her family. Now she had her mother to take care of, even though theoretically it was supposed to be the other way round. Theoretically, many things were supposed to be the other way round, but Emilia knew too well by now that life wasn't always what one thought it should be.

"Danzig it is then." Emilia shrugged and went to tell the head nurse of her decision.

They were given two small bags with some food, very little money and temporary papers, and said their farewells to the staff and patients. After an especially teary last goodbye with Karina, the mother and the daughter went on their way to the nearest train station.

The first thing they saw as they got off the train in Danzig, or Gdansk as it had been renamed once again, was a group of people, sitting on the opposite platform, waiting for the train. There would be nothing unusual in this sight, except the people were guarded by a Soviet military escort and this caused taunts and scornful remarks from civilians on the other part of the platform.

"Go back to where you came from!"

"Where is your Führer now, huh?"

"Gdansk and Poland are for the Polish people!"

"Go back to your *Greater German Reich*!"

"If it was so great, what did you forget here?"

"Bunch of Nazis!"

"Get out and never come back!"

"Say thank you that we didn't kill you all, like you did to us in 1939!"

Emilia and Hannah exchanged wary glances and didn't even notice a Russian soldier, who demanded their papers for the second time.

"What is going on?" Emilia finally realized that he was addressing them, and handed him their papers, motioning her head towards the people on the opposite platform.

"Ah, that. The new government is sending Germans back to their *fatherland*; the ones who Hitler sent here in 1939 as soon as Germany annexed the city." The soldier studied their papers while Emilia looked at the group of Germans on the other side, only now noticing a big swastika drawn with chalk or paint on one man's back. They all sat quietly, keeping their heads low and trying not to provoke any more aggression from the Poles' side. "It says here you're from Munich, too?"

"Yes, but we aren't Germans," Hannah rushed to persuade the frowning soldier, who was ready to whistle to his comrades to herd them together with the rest of the ethnic Germans and put them on the first train to their homeland.

"Munich looks German enough to me." The soldier raised his brow skeptically.

"We're Jewish, she meant to say." Emilia came to her mother's aid quickly. "We're from Germany, but we're Jews."

"What's the difference? If you're ethnic Germans, you should go back to Germany."

"We weren't 'ethnic Germans' when they sent us to the concentration camps!" Emilia took a defensive tone as well.

"Well, I don't know what we should do to you, to be honest." The Russian scratched his head pensively. "There aren't really any Jews here, so I don't know what the law says regarding you... Maybe you should go to the commandant's headquarters; people in charge will help you there."

"Where is the commandant's headquarters?"

"City center. There's only one bus that goes there since the whole city got almost wiped out at the end of the war; you'll see for yourself. So you tell the driver where you're going and he'll tell you when you should get off and where to go from there."

After thanking the Russian, Emilia took Hannah by the elbow and led her in the direction in which the soldier pointed. At least they had escaped forced deportation for now; that was already quite an achievement. Emilia was still worried about the new and always changing laws, and could only hope that the Russians in the commandant's headquarters would be sympathetic to their situation.

In the headquarters of the temporary city administration, consisting of the occupying Soviet forces as well just like in the rest of Poland, there was a lot of further head scratching, shrugging, and murmurs in Russian as different officials studied the women's papers again and again after sending them from one office to another.

"Well, as victims of the fascist regime of the former Nazi Germany, you aren't subject to deportation," one of the higher-ranking officials concluded after several hours of thorough examinations, calls and consultations with the commanding staff. "As for your house, I made an inquiry and luckily for you it is still intact. Due to its position it wasn't touched by artillery fire. However, I'm not quite certain how you can claim it back now... All the documentation was destroyed by the fascists when they were leaving the city, and it would be quite difficult for you to prove your ownership. However, the good news is that a Soviet officer lives there, and not of low rank either, and he is in desperate need of a good maid. He'll no doubt let you live there if you take care of the house and...well...cook and clean for him. You understand."

"That suits us perfectly." Emilia replied with a bright smile, dismissing the officer's concerns in regard to their possible reaction.

"Splendid." The Russian even rubbed his hands together, satisfied with the arrangement. "I suppose you know the address, so… Major Vlasov is expecting you."

"Thank you. We'll be on our way."

With that they shook hands.

———————————

"Where are your suitcases?" questioned the man, who Emilia presumed to be Major Vlasov.

She and Hannah stood in the hallway of their former house, the door to which was opened by a very young, barely eighteen year old soldier, who was probably Vlasov's adjutant, or whatever they were called in the Soviet Army. Unlike Vlasov, he didn't speak a word of German, and it took Emilia quite some time to explain to him who they were and what they wanted. Only when Vlasov himself showed up from inside the house to usher the women in did the young soldier, or Andrey, as Vlasov addressed him, nod in understanding.

"This is all we have." Emilia smiled embarrassingly, pointing at the two small bags they came in with.

"And your clothes?"

"Everything we have on our backs, and that is only thanks to the Red Cross. Without them I'd still be wearing a maid's uniform, and my mother – a striped dress."

That evening they ate a dinner that Emilia prepared, which was consumed by both Vlasov and Andrey with a hearty appetite. It seemed that whatever Andrey cooked for his immediate superior was only just edible enough to get them by, just like all the field kitchen food. Emilia was not a bad cook, having learnt how to make delicious meals in the Kommandant's kitchen; compared to what he had recently eaten it was no wonder that the Major couldn't stop praising her skills.

During dinner Vlasov kept asking Emilia about her past and her days in the camp, to which she answered in clipped, "yes or no" responses. He was very chivalrous and polite with Hannah, moving up her chair and helping her with the red wine, which he told Andrey to open for the occasion. Mostly, however, he ignored Hannah during the conversation, even though it was probably unintentional, as he concentrated all his attention on Emilia. Learning that she had no husband and no POW fiancé waiting for her, his face brightened even more. When both Hannah and Andrey retired to their bedrooms, he insisted that Emilia stay with him a little longer, to share a few more glasses of wine with him. She agreed out of politeness but barely drank anything, explaining that she wasn't used to alcohol. Just like all of them – Emilia knew from her own experience by now – Vlasov made his interest in her obvious from the very beginning, but thankfully didn't press the matter when Emilia once again politely replied that she wouldn't want to rush things, wisely deciding not to give him a straightforward "no." Who knew if he would kick them out of the house and find a "friendlier" maid? Emilia hoped to keep her distance by not promising anything, but not agreeing to anything either before...*before God knew what*, she thought that night, laying in the bed she once again had to share with her mother, in the bedroom that Vlasov let them use. Emilia was too used to life being unpredictable and chaotic that she had learned a long time ago not to make any plans, for it was absolutely useless in the time she happened to live in.

Vlasov, or Maksim, as he asked Emilia to call him, was a handsome enough man well in his thirties, with a mane of chestnut hair and warm brown eyes. He was quite tall and broad-shouldered too, unlike thin as a rail and wheat-haired Andrey, who was even shorter than Emilia. Andrey left the table barely containing a sigh that first evening, clearly interested in the new guest as well, but also clearly being in no position to stand in his superior's way. However, both proved to be rather innocent, as Emilia found out with immense relief throughout the next few days. Except for some harmless remarks and odd elbow squeezing they didn't bother her too much.

Vlasov even gave Emilia some money after the first two weeks, calling it her first salary, suggesting she buy some clothes with it in the only store that stood untouched in the city center, which was generously supplied by the local Soviet administration with "commandeered" goods from neighboring Germany. It seemed that "the Bolsheviks" condemned capitalism from the tribunes, but didn't find anything shameful in indulging in certain aspects of it when it suited them. Learning the little perks of the new regime and the people who represented it amused Emilia more and more. However, when she had just mistakenly assumed that all her hardships were in the past, an incident happened which resulted in much graver consequences that she could possibly foresee.

Emilia walked through the rubble of the city center to the makeshift market, which the local Poles had organized with the consent of the new administration to sell and trade whatever food items they were lucky to secure. After the German army and the officials fled the city, leaving basements stacked with preserves and non-perishable items and also quite decent wine, the Poles got their hands on it and were now selling it as their own, unless the Russians didn't get to those basements first, that is.

Emilia was reading a label on one of the bottles, which she had decided to buy as a present for Vlasov for taking her and Hannah in and paying them for their housekeeping services on top of it, when a long-forgotten, but familiar voice made her jerk as soon as it screeched right above her ear.

"What are you doing here, you little field whore?! Did your Nazi lovers let you go unscathed, instead of murdering you like they did the others?! You must have served them well, if they did!"

Emilia turned around, miraculously catching the bottle that almost slipped from her trembling hand, to come face to face with one of her former tormentors – if not in the physical sense than in an emotional sense for certain. Irene Nemkoff, with several women in tow, stood before Emilia wearing similar scowls reflecting their leader's hateful tirade.

"How dare you come back here after what you've done?!" Nemkoff stepped forward, her hands butting her narrow hips, gaining more and more confidence as she realized that the pale-faced girl in front of her most likely wouldn't say a word in her defense, as she was too startled to speak. "A good, honest woman, my closest friend Idit died because of you, you filthy whore, and you made your way out as if nothing happened!"

"Why don't you leave the girl alone?" The man behind the makeshift counter grumbled, obviously not wanting to lose a customer who was so interested in his wine. "She's just trying to shop, minding her own business…"

"She should mind her own business together with the rest of her lot in Germany! She liked her uniformed compatriots well enough, so she should go back there than to be here instead! On a second thought, why don't the Ivans send her to Siberia together with the SS, so she can keep entertaining them there as well? She seemed to do the job perfectly well in the camp where I was!"

Emilia put the wine back on the wooden counter and stepped backwards slowly, as more and more people started gathering into a small crowd, attracted to the screams of the infuriated woman. All the voices telling Nemkoff to back off were soon replaced by a menacing silence after her latest statement. Encouraged by the supportive rambling growing louder and louder behind her back, Irene made another step towards her victim.

"I want you to all to take a good look at her!" Nemkoff said even louder, pointing a finger at Emilia. "She used to be what the French and the Dutch call 'collaborators'! And not just some 'collaborators'; she and her friend serviced the whole regiment of the SS, in the camp where I had the misfortune to be with them. While all of us were dying by the hundreds, starved and worked to death, they lived a fancy life at our expense. They got the easiest jobs instead of the ones who really deserved it, they always had food, which they never shared with anybody, and they were never beaten, unlike the rest of us, who had to endure it daily. And if that wasn't enough, they told on the only good woman, who supported me and helped me survive through that horror, but who was too outspoken to these whores' taste, and the SS hanged her, hanged her for nothing!"

"This is not true," Emilia whispered, but her meek voice was drowned out by the ocean of indignant remarks that the crowd had started throwing her way, cornering her closer to the nearest wall.

"Oh yes, it is! And you dare come back now, after what you've done! What a spit in the face to all of us! This is our city, and you should get out, back to that hole of a country where all of you crawled out from! But before you go, we should do to you what the French and the Dutch did to their 'collaborators' – that will teach you how to open your legs next time!" Irene Nemkoff turned to the crowd gathered behind her back. "What do you say, shall we give this whore a new haircut and roll her in tar before sending her back to her fatherland?"

Realizing that her destiny would be even worse than the ethnic Germans she had seen on the platform just a couple of weeks ago, Emilia turned around and ran as fast as she could towards the first Soviet soldiers she noticed on the other side of the plaza. Unfortunately for her, her escape only triggered the enraged crowd, which followed her dangerously close, but it also attracted attention of the three uniformed men as well. Reaching them, Emilia grabbed the first one by his tunic, praying that they spoke German.

"Officers, please, help me! These people want to harm me! I live with Major Vlasov, please, take me to him!"

Nemkoff was screaming steps away from her, her face twisted with hatred. "Give her to us, officers! She's a collaborator and an SS whore!"

"I am not!" Emilia shouted back, and pleaded with the officer once again, "Take me to Major Vlasov, please! I'm his maid! I'm a former persecuted Jew! Please, help me!"

"Don't listen to her, she's a Nazi collaborator!"

One of the officers finally stepped between the two shouting women and in broken German ordered both of them to stop screaming. The other two didn't speak any German Emilia realized, much to her disappointment, and therefore it would be pure luck who they decided to listen to, or understand for that matter: Nemkoff kept pointing at Emilia and repeating the word that triggered every Russian Emilia had ever met – "Nazi" - and Emilia, on the other hand, repeated the name of Major Vlasov with probably more zeal than some people use to say their most ardent prayers.

At last, after talking among themselves, one of the officers grabbed Emilia's hand rather rudely and asked her for her address.

"You stay here. We come back," he told Nemkoff sternly, and the small procession of three officers and Emilia trailing behind them started making their way to the Major's house.

Andrey opened the door, smiled at Emilia at first as he always did, but his smile soon turned into a deep scowl after listening to what his comrades reported.

By the time Andrey went to fetch the Major, Emilia had started shivering slightly, anticipating his reaction. Not only must she confess her ugly story now, but she would have to do it in front of all these men on top of it; who knew if they were going to believe it at all.

All three officers saluted Vlasov, who threw a concerned glance at Emilia standing next to them with her head lowered. Her guilty posture only added more credibility to the story that they told him, repeating the words "collaborator" and *"natsist"* – Russian for "Nazi" – far too often for Emilia to have any hope left. If she was lucky, they'd just send her back to Germany. If not... Emilia didn't want to think about the alternative.

"Is it true, what they're saying?" Vlasov asked at last, standing right in front of Emilia.

"I don't know what they're saying," Emilia replied quietly. "I don't speak any Russian."

"They're saying that you were...going with the SS men." Vlasov almost spit out the last two words with utmost disgust.

"No... I mean... That's not how it was," Emilia said, still refusing to meet his eyes.

"It either *was* or *was not*. There is no in between," Major Vlasov raised his voice slightly, giving way to irritation.

Emilia looked up at him at last. The Major frowned slightly, seeing how tired her eyes suddenly looked; not afraid or ashamed, just very tired and indifferent.

"They raped us. Sometimes the whole barrack of SS men did, ten or fifteen people at a time. If it is called 'voluntarily collaboration' or 'voluntarily going' in your language and terms, then I'm guilty. Do whatever you want to me, just don't touch my mother. She's an innocent party in all this."

It was Vlasov who looked away first this time, clearing his throat uncomfortably and murmuring something in Russian to the officers. They started shuffling awkwardly as well after he had obviously explained to them what the full story was, before saluting their superior and leaving, nodding at Emilia on their way out.

Emilia stirred her tea later that evening, silently listening to what Vlasov was saying, her unblinking stare looking through him.

"You have to understand, the people – they will keep talking amongst themselves, and not me, not even comrade Stalin himself, can shut their mouths. But as long as you're under my protection, you won't have to be afraid of them. All of the officers, all of the soldiers will know that you're with me, and no one will say a word to you or harm you in any way. I'll take good care of you as long as I'm here, that much I can promise you. You can live here not as my maid, but as my…companion, if you like. I will hire a maid myself, I'll find someone. You won't need for anything, and I'll treat you like you deserve to be treated, not like they treated you."

Emilia shot him a sharp glare, but he only smiled back, outstretching his arms towards her over the table.

"You just have to say the word, Emilia. One word from you, and I will be your most loyal servant."

Emilia looked at his hands, wondering if he understood it himself, how ridiculous his words sounded when he said that he wasn't like them, the Nazis. No, he was good of course, he wouldn't rape her, of course not, because the Russians didn't do that, most certainly they didn't. No, he had just found her weak spot and would coerce her into a "companionship" relationship, which was nothing like rape in his eyes, because she would have to consent to it, if she wanted his protection, that is. Everything was very civilized and voluntarily. Emilia smirked slightly at the sarcastic voice inside her head, cleaned the spoon on the rim of her tea cup and placed it neatly on the table.

"I want a house after you leave. Legally, with papers and all the necessary documents, which would prove my ownership, previous and present," she said in a leveled and absolutely unemotional tone, with so much coldness permeating the words that Vlasov took his hands away to place them back onto his lap. "And not this house, I want something far outside the city limits, preferably a farm. It doesn't have to be big, but I need land with it, so I can grow my own food so I don't have to go to the city to buy anything. Also, before you leave, I need a weapon, a gun with ammunition, to protect myself and my property if it's necessary."

"We can do all that," Vlasov promised quietly.

After several minutes of uncomfortable silence, interrupted only by the sound of Emilia sipping her tea, Vlasov tried to catch her glance.

"What are you thinking about?"

"What am I thinking about? I'm thinking that this will never end, Maksim."

His brow furrowed as he tried to comprehend her words. "What will never end?"

"Nothing. My life." Emilia gave him a somewhat crooked grin.

Chapter 3

Near Gdansk, Poland, June 1948

Emilia was working in her bedroom when she heard her mother's frantic screams and indignant tone, coming from the front door. It was odd to begin with, since they lived far outside the city limits in a farm house that very rarely saw any visitors. It couldn't be Ivans again, they had all left for the most part a long time ago, leaving the Soviet-installed government behind. But, Emilia still quickly grabbed a gun out of the top drawer, hid it in the pocket of her skirt and went downstairs to see what all the noise was about.

"Didn't you see a mezuzah on our front door?! Didn't you see whose door you were knocking at?! Some cheek you have, coming here and demanding something after all you've done to us, you disgraceful creatures! Go along, get out before I call the authorities on you. I won't blink an eye if you die of thirst on the way! Serves you right! They shouldn't have let your lot go at all, should have hanged you all there in Siberia!!!"

Emilia saw her mother, standing in the doors and shaking her fists at someone that she couldn't see in the dark.

"Mother?" Emilia shouted, to find out what was going on.

"It's nothing, sorry for troubling you," someone replied in a raspy voice from the darkness outside. "We're already leaving."

Emilia moved Hannah out of her way and stepped onto the front porch, squinting slightly in order to make out two figures, who had already started making their way back to the field. "Wait! What did you want?"

The couple turned around and lingered where they stood, shifting from one foot to another with uncertainty.

"Well, what is it?" Emilia asked again, looking the two men up and down.

They were beggars most certainly, because even from a distance the unbearable stench from their clothes reached Emilia's nostrils. The clothes they wore, some unrecognizable shoes and hanging trousers, and the bundles of the rest of their possessions that they held in their hands made them look more like former camp internees than simple beggars.

"We just wanted some water," one of them replied at last and scratched the back of his head violently. "We've been walking all day and it's very hot out, and there's not been one water pipe in sight. But it's fine if you don't want to give us any. We didn't know you were Jewish. Please, accept our apologies."

"No need to." Emilia motioned them closer. "Wait here, on the porch. I'll go fetch you some water."

"Emilia!" Hannah clasped her elbow and pulled her back inside the house. "Don't let them come here, are you mad?! They're the Germans that the Russians let go from the camps! The prisoners of war! The people who started all this!"

Emilia looked at the two men, who stood in the light coming from the open door with their eyes lowered and shoulders hunched. Only now, seeing them a little closer, could she make out the former uniform trousers on one of them. The rest of their clothes were so dirty and worn out that it was difficult to say what they used to be before.

"Are you from the SS?" she asked them at last.

"No, Frau, we're regular *Wehrmacht*." The same one who did all the talking replied.

"Wait here," Emilia said after a short pause. She closed the door, heading to the kitchen.

"Are you really going to give them water?" Hannah asked in amazement, trailing behind her.

"Of course I am. They're thirsty. They can barely talk, didn't you hear?"

She took two glasses from the cupboard and filled them with running water.

"Let them die from thirst, who would cry for them?"

"Their families, probably," Emilia replied in the same calm voice, and put the glasses on a small tray.

"Families! They didn't care about our families when they—"

"Mother!"

Emilia turned around so fast that Hannah almost crashed into her. The look in Emilia's eyes made her just purse her lips and huff.

"It's the *Wehrmacht*, mother," Emilia replied more calmly and went back to the door. "They were regular soldiers only."

The two former POWs were still standing where Emilia had left them and smiled with gratitude at the glasses she offered them. They downed them so fast that Emilia chuckled unwillingly and asked them if they wanted more. The two exchanged glances and nodded a little embarrassingly.

"Maybe you're hungry too?" Emilia couldn't help but notice how emaciated the men looked. It appeared that the Soviet camps didn't treat their prisoners any better than the former Nazi government had treated their prisoners.

"If you have some bread, we would be very grateful," the younger one replied with a shy smile on his unshaven face, and reached to scratch his head again and his shoulder right after. "They gave us a ration, but…"

149

"We ran out of it two days ago," the other one finished his thought.

"You must be starving then!" Emilia was actually surprised they still stood on their feet. She remembered her own hungry days, when she could barely stand without Magda's support during roll call and immediately felt a surge of sympathy for the two men. "You know what? We still have something left from dinner, why don't you come inside and finish whatever's left? And then I'll fix something for you for the road. How far do you have to walk, if you don't mind me asking?"

"Dresden," the young one replied.

"But that's… hundreds and hundreds of kilometers away! All on foot?" she asked incredulously.

"Well, we rode a train to the Soviet border…" The older one lowered his eyes and sniffled. "Then they told us to get out, gave four pieces of bread to each and… told us to go wherever we wanted."

"You walked all this way? Across the whole country?"

They shrugged and smiled crookedly again. "We didn't have much of a choice, really."

"Come inside, I'll fix you something," Emilia opened the door wider and motioned them in.

Hannah rushed to stop her daughter, waving her hands at the two men. "Emilia, have you gone off your head?! Look at them, they scratch constantly, they must have lice all over them! Do not let them in here, God knows what diseases they carry!"

"Mother, will you stop it?!" Emilia shouted back at the woman, getting both annoyed and embarrassed by her words.

"She's right, actually," the young one spoke again, smiling bashfully. "We better not go inside, we do have lice, even though they sprayed us with something before the release… But it wasn't enough to get them out of our clothes, so they're back. Besides, we haven't showered in a while, we really better stay outside."

"Where are you going to spend the night?"

"Right here likely, in a field nearby."

Emilia pondered something for a moment, and then pointed at the bench outside, under one of the windows. "Wait there, I'll bring you some sandwiches for now and then I'll figure out what to do with you."

"What on earth are you going to do with them?" Hannah followed Emilia around the kitchen, where she began cutting bread, ham and cheese in thick, generous slices. "You aren't going to invite them in for the night, are you?"

"Of course I am. Don't worry, I'll clean them first."

"Are you insane?! Two strangers, and not just strangers, soldiers! You're going to invite them inside our house—

150

"It's *my* house, mother," Emilia sternly cut her off and gave her mother a pointed look that made her go silent at once. "If it wasn't for me, we would still be living in some communal housing project. So, I believe this makes me the mistress of the household, and I decide who I would like to invite here or who I shouldn't. Fair enough?"

"They're dangerous men," Hannah muttered under her breath, following her daughter back to the door.

"These dangerous men can barely stand on their own two feet at the moment."

Minutes later, after the two had wolfed down their sandwiches and rewarded Emilia with two beaming smiles on their grimy, bearded faces, Emilia told them to get undressed to their underpants and put all their clothing in a pile.

"Don't worry, I do have men's clothes inside the house. Maybe not your size exactly, but I don't believe that this is your size either." She nodded at the men's attire. "What are your names, by the way?"

"Franz, Frau." The older one slightly bowed his head. "Franz Miller."

"Klaus." The other one smiled. "Nickolas Lemmel, but everyone calls me Klaus."

Emilia inwardly smiled at his surprisingly happy-go-lucky attitude despite the constant bug biting him and the general situation and condition the two were in. After the meal his expression seemed to have brightened even more.

"Emilia." She introduced herself, before pointing her new acquaintances to where they were supposed to pile up their clothes.

Under her mother's concerned stare through the half-opened door, Emilia went to the shed which they used to keep all their farming equipment and came back with a small canister of kerosene. It was a warm night, so the men stood in their trousers only, having thrown everything else in a pile.

"All of your clothes need to be burned. The lice will never disappear if you keep wearing the same things."

They nodded indecisively, still not looking too sure about the idea, but Emilia had already returned from the house with a box of matches and two towels. She poured some kerosene on the clothes and lit the pile. After that she pointed the men towards the bench.

"Do you have something under them?" She nodded at their trousers.

They exchanged awkward glances and replied with embarrassed smiles, "Underwear."

"So, take those pants off then and throw them into the fire!"

After they shuffled for some time without making any attempt to rid themselves of their clothing, Emilia crossed her arms over her chest and shook her head.

"I wish all of your lot were as shy as you two! Get them off, because I won't let you inside the house with those pants on!"

After the trousers were thrown into the fire, Emilia pointed the men to the bench again.

"Sit and lower your heads. I'll put the kerosene on you."

"What for?" They both immediately stepped back, not too enthralled with the idea, obviously wondering if an insane Jewish girl had decided to exact her revenge on them and set them on fire as well.

Emilia chuckled. "Kerosene kills lice, like no other chemical can. Believe me, I know."

After more uncertain looks followed, Emilia sighed and threw the match box on the front porch, away from them. "Feel better now? Come, sit down, keep your heads low and keep your eyes shut with your hands. I warn you in advance: it'll burn, but the lice will be gone in no time."

In five minutes the two scrawny figures sat there with towels wrapped around their heads, smiling again and a little reassured with what her intentions were. She brought them some potatoes and more ham, which they consumed in record time again and with a hearty appetite.

"So, where are you coming from?" Emilia asked after they were done with their meal.

"Siberia. One of the Gulags," Klaus replied, trying to scratch his head under the towel. "We are some of the first ones who they let go. We're lucky that we used to belong to the *Wehrmacht* and not the SS. They don't like those, I tell you. And the officer staff are hated even more. We were just regular soldiers, so they didn't bother us too much. Franz and I worked on a railroad that they wanted us to rebuild, and as soon as we did, they put us on the first train and sent us back home. They said they didn't need too many mouths to feed."

"I wouldn't call it 'feeding' to begin with." Franz grinned, slightly nudging his comrade with his elbow.

"So, they're letting the regular *Wehrmacht* go back home now?" Emilia asked.

"Not all *Wehrmacht*, just a small part, as we understand." Klaus shrugged. "There were barely two hundred of us on that train, all former privates. No officers, no one of any rank at all really. The NKVD people are very serious about who they can let go. We were questioned for a good hour before they approved us."

"What did they ask you?"

Klaus shrugged again. "They asked if we used to belong to the Nazi Party, if we liked Hitler, if we volunteered for the *Wehrmacht* or were drafted, if we had any National-Socialists in our families, if any of our relatives were party members... Things like that."

"Well, how would they know if you lied?" Emilia smiled.

"They had our papers, with which they arrested us, so they did know whether we were party members or not and whether we were drawn into the army or volunteered. But the rest they could easily find out from our comrades: for a piece of bread people would tell them every thought you had expressed while incarcerated in the camp, or the name of every relative you mentioned."

"Reminds me of some other place." Emilia chuckled slightly.

Klaus tilted his head to one side with curiosity, but seeing that Emilia didn't want to elaborate on the subject, he decided not to pry.

"You can take your towels off," she told them after checking her watch. "I'll run the water for you on the first floor, so you can go on and take a shower over there. I think you'd better do it together if you're not shy; that way you can scrub each other off much better."

"We showered with a hundred other men for the past few years..." The two exchanged smiles. "So, we're used to it."

"Good." Emilia motioned them to follow her inside the house under Hannah's disapproving stare. "I'll bring you fresh clothes and put them on a chair outside. You can also use a shaving set that was left by the Ivans, soap and whatever else you might need. We don't use that bathroom for ourselves, only for laundry, so don't be afraid to make it messy. I'll put clean towels for you too on top of the clothes. Take your time, and I'll make some more potatoes for you."

Franz was snoring evenly on the couch in the living room, while Emilia and Klaus sat at the table finishing their fourth cup of tea. After a thorough shower and a makeshift delousing, her new guest had turned out to be much younger than she had originally thought, and his hair, now washed and neatly brushed to one side, was a light golden color and not dirty gray as it had seemed before. The absence of the beard and layers of dust on his face made it possible to make out two dimples on his cheeks every time he smiled, and Emilia couldn't believe how much he smiled for a man who had just came back from a hell that wasn't much different from the one that she had experienced.

He ate everything she put before him, but nodded in agreement as soon as she mentioned that she couldn't give him any more food, not because she didn't want to, but because it could make him sick or even kill him.

"I've seen so many people die after they were liberated from the camps," Emilia said in a quiet voice while putting away the dishes. "I lived and worked in one of the hospitals back then, and it was just so heartbreaking and unfair, the fact that they were free at last, but their bodies just couldn't adjust back to normal life. So many of them, after somehow surviving on tiny portions while in the camp, died after the doctors tried to nourish them back to life. It was really devastating to watch."

"I'm sorry you had to live through that," Klaus replied sympathetically, quickly getting up to help her with the dishes.

You have no idea what I had to live through, Emilia thought, but she didn't say anything further.

"Allow me to help you," he insisted, taking a dirty plate out of her hands and standing in front of the sink. Emilia tried to object, but he shook his head, not having any of her protests. "It's the least I can do after everything you have done for us. I don't know if I would have fed, let alone invited in for a night, anyone of my sort, if I were in your shoes."

"Why is that?"

"Well... You're Jewish," Klaus said softly, lathering a plate with soap. "In the Gulag they showed us films and documentaries about what the SS were doing with the Jews in the occupied territories and in the camps... We, the *Wehrmacht*, together with the *Luftwaffe* and the fleet, we didn't know about any of that, and it came as a shock to us, to be honest... Many of us cried watching it. It should have never come to this. No wonder the whole world hates us all now. We deserve it."

"It's not your personal fault." Emilia shrugged slightly, sitting on the table behind him, only now noticing several scars crossing his back. She contemplated for a moment if she should ask him about them. "They beat you there?"

"Who?" Klaus turned around to the sound of her voice and caught her studying the long white lines across his ribs, just visible under the skin.

"Ach, that." He chuckled and shook his head, much to Emilia's surprise. "Yes, I got it across the back one time. I stole a bone from the kitchen. It was a huge bone, one that you could have killed a man with, I tell you! They used to put such bones in the big pots where they made soup for everyone, so it would at least taste like meat, not that we would get any of the real meat from that bone – all of that went to the Russian officers. So, I stole it from the kitchen while the cook wasn't watching and carried it out under my *telogreika* – that's a Russian jacket, stuffed with cotton. They're really warm, great for winter. Anyway, I hid behind the barrack, with three of my comrades, and we all feasted on that bone; we even broke it in pieces and sucked it dry. You know that sweet, tasty stuff that's inside? Oh, how good it was! The best meal of my life, I thought back then. Of course, we got caught by some guard who happened to be passing us by with his dog, and all of us were put in front of everyone else for public punishment the very next morning. We all got fifty lashes, but let me tell you, it was worth it!"

Klaus laughed under Emilia's incredulous stare. "You're laughing about it? You probably weren't able to lay on your back for a month!"

"It doesn't hurt anymore, so why not laugh about it?" he replied simply, once again smiling at Emilia over his shoulder.

She caught herself reaching for her own shoulder as soon as he turned back to the sink, to touch the long, raised scar under her shirt, one of the many left by Engel.

"Some things you can't laugh about," Emilia said pensively, quickly taking her hand away.

"Yes, you're probably right," he agreed easily. "I'm laughing just because I was lucky, that's all."

"Lucky?" Emilia arched her brow.

"Why, yes, I'm very lucky. Most of my former comrades died fighting, many of them died of starvation or diseases in the camp, and almost all of them are still there." Klaus turned to her, beaming. "And I'm here with you, almost back home. I don't itch anymore, I could finally wash myself and shave, I just had the best dinner I could only dream about for the past few years, and I'm going to sleep on a couch instead of a wooden bunk or even the dirty ground... I couldn't be happier, really. So yes, I consider myself very lucky."

Emilia didn't like that word, *lucky*, but, somehow, in her new acquaintance's case it surprisingly made a lot of sense. She got off the table and picked up a towel to wipe the clean dishes that Klaus was setting aside.

"So you have family in Dresden?" She decided it was better to change the subject, as the conversation had brought up too many uncomfortable memories, despite Klaus managing to make his own experience in the camp sound like a fun summer adventure and not a horrid incarceration. He had some sort of a talent to turn even the most serious situations and subjects into a joke, Emilia had noticed. Not one time had he complained about anything, and this fact fascinated Emilia for some reason. She had barely talked to anyone after the Ivans had left several years ago, and she most certainly hadn't spoken to any man, unless it was some sort of city official stopping by for some reason. The city itself was another place she preferred not to show her face at all, and her mother always went there to do the shopping or to send packages that Emilia had prepared for Friede.

Friede had gone back to her former occupation – working for the newspaper, only this time it was a new and legal one, and not her former leftist publication, for which she had been sent to the camp. After a psychiatrist suggested that Emilia start writing a diary, to put down on paper all those issues she couldn't bring herself to talk about, Emilia decided to share what she wrote with Friede. It helped to talk about it all with someone who was there with her, and was at least partly familiar with what she had to go through. After reading Emilia's diaries, and after the two spent half the night drinking and crying over their past experiences, Friede came up with the idea that her friend should work at the newspaper with her. Emilia didn't want to move to Austria, so the two decided that she should send her writing to

Friede, who would publish it for her and send the money to Emilia. It was a fair enough arrangement, and it worked perfectly for Emilia, who preferred not to be around people that much.

Even now, having just two guests in their big house was a little overwhelming, but having a weapon, secretly concealed in her pocket, made Emilia feel more comfortable in the company of the two soldiers. In her mind she understood that they were absolutely harmless, but her shoulders and back tensed instinctively every time Klaus's hand accidentally brushed hers, even though it was just to pass a dish, without any ulterior thought in his mind. Emilia hated the contradictory signals that her body always exchanged; her brain told her to calm down but her nerves shouted "danger" at any human contact, even when doctors in the hospital checked her right after the liberation.

The Ivans were another story, one that Emilia preferred to erase from her memory once and for all, but they were the new masters of the country now, and she and her mother did need a place to live and something to eat. Major Vlasov, who pestered Emilia from the time she arrived back to Danzig, made it quite transparent that she wouldn't want for anything if she was only kind enough to him.

Vlasov begged her to come with him when it was time for him to go back to his mysterious Moscow, but his begging and hand kissing were all to no avail; Emilia only smiled crookedly and shook her head. She had had enough of all of them to last a lifetime, and now all she could think was that she wanted to be left alone in the house, a house that she had paid quite a price for. *Farewell to you, Maksim. Don't stay in touch, I won't reply to any of your letters. You never existed, and I don't remember your face anymore.*

And now Klaus had come into her life and brought up memories that had been hidden deeply under dusty layers of pain and humiliation. He made her think again about everything that she had done wrong in her life, and whether it was wrong, and where was up and where was down in this life. She felt like no one could possibly understand anymore, and yet she wanted to learn more about him, if only to find out his secret, of how he was able to come out of this bone-grinder of a war, and Gulag, so completely unscathed and cheerful. She wanted to know how it hadn't tainted him like it had tainted her, and hadn't left a scar. Her scars felt like dirt that wouldn't come off no matter how fiercely she scrubbed herself every single day, with hatred, with carefully faked indifference and a well-rehearsed strength that she didn't feel and yet had learned how to show to others.

"No, I don't have anyone in Dresden," Klaus replied, distracting her from her thoughts. Emilia hadn't noticed that he had been quiet for a long time before answering. "I'm just going there with Franz, because he invited me to live in his house before I find a place of my own. The city is almost all destroyed... His wife lives with his parents and her parents and their four children, all in one apartment in a building, half-destroyed by bombing. I don't want to impose on him, but I really have no other place to go."

"You don't have anyone at all?" Emilia asked mildly.

"No. My wife moved in with my parents after our building was hit with bombs. And then they all died during another air raid. It was a hellish night at the end of the war, you probably heard of it. I was on the front then, and I only found out about them when I was put in the camp. Her parents died too as far as I know; I think they starved to death after hunger hit the country right after the war finished. So, no, I have no place to go."

"I'm very sorry." Emilia lowered her eyes. "No children?"

Klaus thought for a moment, washing his hands and shaking them off above the sink. "I do have a son. Walther. He slept that night with a neighbor across the street because she still had breast milk and my wife didn't, so she always kept him there for the night, together with her boy. But he was born after I had already gone to the front. I've never seen him, and he's never seen me. I suppose he's in some orphanage now, or maybe with some adopted family. I don't really know what happened to him."

"Don't you want to go find him?"

Klaus frowned for the first time since the time of their meeting.

"No, I don't," he replied firmly, after another pause. "First, I can't even take care of myself now and will have to rely on my friend and his family's mercy to help me out at least for now, and second... He doesn't know me. Maybe he's better off with his new parents."

"You don't know that," Emilia said, but quickly shook her head in apology. "I'm sorry, it's not my place to say that. It's your life and your business, not mine."

"That's fine." Klaus smiled again, leaning onto the sink next to Emilia. "Do you have any children?"

"No." She replied a little too quickly, but if her guest had caught onto that, he didn't say anything. "More tea?"

"Why not."

"I'm sorry, let me know if you're tired, I'll let you go sleep..." Emilia said.

"Stop apologizing, it's a pleasure for me to talk to you."

Emilia put the kettle on the gas burner, when he suddenly said, "That's a very smart idea, having a gun on you."

Emilia quickly turned around, instinctively putting her hand on top of her pocket. Klaus chuckled softly. "Even though, technically, it's illegal."

"We live alone and far away from everyone." Emilia tried to explain, embarrassed that he had noticed it. "It's not because..."

"No, no, don't worry, I'm not taking it personally in any way. I really do think it's a very good idea. What kind of a gun is it? Russian or German?"

"German. It's a Mauser."

"Can you shoot it?" Klaus asked with a mischievous smile.

"Yes, I can shoot it!" Not knowing why, Emilia caught his barely contained contagious laughter, and after the two were finally through their laughing fit, she asked all of a sudden, surprising even herself with her question, "Do you want to stay here?"

"Stay here?"

"Well, yes… I just figured that if your friend is in a tough situation as it is, and you have no one in Dresden anyway… Maybe you should stay here. The house is big, and we could really use a man's help here on the farm. Only if you want, of course."

Klaus looked at her, his smile getting wider and wider. "Really?"

"Why, yes… If you want to."

"Aren't you afraid to invite a complete stranger inside your house?" he asked, his dimples becoming more prominent.

"I have a gun." Emilia smiled cheekily, and started giggling with him, wondering how he could possibly make her laugh so effortlessly. "You still don't believe me that I can shoot it, do you?"

"That's quite fine, I'll teach you how."

That night, laying in her bed on the second floor with the above-mentioned gun, Emilia couldn't believe what she had done. For some reason, however, the decision seemed right, both in her mind and her heart.

Chapter 4

The following morning, Emilia announced her decision to her mother, that she had decided to let Klaus stay. She cut short all of her mother's objections, calmly pointing out that Klaus and Franz were just the first small portion of POWs, released by the Russians, and that more would most certainly follow, and no one knew how friendly those would be.

"It's always useful having a man in the house. He'll be of great help with the farm, too." Emilia tried to pacify her mother, who was wringing her hands, obviously not too reassured about the new living arrangements.

"He's all skin and bones," Hannah grumbled in response. "What kind of a worker will he make?"

"He'll be just fine in a couple of months. We'll feed him well."

"More food going to waste! Even his comrade's family wouldn't want him, so why would you?"

"He has no family and no place to go."

"Some stranger living under our roof with us! God knows what will come to his mind one day! What if he decides to kill us both and run away with our money?"

"That would be highly unpractical of him. Besides, we don't have much money."

"I still don't know about this, Emmi…"

"You don't have to 'know' anything, Mama. He's staying."

After all four had their breakfast, Emilia made several sandwiches for Franz and filled an empty bottle with water.

"That should last you till you reach Gdansk, and over there you can refill it at a pump." Emilia reached into her pocket and handed the man several bills. "Here, take this, too. It should be enough for you to buy a train ticket to Dresden, so you don't have to walk."

Franz looked at the money in Emilia's hand and shook his head slowly.

"No, Frau, I can't accept this."

"Why not?"

"No, it's just… It wouldn't be right. Thank you from the bottom of my heart, but I can't. You've done enough for us as it is."

"You'll do me a favor if you take it, really. And it's not an imposition in any case, we're not struggling here." Seeing that he was still not sure, Emilia gave him an encouraging smile. "You can give it back, if you want. As soon as you're back on your feet and working. Let's consider it a loan, how about that?"

Franz beamed her, finally accepting her offer. "You've talked me into it, Frau. I'll send it all back to you the first chance I have."

"Don't be in a rush."

Emilia gave the two men time to bid their farewells outside, leaving them to the privacy of the front porch. A few minutes later, Klaus walked in, trying to hide his eyes which were slightly clouded with tears under wet eyelashes, and asked Emilia what needed to be done around the house.

"Just rest for a while." Emilia grinned at his eagerness while gathering up the blanket and pillow that Franz had used. The other cover and pillow she folded and put on the corner of the couch that would become Klaus's bed for now. "We'll go together to the field later, and I'll show you what we plant and grow. That's so we don't have to go to the city that much. Lay down, read a book – we have quite a library over there. I have to go upstairs and finish an article I'm working on, but you can call me if you need something."

Klaus nodded and obediently went to the bookcase, which occupied a big part of the wall next to the window. An hour later, Emilia noticed that some other sound was interfering with the sound of her typing machine. She looked out of her bedroom window and saw her new housemate sawing a big piece of wood outside. Wondering what he was doing, she went downstairs and noticed one of the books, laying on a side of the couch, where he had left it.

"What about that rest time?" Emilia chastised him with a smile, stopping besides Klaus.

He turned around quickly, just now noticing her. He gave her an apologetic smile, wiping the sweat off his forehead.

"I'm sorry, did the noise bother you? I'm almost done, I promise. I noticed this morning that the middle step on your porch is all rotten and it might collapse when someone steps on it. I thought of changing just that one, but then realized that it will be different in color from the other ones, so I decided to change them all. I found these planks in your shed, and they'll fit perfectly. You didn't need them for something else, did you?"

"No, I don't even know about half of the things that are in that shed," Emilia confessed. "Thank you. It's very thoughtful of you. But you really should rest more now, you still have a long way to go before you're back to normal, and overworking yourself is really not good. I'm telling you as a former nurse."

"Oh, don't worry about me, I feel great. Really!" Klaus replied cheerfully. "And besides, I can't sit still, I'm used to doing something all the time. A Gulag habit."

"I understand. I couldn't spend a day without a purpose, too, after we had been liberated."

Klaus blinked a couple of times, taking in the new information. "You were in a camp too? I'm sorry, I didn't know…"

"How would you know?" Emilia smiled slightly.

"They showed us in those films that all of you had numbers on your arms…" He quickly glanced at hers.

"Not all of us. Only the Auschwitz people. They didn't shave our heads either."

"I'm sorry," Klaus muttered again.

"For what?" Emilia shrugged slightly. "It's not your personal fault."

"We were fighting along with them in the front. We were on the same side…"

"For the Führer?"

"No." Klaus frowned. "For Germany."

"That's the difference. They were fighting for the Führer."

Klaus was quiet for some time, brushing the sawdust off the wood. Suddenly, he raised his eyes back to Emilia and said firmly, "I didn't volunteer for the army. They drafted me."

"You don't have to explain yourself to me, I don't blame you for anything," Emilia replied calmly.

"But I still want you to know. I was always against those kinds of policies, and against the war itself. He should have never gone further than Austria. Look what he did to our country! And all because *he* wanted something. It wasn't for the people, but was all for himself. The best thing he did for all of us was shooting himself."

"Too bad it didn't all end there."

Klaus looked at her inquisitively.

"There are still evil people out there. Angry people, jealous people, destructive people, who prey on other people's misfortunes," Emilia explained pensively. "People like that killed my best friend a long time ago, and almost killed me as well. Even now that the war has been over for a few years, they still… Ach, I don't want to even talk about them. They're far away, and let them stay that way."

She walked away with a pensive look on her face. He didn't call her back, instinctively knowing she needed her space.

———

In only a few days Klaus had managed to completely change the atmosphere in the house. He seemed to never stop talking and even if his female audience, which was too used to silence, was at first a little reluctant to engage in the conversation, it didn't discourage him in the slightest from entertaining both Emilia and Hannah with his cheerful banter.

"No, no, no, Frau Hannah, that's not how you make good mashed potatoes." Not only would he entertain the women with his stories while doing something next to them, Klaus would leap up from his chair and offer to help at every opportunity he had. "Here, let me show you. The secret – it's a Ukrainian secret, so don't tell anyone – is to put a lot of butter in it, and instead of water, like you just tried to do, you pour milk in it. It makes the best mashed potatoes, fluffy and soft, like a cloud, and the taste – ach! Here, I'll just finish mixing it and let you try it. You'll never have your mashed potatoes any other way from now on that much I can promise you!"

"And who taught you this secret?" Emilia grinned from her chair, where she was busy cutting ham.

"One Ukrainian woman, in whose house we were stationed for a few weeks. She was the best cook I've ever met, and always fed us so much that we couldn't move. Our commanding officer always joked that she did it on purpose, so when the Red Army came, we wouldn't be able to fight them!"

Both mother and daughter couldn't help but chuckle at that.

"Anyway, Tosya – that was her name – showed me how to make the best mashed potatoes, because before that the only mashed potatoes I knew were regular potatoes that you bake in the fire, peel with your hands, and they become mashed in your mouth later." He stole a mischievous glance at Emilia, who was giggling enthusiastically. "What?"

"Nothing. Well, it's your story, it's funny, but I'm laughing about something different."

"About what?" He grinned wider, stopping at his job of mixing the potatoes.

"About your division being lucky that the Russians didn't catch you one night as a 'yazik' as they call it. You know, when they snatch up an enemy soldier at night and interrogate them about the position of enemy forces, their ammunition stashes and their plans. Well, they wouldn't even have to interrogate you: you would tell them everything without them even having to ask." Emilia lifted her eyes from the cutting board, making sure that she didn't offend him with her remark, but Klaus only laughed kind-heartedly.

"You know, you're not the first person who has told me that."

"Who was the first one?"

Emilia waited as Klaus offered some potato from the pot for Hannah to try. Judging by her mother's bright smile and big eyes, Klaus didn't lie about "the Ukrainian secret."

"My commanding officer." Happy with impressing Hannah, who was still on guard with him and wasn't so easy to impress, Klaus put the pot in the middle of the table and proceeded to put potato on their respective plates. "He awarded me with two Knight's crosses for bravery, but he refused to promote me to officer rank. He even said it himself: 'Lemmel, you're a great guy and a faithful comrade, but you'd make the lousiest officer in the whole of *Wehrmacht.*'"

"Why would he say that?"

Klaus shrugged a little awkwardly. "I didn't like the actual fighting and I didn't like shooting at people. I was a great shooter, so I would shoot them in the arms or legs, so they wouldn't be able to carry on fighting, but I made sure I kept them alive at least. He knew about that. He chastised me for being too soft many times, but never, not once, reported me. He only told me to watch for the SS when they were near."

"Why?" Emilia raised her eyes from her plate, for a second forgetting the taste of the potato, which was indeed heavenly.

"Ach, they weren't the nicest fellows, let's just put it that way. Not the *Waffen-SS*, they were quite decent guys by the way. These ones were different SS, political ones or from some state organization perhaps, I'm not even sure what they were. They would move from one division to another and supervise us during the battle, and if you did something not to their liking – you were investigated, and even court martialed in some cases."

"Really?" Even Hannah raised her brows, for the first time hearing that the dreaded SS used to harass their own people, and not just those they proclaimed were *Untermenschen.*

"Oh yes! And they took their tasks seriously to the point of ridiculousness. I remember one time when I was sitting in my fox hole – it's a one man or sometimes two man hole that you have to dig in the ground when you're getting ready for an offensive, from where you can shoot at the enemy; a sort of a personal trench so to say. So, here I was, sitting in my hole, and one of these 'supervisors' jumps inside and stays with me throughout the whole shootout. And every time I turn my head, he pesters me: 'Why are you looking back? Are you thinking of deserting?' I kept saying, 'No, I was only checking on my comrades and their positions.' The next time I craned my neck a little too much and looked at the front line a little too long, he goes again, 'Why are you staring at the enemy line so eagerly? Are you thinking of making a run to the Reds?' I said, 'No, I was trying to make out their positions and find new aims.' He spent the whole day with me in that hole, asking all these nonsense questions and simply distracting me from my duties. At last, I finally lost my patience and asked him in jest to yet another one of his remarks, 'So where should I look? Under my feet? But then you'll decide that I want to dig a tunnel back to Germany and call me a deserter!'"

Both women couldn't suppress their laughter once again.

"And what did he do?" Emilia asked.

"Walloped me on the head. Good thing I was wearing my helmet, as he hit his hand pretty hard, too, and cursed me out as if it was my fault."

Later that evening, while washing dishes together with Klaus, an event that had already become a sort of tradition for Emilia and Klaus while Hannah went outside to enjoy some cool night breeze on a bench, Emilia caught herself thinking that she not only didn't mind staying alone with her new housemate, she was longing to be in his company. Although they had only known each other a few days, he had the ability to make the most terrifying events seem so laughable and easy.

The following day she decided to stay in the field with him, instead of locking herself in her stuffy bedroom with her typing machine. The sun was stinging the back of her neck and her exposed arms and ankles, but she didn't even notice, as she dug into the ground next to her new farming partner.

"What did you get your two Knight's Crosses for?" Emilia asked, surprising herself with her bravery. Normally she wasn't the one to initiate conversation, but with Klaus everything was different, simple and without any hidden motive. With him she could just talk, and he wouldn't interpret her interest in him as an invitation to something more; that was a very welcome change.

"It was nothing, really." Klaus hid his bashful grin as he always did when someone praised him or if he had to admit something remarkable about himself. Emilia had noticed that habit of his on the very first night when his comrade Franz was still with them.

"It should be something. They don't give those crosses for nothing."

"Well, one was for saving my comrade," Klaus replied after a pause. "He was in his fox hole when the Russian tanks appeared out of nowhere to back their men. He had nowhere to run, and he would have been shot at once anyway, but, moreover, he was one of three men we had with anti-tank guns, so knowing that his conscience wouldn't allow him to leave his post. After my comrade shot and stopped two of their tanks, one of the remaining tanks drove right up to him and started burying him in his hole. You know how they do it? They drive on top of the hole and start turning around themselves several times, before they level the hole and the man in it to the ground. Rarely did someone survive such a tactic; not because the tank would mangle them, they were too deep down for that, but because they suffocated from the lack of oxygen if no one dug them out in time. As soon as the tank turned its back on the hole and started driving to one of our trenches, I jumped out of my hole, lit a Molotov cocktail, threw it on the back of the tank – where the engine is, the only part that catches fire like dry paper – dropped to my stomach and started digging out my comrade with my bare hands, not even paying attention to the fighting around me. I was just in time to drag him out of there, thanks to my comrades who covered us both with their gunfire, and I carried him on my back to the medics in the nearest trench. He was more scared than hurt." Klaus snorted with amusement at the memory. "That's how I got my first Cross."

"And the second one?"

"No, it's your turn now." Klaus threw an impish glance at her over the plants. "You tell me about your 'front life.' How were your SS since you asked about mine?"

"My SS?" Emilia caught herself smiling as well, even though she didn't know why. "Well, let's just say that the one who walloped you on the head would be considered the nicest man in our camp, to whom everyone would go to for protection."

"That doesn't sound too good."

"No, it doesn't."

"That's all right. One day you will even laugh about it, just like I told you to."

The first time he had said that Emilia had replied sternly that certain things couldn't be laughed about, but this time she thought about his remark for a moment, and said simply, "Maybe I will. One day."

A week had passed since Franz's departure, when Emilia found Klaus writing a letter in the kitchen, to his friend as she assumed.

"To my comrades in the Gulag," he corrected her, surprising her greatly. "I'll write to Franz, but later. He's home already, with his family. My other comrades need this letter more than he does."

"That makes sense." Emilia agreed and, after making herself tea, started walking away to give Klaus his space.

However, he stopped her with an unexpected question.

"Do you want me to read it to you? I'm almost finished."

"Oh, if you'd like."

Feeling pleasantly surprised that he trusted her so easily, so as to read his private correspondence to her, Emilia sat on the chair across the table from him, cupping her mug with her hands.

"Dearest Wilhelm! It is with the greatest pleasure and relief that I write to you, just like I promised before we shook hands for the last time, that I am safe and sound, and back home. Well, almost home, because my real home, as you know, was long ago destroyed by the bombing. Franz and I made it to Danzig, or Gdansk as it's now called after it became part of the territory of Poland after the war. To be truthful, we were making our way through Danzig in the hope for some shelter and bread as the Polaks didn't take to us too well as you can imagine, however we didn't know that all the Germans have been deported from here as well. Just when we thought that we would die of thirst and hunger without making it to the German border, we stumbled on a farm house, the owners of which happened to be German. Well, almost German. They are a mother and daughter; former persecuted Jews that were lucky to survive the hell that we saw in those documentaries. And what do you know? It was them who took us in, gave us water, fed us, gave us clean clothes and let us in for the night, after we had been turned away from every other house with nothing else but scorn and curses. If it wasn't for them, who knew if we would have woken up the next day…

"Franz left for Dresden the next day, but Emilia – that's my generous hostess whom I owe my life to – offered that I could stay with her and her mother. I thought I was dreaming when she asked me! Of course I said yes, before she could change her mind and throw me out. Frau Hannah didn't take too well to me at first, but now she's getting used to me, and all thanks to the Ukrainian potatoes I made for her.

"My generous hostess tries to make me rest all the time, and even took the garden tools from me once and sent me back to the house. She is a former nurse and keeps almost force-feeding me every time I take my shirt off in the garden and she sees my bones. I don't know what I would do without her."

Klaus noticed that Emilia was grinning widely without lifting her eyes from her mug, her cheeks slightly colored with a just noticeable blush. He smiled, too, and looked back at his letter.

"I described you in my letter, so they would know what you look like. I hope you don't mind? I can re-write it if you do," he added quickly, making sure that he hadn't offend her.

"No, no, it's fine. I'm sure your friends are curious."

"Oh, you can't even imagine what a breath of fresh air every letter from the outside was for us! We always read them aloud, for the whole barrack to hear, especially the ones written by family, or wives. Those letters were more important than bread for us. You know what it is? It was a reminder of a real, good life outside that we hoped we would go back to one day. These letters help the soldiers to survive."

They locked their eyes once again and just looked at each other for some time, before Klaus remembered about the letter in his hands.

"She has blonde hair that she wears pinned from both sides, or sometimes she puts it up when she writes her articles. She's a very good writer. I have read some of her articles in the newspapers she has stored on the very bottom shelf of her bookcase, even though I didn't tell her that. One day I'll muster up enough courage to confess to her that I read her works and that she should write a full-length novel, but not now, or she'll get mad and throw me out."

Emilia couldn't help herself and burst out laughing, her laughter joining together with the mischievous sound of Klaus's laughter.

"She has very beautiful grey eyes, and sometimes when she stares in the distance, I wonder what secrets she hides behind them... She gets sad too often, from her memories I suppose, and I try to make her laugh as often as I can. She laughs, but sometimes I think she does it out of politeness and pity for me, because I'm trying too hard. But I won't tell her that either."

Emilia hid her face from him, laughing out loud again.

"Did you write this letter for your comrades or for me?" she asked at last, wiping the tears from the corners of her eyes.

"For my comrades of course. I didn't think I would read it for you," he admitted, chuckling as well. "It just happened...a spur of the moment decision."

"Just like when I invited you to live with us?"

Klaus shrugged with one shoulder. "Sometimes the best things happen on the spur of the moment, don't you think?"

"Yes, they do. They most certainly do."

Chapter 5

About a month later, the local authority representative knocked on Emilia's door while she was busy making an apple pie in the kitchen.

"Good afternoon, Panna Brettenheimer." The short, pudgy man tipped his hat slightly under her unemotional stare. He never showed up for a reason that was positive. "May I take up five minutes of your time?"

"What's the matter?" Emilia crossed her arms over her chest, not making any motion to move from the door to invite the man in.

"The matter is quite delicate, to be truthful." He set his glistening eyes on Emilia, wiping his forehead with his handkerchief. "You see, your neighbors have noticed...a certain man, who is apparently living in your house, according to the reports that we received..."

"And how does that concern them or you? It's my house and I can invite whoever I want to live with me," Emilia replied coldly.

"Not quite, Panna Brettenheimer. According to the law, if someone takes up permanent residence in our city or its surrounding areas, they need to be registered with the magistrate. And besides, you can't rent your house and not pay taxes from your income, that's another law you're breaking."

"I'm not breaking anything, because I'm not renting anything. He lives here as my friend. I'm not making any profit from him."

"I will have to ask you to show me his papers then, Panna Brettenheimer."

"What for?" Emilia frowned contemptuously.

"As I mentioned before, we need to know the identity of every person who lives in our area."

"Wait here."

Emilia barely contained herself from slamming the door in his face, and went to get Klaus's papers, which he had handed to her without a second thought, so she could keep them in her room together with hers. He had asked her a few times if she wanted him to go and try to find a job in the city, but Emilia shook her head each time, pointing out that, number one, no one would most likely hire him, and, number two, he was not an imposition on the household at all, which was the thing that he was most afraid of. He accepted his hostess's wishes and busied himself with the garden and fixing the house. A couple of weeks ago he had pointed out to Emilia that the roof needed to be patched up, and he had spent days re-roofing it, his cheerful singing audible in Emilia's bedroom, breaking her concentration from work; yet, she never told him to stop his singing – he did have a beautiful voice.

Collecting his military card and his release papers out of the drawer where she kept all the documents, Emilia went downstairs and handed them to the city official.

"He's a former soldier?" he inquired, after carefully studying them.

"Yes. The Russians released him from the camp. His papers are all in order as you can see."

"He can't stay here," the man concluded, handing Emilia the papers back after copying all of the information into his notebook.

"Why the hell not?" Emilia started getting angry.

"He's not a relative of yours and you're not renting him a room since he has no job. He can't stay here for free and without proper registration."

"He doesn't have a place of his own, it was destroyed in the bombing! And he has no living relatives! Where do you suggest he goes?"

"It doesn't concern me, to be truthful, Panna Brettenheimer."

"Of course it doesn't." Emilia pursed her lips.

The man started saying something about the law, spreading his arms in a helpless gesture, when a sudden thought crossed Emilia's mind.

"Wait. You said he's not a relative of mine. What if we were to be married?"

The man stopped his speech mid-word, blinking at her in utter astonishment.

"M-married?" he uttered at last.

"Why, yes. Or can't I marry him either, according to one of your constantly changing laws?"

"Well... If you were indeed to be married then I suppose... There wouldn't be any legal objections to your living arrangements..."

"Fine then. We'll come to the magistrate tomorrow with our papers. He can get a new passport there as well, as I understand?"

The man just nodded, obviously wondering if the young woman was indeed not right in her head, and that the Gdansk people had shunned her for good reason. After all, it was something utterly unheard of – that a former camp internee would want anything to do with a former soldier, let him be from the regular *Wehrmacht* or the SS.

The city official cleared his throat once again, looked the girl up and down and went back to his car. Emilia stood on the porch, looking at the dust settling after him, when Klaus called out to her from the roof.

"Who was that?"

Emilia lifted her head and covered her eyes, so she could see him against the sun. Her always smiling housemate was laying on his stomach, still holding a hammer in his hands. He always took off his shirt while working on the roof, and had obtained a golden-bronze tan, while his hair had become lighter, burnt out with the summer sun. Emilia noticed, with some inner satisfaction, that he was getting a nice shape, with lean muscles slowly replacing the emaciated form she had first seen on him.

"A city official. Can you come down for a moment? I need to talk to you."

"Just a second."

With those words he easily flung himself over the edge of the roof, stepped on the ledge and before Emilia could start shouting her protests, he quickly jumped down, laughing at her terrified look.

"Are you mad?! Do you want to break your neck now?!"

"Don't worry." Klaus combed his hair with one hand. "We did worse in the army. What did you want to talk about?"

Emilia sat on the steps and patted a spot next to her, inviting him to sit. After she had explained the situation to him, stopping after the marriage part, Klaus just looked at her inquisitively, not replying.

"You don't have to do this if you don't want to." Emilia shrugged dismissively with one shoulder, becoming a little irritated by his silence. "I only suggested it because it seems to be the only way to keep you here. Trust me, I'm the last person to want to get married."

"No, it's not that." Klaus lowered his face, trying to hide yet another mischievous smile. "I just didn't expect that you would do something of the sort for... someone who's basically nobody to you. What if you meet someone in the future and want to marry him?"

Emilia barely suppressed her bitter laughter. "That is most certainly not going to happen. You, on the other hand, may feel free to divorce me as soon as you find a girl more to your taste."

"We aren't even married yet, and you're already kicking me out?" Klaus asked with a mock-upset expression on his face.

"No, I am not. I'm just saying that the marriage will be purely fictitious so you can keep living here until you want to start a family of your own. A real family, that is."

Klaus arched a brow, looking more and more amused by her words. Emilia started feeling embarrassed for some reason.

"I just want you to know that you are absolutely free to go and pursue your own life whenever you want. I don't want you to think that you're a prisoner here. You can go to the city and find yourself a girl if you want."

"I'm fine right here." Klaus gave her another smile.

Not that he was making his interest in her obvious, but since the very first day Klaus always seemed to be making a big effort to try and make the best impression he could on both Emilia and her mother. Even Hannah was slowly giving up some of her mistrust and resentment toward the young man, especially after he had made a birdhouse and put it right across from her window, after overhearing her say that she felt bad about how the poor things had just nested on the exposed roof and how nice it would be if they had a birdhouse, so they wouldn't have to leave their baby-birds alone, in a dangerous position on the roof, while fetching food. Klaus had also adopted the habit of getting up earlier than the women and making breakfast for everyone. He revealed that he had been an assistant to the cook in the Gulag, before he stole the bone and was banned from working in the kitchen. He knew his way around cutlery and pots, just like he knew his way around the garden and tools.

He brought Emilia cherries that he had gathered from wild cherry trees, or fresh strawberries, quietly knocking on her door and apologizing for distracting her from her work. She very much appreciated all the little signs of thoughtfulness and attention, but she didn't want him to get the wrong idea, even though he never crossed the line from displaying the utmost respect for her and her mother – a line that he had obviously set for himself from the moment he had stepped through her door.

Emilia rubbed her eyes with one hand, deciding to say it in a straightforward manner to make sure that they were both on the same page concerning their marriage arrangements. "There will never be any relationship between us except for friendship, whether we marry or not."

"I know. You made yourself very clear." He smiled again, confusing Emilia even more with his reaction. "I'm very happy with my life as it is now."

Emilia frowned slightly, to which he just replied with yet another smile, before he got up and trotted to the ladder, leading to the roof.

"And I'm very happy that we're getting married!" he shouted from the top of the house, making Emilia chuckle. She couldn't explain why, but for whatever reason the thought that he didn't want to look for comfort someplace, to satisfy needs that she couldn't help him with, gave her some inward pleasure.

Later, she sat before her typing machine, recalling the old, frightful times when she still nurtured the hope that one day she would leave the gates of that hell, get married to some wonderful man and live happily ever after. But, a few months into her incarceration she was convinced that no one would want her, that she was spoiled goods. No one would want to taint his good name by taking someone of her sorts as their wife. And now she would have a husband after all, even though a fake one. Emilia smiled again, wondering what would have happened if the two of them had met in different circumstances. What if she didn't have all those years of nightmares, what if the war didn't start...

A soft, polite knock woke her from her daydreaming and there he was of course, standing in the door with a cup full of raspberries.

"For my future wife." Klaus winked at her, set the cup on her desk, pressed her hand for less than a second and left, as if letting her understand that he would never cross any lines she wished to have between them. He would still knock on her door and wait for permission, he would still care for her without asking for anything in return and leave her in her privacy, until she decided otherwise. For the first time in several years Emilia felt something faintly resembling happiness.

Gdansk, Poland, the following day

Emilia always dreaded going to the city and was stalling as much as she could by brushing her hair in front of the mirror with an unblinking stare fixated on something in the distance. Deep inside, she hoped that maybe this time she would be lucky to escape the people who always found some perverted pleasure in taunting her and humiliating her in front of anyone who listened, as if the very fact that she had stayed alive was a huge thorn in their side. Before she had dreaded going into the city because it would bring up a past that she so desperately wanted to erase from her memory; now she dreaded it because Klaus would be with her to hear all of the taunting. It took a lot from her just to confess to him that she was a former camp internee, but what if today he learned all the gruesome details of her incarceration? Emilia didn't know why she feared his reaction so. Perhaps it was because he had always treated her with the utmost respect, probably imagining her to be something different from what she was. But, after today he might start looking at her with the same disgust as the rest of them did...

Emilia covered her face with her hands, taking a deep breath. Well, if he did than he did, and there was nothing she could change about it. It was his right to do so. She would still help him with the papers and then she would set him free as soon as he decided to go. It wasn't that he would stay with her anyway – she simply had nothing to offer him.

Emilia went downstairs to Klaus, who was already awaiting her on the first floor in a freshly washed and pressed shirt (he always washed all of his clothes himself, despite Emilia and Hannah's many offers to put his dirty clothes in the common pile), with his hair sleeked back and his usual beaming smile.

"You look very pretty," he said instead of a greeting, looking over her blue dress.

"It's our wedding after all." Emilia joked more to cheer herself up than to make him laugh.

Hannah came out of the kitchen and quickly whispered a blessing, before kissing Emilia on her cheek, while trying to hide an anxious frown on her face.

"Don't worry, Frau Hannah, I'll bring her back in one piece, I promise." Klaus smiled at the woman as if sensing her uneasiness.

He opened the door for Emilia, and Emilia heard her mother whisper to him behind her back, "Don't listen to anyone. Emmi is a good girl."

"I know," he simply replied, before he caught up with his "bride" and offered her his hand. Emilia took it.

They had to walk all the way to Gdansk since they had no car, but Emilia didn't mind the long walk, because it meant not rushing to get to the city and its habitants. She was very quiet, and Klaus did most of the talking, telling her amusing stories from his *Wehrmacht* days: about milking a cow in one village, chasing chickens with his comrades while the local peasants were laughing secretly at their attempts to catch their dinner, about drying their clothes on a tank cannon after crossing a river and about letting local children try on their helmets.

"You don't even make it sound like a war." Emilia chuckled at last, grateful for his cheerful chatter that distracted her from her brooding.

"Well, that's the part of the war that's good to remember – the comradery, the laughter, the jokes, all these stories, just like a summer is a part of the year that you like to remember when the winter comes. Without winter you wouldn't appreciate the sun, the flowers, the green grass, and it's the same with war. Without shooting and watching your comrades die you wouldn't appreciate being alive every day. You don't take it for granted anymore and meet every morning like a new miracle. Of course it's always easy to concentrate only on the bad part, but I guess for us, the young ones that is, it was easier to overlook it all and goof around right after another bloody battle was over. We kept our sanity that way, you know? And I prefer to keep only good memories of those times, just like the good memories of my POW days."

"You have good memories of Gulag?" Emilia raised her brow skeptically.

"Of course I do. I told you about the bone, didn't I?"

"Yes, and you got beaten for that."

"That was after. But the stealing and eating part was fun." Klaus winked at her. "Also, sometimes we would trick our guards and change clothes with markings on them, so some of us would go and do easy work one day, and others substituted to do something hard. We would make them trade us bread for pictures of pretty women that our relatives or friends would send us from home in letters. Ivans go crazy for those pictures, even if it's just an underwear or stockings advertisement from an old magazine; they don't have anything like that at home and would almost fight for those pictures, can you imagine?"

Emilia hadn't even noticed that they had reached the city limits. She tried to keep her head low all the way to the magistrate in the city center, and breathed out in relief after they stepped through the doors and stated their purpose to the secretary.

"Wait over there." A young woman pointed at the chairs near the wall after studying their papers for some time. She soon returned and told them where to follow her.

The civil judge studied their papers even longer and after that finally handed them two papers to fill out.

"It's a request for your marriage certificate. After you sign it, I'll issue a certificate and after you sign that as well, you'll officially be a married couple."

Less than half an hour later, Emilia signed her new name on the certificate, and she and Klaus officially became Herr and Frau Lemmel.

"We should go and have a glass of champagne, or at least a beer to celebrate!" Klaus suggested as soon as they exited the magistrate building.

"No, let's go home, we can celebrate there just as fine." Emilia tried to pull her new husband's sleeve, but he would have none of it.

"Oh come now, it's our wedding!" He caught her arm and started pulling her in the other direction, towards the closest café. "Just one glass, please! It's not a real wedding without a toast!"

"It's not a real wedding to begin with. Let's go." Emilia tried to worm herself out of his hand, but Klaus made his best begging eyes at her.

"Just one glass, Emmi, please? I'll give you money back as soon as I get a job, I promise!"

"Don't be silly now, it's not the money issue."

"Well what is it then?" He slightly pulled her hand again, smiling wider. "Come, please. One toast to our happy married life, and we're gone, I swear!"

Emilia threw a side glance at the dark entrance of the café, quickly looked around and thought that one glass, that they could finish in five minutes, perhaps wouldn't really do any harm. No one seemed to be paying them any attention so far.

A little reassured by this fact, Emilia allowed her new husband to sit her at a table outside to order two glasses of champagne and an apple strudel which they decided to share. Ten minutes turned into twenty and two glasses into four. Emilia was laughing at yet another Klaus's story, when she heard a voice that she would recognize out of a million, and she turned her head just in time to see Pani Nemkoff's scornful sneer. She had her three friends with her as always.

"Well, well, well, look who showed her face again! I almost didn't believe my ears when Marika told me that our Emmi had gathered up enough audacity to walk around our streets, as if nothing had happened!"

Klaus frowned, observing the women gathering near their table, while Emilia quickly took her wallet out, and counted several bills with slightly shaking fingers.

"Come, Klaus, let's go," she told her husband quietly, without looking at Nemkoff.

"Look at her, she brought a German with her on top of it!" Another one of Nemkoff's circle snorted. "What, you didn't get enough of their lot in the camp? Missed your little Nazis so much that you grabbed the first one who agreed to look at you?"

"Why are you talking in this manner to my wife?" Klaus also got up from his chair but wouldn't move away from the cafe, no matter how much Emilia tried to pull him away from the scene.

"Oh, you were stupid enough to marry that whore? I guess you don't mind that she opened her legs for the whole squadron of the SS for a couple of years," Irene Nemkoff cackled, while Emilia stood silently with shame burning her cheeks, cursing her decision when she agreed to that glass of champagne.

"I don't even think he's from the regular *Wehrmacht*," one of her friends added. "Probably one of her former SS lovers, who didn't get enough of her in the camp."

"Klaus, please, let's go, I'm begging you." Emilia pulled his sleeve once again, already on the verge of tears.

"Do you know what your lovely new wife was doing in the camp while most of us were dying of starvation?" Nemkoff continued. "Living a fancy live in the SS quarters, serving all of them every day, prostituting herself, together with her friend, for nice meals and easy work."

"Oh, they had it nice, the two field whores! While for us it was a struggle to stay alive every day, for them it was a vacation!"

"And on top of it, when the Ivans came, she turned to them after we threatened to do what the French and Dutch were doing with their whores!"

"Yes, how do you think she got herself that nice little house? One Major wrote it off for her as payment for her services!"

"Better you go to the magistrate and ask for a divorce before they close for the day, soldier boy, because you married the biggest whore in town!"

"I wouldn't kiss her on her filthy mouth if I were you, you have no idea what's been in it!"

"The only filthy mouths I see so far are yours," Klaus replied in an ice cold tone that made all the women blink at him in stunned silence, after which he took Emilia by the elbow and led her away.

They walked in silence for some time, Emilia wiped away her tears quietly, until Klaus saw a quiet narrow street between two houses and pushed Emilia inside, pressing her against the wall.

"Come now, why are you crying? Because some old hags said something to you? You can't let them get to you!" He was speaking in a comforting, hushed tone, holding Emilia's shoulders with both hands. "Who cares what they say? They should be ashamed of their words, not you!"

"It's not the words I'm ashamed of," Emilia finally said in between sobs. "It's the fact that they're right about everything. I am a dirty and disgusting person and I shouldn't have survived back then. I should have died together with the rest. I never wanted to do any of those things, but they raped us anyway, so why couldn't we at least get some food out of it?"

Emilia was both laughing bitterly and crying at the same time, all the words that she could only confine to her diaries finding their escape on this man's chest, against which he was pressing her now instead of pushing her away as she had expected him to. She couldn't stop the words now that they had broken the carefully constructed walls she had built around her perfectly calm demeanor. She told him everything, every shameful, hurtful detail, starting with Richter and ending with Engel and his belt.

Klaus listened without interrupting, only rubbing her back and hair slightly. He turned her away from the street and from any curious stares of possible passers-by, sheltering her from the rest of the world with his body. He even seemed glad that she had confessed her story. He had always imagined that there was something different in her past, some heart-breaking love story with her husband or lover dying tragically, whom she still mourned to this day and refused to let go of his memory for someone new. This – this he could deal with easily, with the right amount of patience and time.

"It's not your fault," he whispered to her softly, after she had nothing else to tell him. "And you have absolutely nothing to be ashamed of."

"Yes, I do."

"No, you don't. You didn't kill anyone at least. I used to take human lives, I'm a murderer, even though it was against my will. That's much worse. You're just a victim of the war, and you did what you could to survive. And you know what? I'm glad you did, because I can't imagine not having met you, honestly."

"Klaus—"

"No, I just want to tell you something. I've been in love with you, Emmi, from the very first time I saw you. Not because of how you look, even though you're a beautiful woman, but because you opened your door to two dirty strangers who fought for the regime that wronged you so, for caring for us when you had every reason not to, for allowing me to stay in your house when I had no place to go and for not once reproaching me for who I was. I don't care if we'll be sleeping in separate bedrooms for the rest of our lives, I just want you to know that I do love you, and I love you even more now, after learning what you had to go through, yet you still allowed me into your life. I will never bother you, I promise. And I also promise that no one will ever say a word to you, neither here, nor anywhere else, while I am around. I promise they'll treat you with the respect you deserve. It's them who should be ashamed, Emmi, not you."

Chapter 6

After a week of fruitless attempts of getting a job, Klaus listened to Emilia and agreed to stay on the farm with her. He never procrastinated, and after nothing inside or outside the house could be fixed or redone and all the little crops in their small garden were taken care of, Klaus disappeared somewhere one day and came back by dinner time with a beaming smile and a sack of potatoes on his back.

"Where did you get that?" Hannah gasped, probably imagining her new son-in-law raiding some of their neighbors' farms.

"I earned it," Klaus replied proudly and dropped the sack on the floor. "Since no one in the city wants my services, I figured that some of our neighbors might. You aren't too friendly with your fellow farmers, are you?"

"We don't know most of them," Emilia confessed, holding a plate in her hands.

"I figured as much. I bet you also didn't know that most of them are also women, whose men are either dead from the war or still missing?" Klaus asked with a mischievous smile.

"Really?"

"Of course. And all they need is a pair of working hands." With those words, Klaus produced some bills out of his pocket, and handed them to Emilia. "Here, here's my first salary."

"No, no, it's yours, I don't—"

"Emmi, take it. It's only a tiny part of the debt that I owe you."

"You owe me nothing."

"Well then, let's set a family fund and start putting all of our money in it," Klaus suggested. "Maybe with time we'll buy a cow, some sheep, or chickens and have our own farm."

"A farm?" Emilia asked, laughing. "I don't know how to take care of domestic animals!"

"I do." Klaus took a plate out of her hands and started helping Hannah set the table.

"How come?"

"I grew up on a farm before I moved to Dresden with my wife. I believe the farm is still intact, looked after by our neighbors. That's the last I heard of it at least."

"You'll have to teach me everything then. I'm afraid of cows."

"I will, big, Munich city girl." Klaus teased her, making her chuckle.

"I used to like cities," Emilia murmured pensively.

"Not anymore?"

"Too many people." Emilia threw a glance in the direction of the kitchen, making sure Hannah couldn't overhear her. "Too many people who talk a lot."

"Don't worry yourself about that," Klaus promised in a strangely cool, firm tone. "They won't be talking anymore."

Emilia had just opened her mouth to ask him what he meant by that, but Klaus had already turned to Hannah, who had entered the room with a steaming pot of ragout in her hands. "Mmm, that smells delicious! I'm starving."

Klaus turned out to be right about the farmers and their need for the good pair of working hands. Local women seemed to spread a surprisingly quick word about a handsome German, who could fix or do almost everything, and soon some of them even started wandering onto Emilia's farm, asking for her husband. At first she didn't pay any attention to it, only called him from the garden in the back, where he spent most of his time; but one day she came out to the porch to notice one of the locals, watching Klaus fish something out of the shed, almost holding her breath, without blinking.

"Can I help you?" Emilia said loudly to startle the woman.

The latter let out a nervous giggle, obviously caught off guard, and blushed immediately.

"I'm sorry, Pani, I was just waiting for Pan Klaus to find the ropes for a swing. I have two children, you see, and he offered to make a swing for them, so they don't spend all of their time just playing in the sand pit. He's so thoughtful! And he did such a great job with our roof. He really does have golden hands!"

Emilia couldn't hide an amused smile when the woman looked back at Klaus, who had come out of the shed, squinting at the sun with his long blond bangs falling onto one eye and fixing a rope on his shoulder. The woman couldn't suppress a sigh of admiration and whispered to Emilia, "You are so lucky!"

Apparently, even if the Gdansk population resented both of them, the local widowed women didn't find anything shameful about hiring a handsome former enemy to help out around their house, as long as he climbed their roofs without a shirt on. Emilia tried to persuade herself that she wasn't even a bit jealous.

One day Klaus came back from his work at a neighbor's house, barely suppressing his laughter.

"You have no idea, what kind of indecent proposal I got today!" he exclaimed, as soon as he stepped through the door, bringing in the smell of freshly cut grass and sunlight. "You know the Hirsch widow, you must remember her, she's the main milk-lady here, well, today I was fixing the shed for her cows. Anyway, she brought me milk and cream all day, circling me like a vulture, and when it was time for me to go home, she says, 'Why don't you stay for a half hour more? I'll pay you twice as much if you do.' I tried not to laugh too much, because if you remember she weighs about a hundred and fifty kilos and is about my mother's age. So, I say, trying not to offend her, 'I would love to, but I really can't, I have to go home to my wife.' She goes, 'She's too skinny, that wife of yours, you come here and I'll show you what a real woman looks like.' And then she starts walking over to me, herding me into a corner. I said, 'I appreciate the offer, but I really do like my skinny wife, and I really do have to be home by dinner.' She stepped closer, completely cornering me, and said, 'Just for a half hour, soldier, I'll pay you three times more!' I barely got away from her! Can you imagine that?"

Emilia laughed so hard that tears started forming in the corners of her eyes.

"I almost got raped by a milk-woman." Klaus sighed with a theatrically grave impression on his face, making Emilia laugh even harder. "Now I know how you feel!"

She didn't believe him when just a couple of months ago he promised her that one day she would laugh about her days in the camp just like he did, and today she was laughing, laughing for the first time in years, feeling how the past nightmares were starting to lose their colors little by little, and all thanks to this grinning man with golden bangs, who seemed to know more about life than all the psychiatrists put together.

That night, Emilia was woken by noises coming from downstairs. Normally, after a hard day's work Klaus slept like a child and the house was always immersed in absolute silence. Without thinking twice, Emilia pulled the gun from under her pillow where it always lay, quickly put on a robe and tip-toed downstairs, squeezing the weapon tight in her hands.

"Don't shoot." Klaus smiled at her, drying his wet hair with a towel.

A faint smell of kerosene still lingered in the air and Emilia scrunched her nose slightly.

"Were you showering? I thought you were sleeping already. And why do I smell kerosene?"

"I was asleep, and then my head got itchy. I was afraid that the lice were back and went outside to put some of it on my hair," Klaus explained, pointing at his wet head. "I took a shower afterwards. Did I wake you? I'm sorry."

"That's fine," Emilia replied reluctantly, putting the gun back into her pocket. "Where would you get lice?"

"I don't think it is lice, but taking some measure of precaution never hurts, right?"

"I suppose." Emilia agreed at last and then added, "Do you want me to cut your hair maybe, since we're both up? It's getting a little too long."

"That would be great!" He beamed at her as he always did and sat obediently on the chair that Emilia pointed him to.

She fetched the scissors and the brush, and started clipping his golden locks carefully, making sure it was even on each side. Klaus sat without moving, only lowering or turning his head when Emilia asked him to. And then it suddenly hit her.

"Your hair doesn't smell of kerosene at all."

"Really?" Klaus asked, still looking straight ahead, even though Emilia could swear that she saw a glimpse of a grin that he was obviously trying his best to conceal. "I guess I washed it very well then."

Emilia's hand with the scissors still hovered over his head. "It usually smells of it for a good week, no matter how well you wash it."

"What can I say? I guess smells don't stick to me."

Emilia glanced at him once again, but decided to dismiss all of her suspicions. After all, what he could really do with kerosene besides that?

"I don't see any lice or their dead eggs though. Better ask me next time to look before you put more of that stuff on yourself."

"I will," Klaus agreed easily and with that the matter was dropped.

In two days' time, however, two policemen knocked on Emilia's door, asking her about the whereabouts of her husband. Irene Nemkoff stood behind their backs, which wasn't good to begin with.

"He must be working at someone's house around. What do you need him for?" Emilia asked, all the while eyeing the woman, who seemed to be fuming for some reason.

"Your bastard husband burned our store!" Nemkoff yelled in response, almost pushing two policemen out of her way to get to Emilia; they wisely held her in place.

"Klaus would never do anything like that." Emilia immediately took on a defensive tone. "He's a kind young man. He wouldn't hurt a fly, leave alone burning someone's store!"

"He?! Wouldn't hurt a fly?!" Nemkoff huffed with contempt. "He was killing people in the front, darling, wasn't he?!"

"And that's why you assumed he's at fault?" Emilia felt more confident on her own ground, and some unknown defensive mechanism had awoken in her, finally allowing her to bite right back at the woman, who used to take such pleasure in humiliating her all the time. "Just because he's German and a former soldier?!"

"Everything was fine in our city before he showed up!" Nemkoff wouldn't give up either. "You two are a pair: one is an immoral whore and the other one is a murderer and an arsonist! Arrest them both, officers!"

"On what grounds?" Emilia put both fists on her hips. "My husband doesn't leave the farm at all, because none of your lot don't want him in the city! The only places he goes are neighboring farms, and there he is always in everyone's sight! So stop badmouthing both of us and get off my property!"

"You better wait inside the car, Pani," one of the officers addressed Nemkoff, clearly not in the mood to listen to the village gossip. "Let us do our job."

"Pani Lemmel, isn't it?" The second one addressed Emilia, quickly showing his papers. "Could you tell us where your husband was exactly two days ago, on the night of August 12?"

"He was home, with me." Emilia even shrugged slightly, as if stating the obvious.

"Does he always spend every night at home?"

"Of course he does. What kind of question is that?" Emilia's tone took on a slightly indignant shade.

"I'm sorry, I didn't mean to insult you or your husband. We're just investigating an arson that happened two days ago, and Pani Nemkoff, the owner of the grocery store that was burned down, was very insistent that it was your husband who did it."

"Naturally." Emilia snorted in disgust. "Did you hear her? She hates us both. I assure you, officers, my husband is the nicest man and would never do anything of the sort. And why would he anyway? He doesn't even know Pani Nemkoff well enough to wish her any malice, and certainly not something as serious as burning her store. He met her only once, when we went to the city to get our marriage license. Why would he burn her store?"

The two policemen exchanged glances, one of them sighing slightly, as if apologizing that they had to come here because of the insane woman in the back seat, to just listen to her accusations against a German lad who had had the misfortune to cross her road somewhere. They both agreed with Emilia on everything that she had said, and once again in the apologetic tones asked her when Pan Lemmel would be home so they could speak to him, more for the paperwork than because they indeed suspected him.

To their luck, Klaus appeared, walking back home with a local widow in tow, a silly grin plastered on her face as he was joking about something with her. Noticing the policemen he walked right over to them with a slightly concerned smile, extending his hand and asking if something had happened. He took his place next to his wife.

"You burned my store, you Nazi *szkop!*" Irene Nemkoff jumped out of the police car. "I know it was you! I saw you strolling around it several times three weeks ago, you bastard! Arrest him, officers, it was him, I'm telling you!"

In contrast to the red-faced woman, Klaus remained as calm and poised as before, offering yet another apologetic smile to the officers.

"I'm sorry, Pani, but I don't even know which store you're talking about. I apologize if you had the displeasure to see me pass it by, but you see, I was trying to solicit some work in the city and took the same route every day, before my wife persuaded me to give it up and work at the home with her. I understand perfectly well, too, about the local people's sentiments towards us; no one wants to hire a German, especially one who used to fight in the war, even though I was just a regular soldier in the *Wehrmacht*. They have all the right to feel this way, that's why neither my wife, nor I, decided not to bother them anymore with our presence and to just stay here, in our quiet farm, where I can do odd works for some of our neighbors, who don't mind paying a former soldier for work."

Both policemen shuffled uncomfortably after such a humble, moving speech and barked at Pani Nemkoff, who started shouting once again that the Nazi was most certainly lying and needed to be arrested.

"Get back inside the car, or we will arrest *you* for public misconduct!"

"I'm sorry, officers, may I speak a few words with Pani?" Klaus addressed the policemen with his most disarming smile. "I believe that we might have started on the wrong foot when she confronted my wife on the day of our wedding, and I would appreciate it if you gave me the chance to apologize to Pani, if I ever happened to offend her in some way, to make sure that we put the past at rest between us."

"Most certainly, take your time." The policemen gestured Klaus towards the woman, and gladly took Emilia's offer of some lemonade, leaving the two outside.

They satisfied their thirst inside the kitchen, all the while listening to the widow, who Klaus had brought with him so she could choose a cherry tree from their garden, a branch from which he would later plant in her garden. She couldn't stop singing the praises of the young man, saying what a godsend he was for all of them and how evil that other woman must be to badmouth such a good man with her insane accusations.

"He always hurries home to his Pani." The widow smiled at Emilia, handing her an empty glass. "He never wants to be late for dinner; no, he would never lurk around at night, leave alone going to the city to do something of the sort! We can all speak in his defense. No, he's a good young man, so what does it matter if they're both German?"

She gave a nod in Emilia's direction.

"It's not their fault, is it?"

The two officers smiled in agreement. When all four of them emerged back onto the front porch, Pani Nemkoff met them with unusual silence and a very pale face, mumbling something in reply to the policemen's questions as to if she wished to insist on pressing charges against Pan Lemmel.

"So, I guess we're done here then." They tipped their hats to Emilia and exchanged heartfelt handshakes with her husband. "Sorry for the bother. You have a nice day."

When the police car left and the widow was sent to the garden to select her tree, Emilia slightly nudged Klaus with her elbow, motioning her head in the direction to which the police car had disappeared.

"What did you tell her that she became so docile all of a sudden?"

"Nothing." He shrugged nonchalantly. "Just told her that the store was only the beginning and that if she opens her filthy mouth about you once again, I'll burn her house to the ground, with her inside, tied to the bed and doused with kerosene first."

Emilia looked at her sweetly smiling husband with her mouth agape, unable to form any questions.

"Not that I would do it, of course," he rushed to reassure her, "but she doesn't have to know that, does she?"

Another innocent smile followed in tow with sky blue doe eyes.

"It was you, wasn't it?" Emilia whispered at last, finally putting two and two together. "It was really you! You burned her store that night when you came back smelling of kerosene! That's why your hair didn't smell of it! Your hands did though!"

"Shhh!" He pressed his finger to his lips with the look of a conspirator, nodding at the widow not too far away. "We don't want her to learn our little secret, do we?"

"Klaus! You shouldn't have done it!" Emilia whispered back, making big reproachful eyes.

"I promised you that they will never offend you again." Klaus grinned again. "And I always keep my promises."

Chapter 7

Emilia had been pondering something for a long time, and had finally made a decision: today she would write to the orphanage that Klaus had mentioned once before and inquire what had happened to his son and whether he was still with them or if he had already been adopted by some family. She decided not to inform Klaus of her decision so as not to disappoint him in case his son had indeed been adopted, but she herself just couldn't leave the question unresolved, even though she couldn't quite point her reasons for it.

Coming back from the local post office, Emilia found her husband outside the house, waiting for her.

"You will not believe what I found!" he declared in an excited tone, getting up from the porch, on which he had been cutting a whistling toy out of a piece of wood for one of the local children. Emilia caught herself thinking that maybe discovering this latest talent of his and seeing how good he was with children had somehow influenced her decision to find his son. "All the way behind the cemetery, across the field there is a beautiful lake! I bet you didn't know about it either!"

"No, I don't wander off far from the house," Emilia admitted with a smile.

"I thought so. Go get your bathing suit and let's go for a nice swim. The water is so clean there, it's unbelievable! And it's absolutely deserted, there's no one there!"

"No, Klaus, I can't."

"You can't swim? I'll teach you in five minutes!"

"No, it's not that." Emilia shifted from one foot to another, avoiding his eyes. "I just don't... I don't like water."

Klaus sensed insincerity in her words, but decided not to ask her for the reason why she had decided to lie about it. Instead, he just shrugged and smiled. "You can stay on the bank then. The weather is beautiful today, and the summer will be over soon. Who knows if we'll ever get a warm day like this one again soon? Come on, stop locking yourself in your bedroom, life's too short to be a hermit. And you're far too young to enjoy all this solitude, and don't even try to lie to me."

"Maybe I really do."

Klaus only arched his brow skeptically, making the Emilia grin.

"All right, maybe I like your company, but that's about it."

"There will be only two of us there, I promise."

"You won't leave me in peace until I agree, will you?"

"No, I won't. I'll carry you there on my shoulder if I have to, but you have to see that lake."

Emilia shook her head, hiding her smile. "Fine, you win. Let's go."

"Go get your bathing suit. We'll catch some sun over there."

"No. I don't like the sun."

"Who doesn't like the sun?"

Emilia took a deep breath, trying to think of some story, but then just decided to say the truth. "I don't like taking my clothes off in front of the other people. My back... I have scars all over it. From the camp. It's quite an ugly sight. I don't want you to see me like that."

"I have scars on my back, too," Klaus replied softly, as if a little relieved that she was at least trusting him enough to tell the truth.

"Mine are much worse."

"Let me see."

"No! I told you, I don't want anyone to see them."

As soon as Emilia raised her voice a little, Klaus quickly put both hands up in the mock surrender, showing her that he wouldn't press the matter.

"Wear your dress, if you like. Just come with me. I've already packed some sandwiches and water, so we can have a little picnic over there."

"So, you were quite sure of yourself that I would agree?" Emilia crossed her arms over her chest in mock contempt. Klaus just laughed and ran inside, coming back in less than a minute with a small basket and a blanket under his arm. Emilia had nothing else to do than follow her husband.

"I thought you said it was behind the cemetery?" Emilia asked after they started to stray in a different direction.

"It is, but I want to show you something else first."

"You've lived here for a little over two months and know the village better than I do, and I've been here for years." Emilia couldn't help but chuckle.

"What can I say? I like discovering new places," Klaus replied cheerfully.

"All right, where are you taking me now, Columbus?"

Klaus only smiled mischievously. "You'll see."

After they walked uphill for some time and stopped on top of it, Emilia saw a church at the other bottom of the hill, which she never even knew existed. From their vantage point, it was visible that the church was ruined, either by bombardment or artillery fire, for it lacked a big part of its roof and they could see the broken pews inside.

"Come." Klaus slightly nudged Emilia.

They both went down the hill and entered the old temple, the floor of which was still covered with war-time rubble, with parts of the stone walls laying in the middle of the formerly exquisite mosaic floor. Statues of the saints, pockmarked with bullets, still remained standing in their respective places, like martyrs refusing to succumb to the horrors of the war.

Klaus sat on one of the pews and patted the spot next to him, inviting Emilia to sit down.

"Do you like it?" he asked her quietly, lifting his hands under the multicolored sunlight that was shining through the partially shattered stained glass above their heads.

Emilia also lifted her hands and they were immediately colored like rainbows, just like Klaus's were. She smiled. "It's nice. Why did you bring me here?"

"Why do you think I brought you here?"

"I don't know." Emilia looked around once again, taking in the surprisingly quiet, serene atmosphere. "I'm not actually supposed to be here. I'm Jewish."

"And I'm an atheist. It has nothing to do with religion." Klaus smiled softly once again, catching more sun bunnies with his palms. "I just wanted to show it to you."

"Why?" Emilia asked once again.

Klaus looked around and Emilia followed his gaze.

"Do you like being here?" he asked her instead of answering.

"Yes, I actually do. It's very quiet, peaceful."

"You don't mind all the rubble inside?"

"Not really, no. I even like it better this way. I don't think I would have dared to enter it if it was an intact, functioning church. I always found them to be too overpowering. Now, this…this is more…" Emilia went quiet, looking for the right word. "More true to life, more unpretentious. And yet still holy. Think of it, it went through the war, it almost got destroyed, but it never fell. Parts of it are ruined, yes, but the rest, the rest is still there, stubbornly and defiantly. You know, maybe you think I'm mad, but I think it's more beautiful now than when it was before. It has character now. It didn't give in. So no, I don't mind the rubble. Certain things are even better when they're broken."

"Exactly." Klaus was beaming at her, even though she wasn't sure of the reason why.

"Exactly what?"

"Don't you understand it, you silly girl? You are this church. This is you. You and your scars that you are so ashamed of, your memories and your fears. Look around. Do you think this church cares that much about what others might think of it? It stands proudly, because it should take pride in itself; it survived the gunfire, the troops marching through it, trying to wreck it and burn it down. And yet it stands and proudly displays its wounds, for they're the marks of bravery, not humiliation. It didn't lose its sacredness after all the horrors it had to endure, you said it yourself, it stayed serene and holy; only certain parts are broken, but the spirit is still there, it's still a church, no matter what they tried to make out of it, all of them, first the German troops, than the Russian ones and finally the locals, who simply gave up on it. And it still remains my second favorite place in the world."

"What's the first one?" Emilia asked just to fill in the pause. She was biting her lip and looking under her feet, not too sure what to make of all this.

"Home, with you."

Emilia was afraid for a second that he might interpret her silence in some other way and try to kiss her, but Klaus just took her hand, intertwined their fingers together and turned his face back to the stained glass. Emilia felt both relieved and disappointed for some reason.

She wanted to say something, to explain her reluctance somehow, to make him understand that she was afraid of so many things, of revealing that ugly, damaged side of her that he could find repulsive because even she couldn't look at her own back without turning away in disgust. To show the physical proof of what had been done to her might scare him away, and even though she didn't want him too near, she was still terribly afraid to lose him at the same time. All of these feelings that she didn't understand, so contradictory and confusing, were overwhelming and she didn't know what to do with herself anymore.

"Come." Emilia got up suddenly, having made a decision, and pulled at her husband's arm. "Come, take me to the lake. I want to see it."

Klaus silently obeyed, and the rest of their way to the lake, which was indeed absolutely deserted just like he promised, they talked about completely irrelevant things, as if Klaus was trying to take Emilia's mind off her old wounds, which he was probably sorry that he had reopened. Emilia, on the contrary, was in some strange state of excitement, the same feeling that she had experienced as a little seven year old girl, when she was taken to the dentist to have one of her teeth pulled out, terribly fearing the pain. However, it turned out to be not half as bad as she expected, and being highly praised afterwards, she felt as if she had done something utterly remarkable.

This time, as Klaus spread out the blanket, she decided to be brave too, and before she started doubting herself, she quickly opened the zipper on the side of her dress and pulled it over her head, to stand only in her underwear.

"Klaus," she called to her husband, who turned around and froze on his knees, trying his best to keep his eyes on her eyes. "Look."

She turned her back on him, still holding her dress in her hands, anxiously waiting for what he would say. After several agonizing moments, Emilia felt his hands on her shoulders, and the soft kiss that he planted on one of the raised scars on her shoulder blade.

"Thank you," she heard him barely whisper, in between the gentle strokes of his soft fingers on top of every cut.

"For what?"

"For showing me."

"Thank you for not calling me beautiful after you saw them." Emilia caught herself chuckling slightly. Klaus was still slightly nuzzling her shoulder and Emilia hoped that he wouldn't move away any time soon. His warm breath on her skin suddenly felt as essential as her own breathing.

"You are. It's just such a corny thing to say. I love you for what you are, not for how you look."

Emilia turned to Klaus and wrapped her arms around his neck, burying her face in his shirt, barely breathing after her own impulsive desire to hug him. She froze at once, realizing that she stood next to him, barely dressed, and feverishly trying to figure out what she should do next; if she should do anything at all. No matter how much she hated to admit it, she was jealous of all those widows, even though Klaus only laughed at all of their efforts to woo him and calmly answered any of Emilia's questions as to why he didn't make use of the situation with them, for he must have some sort of needs that she couldn't help him to satisfy, he had only responded that he wasn't an animal who couldn't control its urges, but a human, and a human who had spent several years without any female companionship, and he could easily survive some more. 'Until...?' Emilia asked him then. He just shrugged and gave her another impish grin. Until she would be ready to give herself to him, Emilia understood it now. He didn't want those other women, he wanted her. For the first time, Emilia admitted to herself that she wanted him too, and not in a purely physical way. That part still frightened her quite a bit, since she never saw anything from it other than pain and disgust right after, maybe indifference at the most if she was lucky. She wanted to be close to him, with him, and if offering him her body would make him stay with her for the rest of her life, she could live with that. Besides, he wouldn't hurt her like the others did, she knew that already, and so she lifted her head and kissed him, still very fearfully and breathlessly, barely parting his lips with hers.

"Will you stay with me?" she whispered, hiding in his shirt again, too afraid to look him in the eye.

"Of course I will," he replied softly, holding Emilia against his stiff body. "But don't kiss me to make me stay. I don't want it to be this way."

"That's not why I kissed you."

"Why then?"

"I just wanted to." Emilia finally looked at him, with determination this time. "Klaus, make love to me."

"Emmi—"

"No, please, Klaus, I know what I'm asking for. Since you dragged me here and made me show you my scars, we might as well go all the way to the end." She giggled nervously, already taking his shirt out of his pants, even though he was still half-resisting her, trying to mumble something reasonable in protest. "I'm not afraid of anything today, and tomorrow I might change my mind and will be too terrified to let you close to me again. No, since we're here, let's do it. I need to go through all this today, so please, don't try to reason with me, and I'm begging you, don't push me away, because I'm feeling stupid as it is, undressing you when it should be the other way round, and when you're fighting me on top of it—

He chuckled, took her face in his hands and covered her mouth with his, making her stop her nervous talking.

Emilia took a deep breath and tried not to shiver as he lowered her onto the blanket after shedding the rest of their clothes, but Klaus still noticed it.

"We don't have to, if you don't want to," he told her once again with an unusually stern face.

Emilia knew how hard it must have been for him to contain himself after such a long time of not feeling a woman's body next to him, and yet she knew that if she only said one word, he would get up, get dressed and leave her alone. She shook her head slowly.

"I do. I'm just scared."

"I won't hurt you."

"Yes, I know."

"You tell me to stop and I'll stop."

"Yes." Emilia nodded and couldn't suppress another nervous giggle. "We're talking as if it's my first time."

Klaus laughed softly somewhere in her hair. "Yours and mine both. It's been so long I hope I didn't forget how it's done."

He started kissing her neck and collarbone, but Emilia stopped him. "No, don't kiss me, it's better if you do it like with cold water: one jump and you're done. That way it's not too terrifying."

"Are you sure?" Klaus asked her for the last time.

"Yes," Emilia replied firmly and held onto his shoulders.

It wasn't terrifying at all, just very different from all the other long forgotten times, when she had no control of anything that they chose to do with her body. This time it was Klaus, her Klaus, who she knew and loved. She admitted to herself that she loved him, even though she didn't want to tell him yet. Even if for her lovemaking was far from the magical event that Magda had once described to her, knowing how much Klaus enjoyed her body caused Emilia an unexplainable feeling of excitement and satisfaction. She didn't even mind it when, without noticing, he started moving much harder that in the beginning, whispering to her something undistinguishable in between short, hectic breaths. Emilia caught her own breath synchronizing with his, and she felt that whatever made it better for him, made it better for her, so she let him take all the pleasure that he wanted.

She was right in a sense, when she had commented that it felt like the first time for her. At least, for the first time she didn't feel empty and used after Klaus clenched her tightly for the last time and buried a loud moan in her neck, pulling her close right after and murmuring how much he loved her while trying to catch his breath. She knew that he did, and she was happy that he was happy. For the first time someone didn't discard her when she was of no use anymore, but instead a thoughtful hand pulled the side of the blanket, covering them both and she slept, pacified by the strong heartbeat of the man, who refused to let her go even when he fell asleep.

Chapter 8

Emilia kept squirming in her seat more and more as their train approached Dresden. As if sensing her nervousness, Klaus took her hand and squeezed it slightly, offering her a reassuring smile. He should have been nervous, not her, she kept telling herself, because who she was in the whole situation? No one, just a stranger basically, and yet it felt like the most important meeting of her life.

Emilia had been afraid at first to show the letter to Klaus that she received from the orphanage, fearing that he might get upset with her for putting her nose in someone else's business. After all, he'd made it clear from day one that he didn't want to even inquire about his son, since Walther had never seen him and would probably be better off with his new adopted family.

Only, there wasn't any new adopted family, as Emilia found out from the letter from the third orphanage she wrote to. Walther was still with them, and the head nurse wrote to Emilia in an excited tone about how the boy kept asking about his mother and how wonderful it was that his parents were finally found, and when did she, Emilia, think, would be the best time to take him home.

For a couple of days she kept tip-toeing around her husband, thinking of how to bring up the news. He noticed, of course, like he always did, that there was something bothering his Emmi, and asked her in a straightforward manner what it was.

"I found Walther," Emilia admitted at last and searched Klaus's face for signs of an approaching storm.

"You did?" he asked at last, seeming to be a little bit at a loss.

"Yes. He's still in an orphanage in Dresden."

"Oh."

Emilia watched her husband trace the lines on the wooden table with his finger, obviously deep in thought.

"They're asking when we can take him," Emilia continued warily, still not sure of what he was thinking. "Do you... Do you want to take him at all?"

"Take him home?" Klaus lifted his eyes to hers for the first time. "For good?"

"Well, yes, of course for good." She smiled.

Klaus went silent for a while again and then asked Emilia quietly, "And you will be all right raising someone else's child?"

"He's not someone else's, he's yours." Emilia's smile grew wider together with Klaus's.

"Really? You want him?"

"Yes, of course I do. I told you that I can never give you our own children. So Walther is the closest thing to having my own child. I was so happy when that letter came. Yes, I do want him, Klaus, very much."

What if he doesn't want me though, Emilia kept thinking as their train approached the station in Dresden, which had still not been completely rebuilt after the horrifying bombing of 1945. *What if he rejects me and says that he wants his mother, and not me? He's four, he's not a baby anymore after all...*

"Do you think he's indeed waiting for us?" Klaus interrupted her thoughts as they were riding in the back seat of a hired cab. "Or maybe the orphanage is so overflowing with orphans that the nurses just try to get rid of any of them as soon as they can?"

"I don't know, Klaus." Emilia sighed for the millionth time. "I'm so nervous myself."

"Me too," Klaus admitted. "I don't even know what he looks like."

They both sighed again and turned to their windows, watching the traces of the former devastation outside. The city was slowly being rebuilt, but it still seemed inconceivable what it must have looked like just three years ago.

The orphanage was hidden behind tall concrete walls, on which someone had painted animals dancing and smiling. Somehow this made the building look even more gloomy and depressing. Everyone knew perfectly well that places like this one, just like hospitals, were far from something even remotely reminiscent of happiness. After they were admitted through the black iron gates, which made the place look even more like a prison, they were escorted to the reception, where they showed the letter from the head nurse.

The elderly receptionist nodded several times, smiled, and took them to the head nurse's office. After the latter barely checked their papers to verify their identity, she took them to the back of the building.

"They're playing outside, getting their daily exercise," she explained, opening the door to the backyard. "I take it you want to take him home right away?"

"Yes, we do," Klaus and Emilia replied in unison.

"Splendid." The woman stepped outside and yelled in a mighty voice, "Walther Lemmel! Come here, your parents have come to take you home."

As if hearing the magic words that they normally only dreamed about, all the children stopped their fussing at once and turned to the door, observing the three people in stunned silence. Emilia scanned the crowd of children trying to figure out which one was Walther. She saw all of them watching both her and Klaus with big hopeful eyes full of desperation and unspoken pleas to take them along as well. They all looked the same to her, dressed in some sort of gray uniform, some too big on their small frames, some obviously outgrown, with their hair cut short and desperate eyes; eyes she would never forget. They reminded her of the eyes of the inmates watching the Red Army step through the gates of the just liberated camp, with both fear and hope.

"Mutti!!!" A shriek pierced the silence at last, and one of the boys broke off the gray crowd and ran towards Emilia, with his arms outstretched and his big eyes wide open. He almost knocked her off her feet, crashing into her legs and squeezing her as tight as he could with his thin frail arms, to press his blond head to her stomach and clenching her clothes as if his life depended on it. *"Mutti,* I knew you would come back for me! I knew you weren't dead, I knew you would come!!!"

Emilia turned her head to Klaus, her eyes full of unexpected tears, as if asking what she should do. The boy obviously thought she was his real, biological mother, who had survived despite all the odds and came for him at last, after he begged God every single night before going to sleep to return her to him. Sometimes God answers prayers. Klaus nodded slightly to her, and Emilia lowered to her knees to hug the boy tightly.

"Papa!" Still clinging to his newly found mother, Walther twisted himself to outstretch one hand to Klaus. "I knew you would come too! I told them all that you would come, but they didn't believe me! I told them you were alive, I knew you were both alive, and that you would come for me one day!"

Walther turned out to be a chatty boy, just like his father was, and wouldn't stop telling Emilia and Klaus about his days in the orphanage, about his friends, about how well he did in the nursery school and that he already knew how to read and even write a little, and that he was studying so hard because he wanted to write a letter to his Papa, who was in Siberia as Frau Kohl told him, and ask him about his *Mutti,* who he knew wasn't dead, but who had probably followed his Papa to Siberia and lived there with him. Both Klaus and Emilia somehow silently agreed to just go along with Walther's version, and not complicate his life even more with long explanations as to who Emilia really was. He obviously didn't remember his real mother, so why disillusion the boy, who had to go through so much in his short life already?

The three of them stopped at some café nearby for lunch, and Emilia and Klaus kept exchanging half-hidden smiles and glances at Walther's hearty appetite, with which he attacked everything that was put before him. He fell asleep in Klaus's arms barely ten minutes after he finished dessert, and Emilia couldn't help but notice how alike the two of them looked.

Emilia watched Klaus sleep every morning, still not believing that she had invited him to share her bed since that day on the beach, the bed, which she swore some years ago that no man would ever sleep in. Only, Klaus wasn't an ordinary man; he was everything that she thought didn't exist anymore, and he was everything she had prayed for when yet another heavy boot had stepped on her very soul; a soul already torn into a million of pieces. Yes, sometimes God answers prayers.

"Shall we head back to the station?" Klaus whispered, so as not to wake his son, who was sleeping peacefully on his shoulder.

Emilia nodded, but after they had already paid the bill, she suggested, also in a hushed whisper, even though gunfire probably wouldn't wake Walther at that point, "Since we're already here, do you want to go see your old farm?"

"The old farm?"

"Yes, the one that you said was still intact."

"I suppose we can."

Walther slept the whole hour that it took for them to get to the village in the suburbs of Dresden, and only mumbled something in his sleep when Klaus shifted him to get in and out of the taxi. They paid the driver and asked him not to leave, for they wouldn't be long.

"Is this your house?" Emilia asked her husband, as they approached the front porch, freshly painted and decorated with potted flowers.

"No, the one next to it. The family who takes care of it lives here."

Klaus knocked on the door, and they heard hurried steps and a voice from inside, "Coming, coming! Just a second."

A woman well in her sixties opened the front door and gasped at once, clasping her hands on her chest.

"Klaus! Is that really you, my boy? Oh, my Klaus, we thought you were long dead on those Siberian steppes! Oh, thank God, you're alive!"

The woman rushed to hug him gently so as not to disturb the sleeping boy.

"I'm alive and well, Frau Seidel. They released me not that long ago."

The woman turned her head to Emilia. "And this must be your wife?"

Klaus looked at Emilia, grinning impishly. Frau Seidel seemed to also take Emilia for Klaus's first wife, just like Walther did. Once again, they silently agreed to leave it that way.

"Yes, she is. This is my Emmi, and this is our son, Walther."

The woman smiled at Emilia and gave her a tight hug.

"You've been waiting for this little rascal this whole time?"

"Yes, I have." Emilia and Klaus exchanged another glance like two conspirators. "I would have waited for him my whole life if I had to."

Frau Seidel, still beaming uncontrollably, ushered them inside the house and started fussing about tea, leaving the three of them in the small dining room next to the kitchen.

The decision to move to Klaus's old family farm came to them both clear as a day, and barely giving it a second thought on the train back home, the couple was already looking forward to starting a new life. Emilia wiped away her tears silently that night, while lying in bed next to her husband who was snoring softly. No one knew her there, to all of them she was just an ordinary woman, Klaus's wife, and not some former camp internee, who was afraid to show her face in the nearest town, forever branded and shamed for something she never had any control of.

No one knew of her past in that small village; she could finally bury all of her demons, which wouldn't come back to haunt her dreams each time another poisonous tongue spilled more venom on her old wounds. She would be just an ordinary wife and a mother, something she had never believed she could be. And the scars? The scars were from the bombing, but she had survived it. Emilia was sure, with time, that the old, mortifying memories would eventually be replaced by new ones, and the nightmares would finally lose their power over her completely.

Thank you for reading "Emilia." I hope you enjoyed it! If you liked the story, the author and all the people who worked on the book will really appreciate it if you leave a review on Amazon or Goodreads.

Feel free to connect with the author on Facebook and ask any questions you may have left after reading "Emilia." I will be more than happy to answer all of them.

Also by the author:

"The Girl From Berlin" series:

"The Girl From Berlin: Standartenführer's Wife" (book 1)

"The Girl From Berlin: Gruppenführer's Mistress" (book 2)

"The Girl From Berlin: War Criminal's Widow" (book 3)

"The Austrian" series:

"The Austrian"

"The Austrian: Book Two" (book 2)